I0586829

Wherever He Goes

VANIA RHEAULT

E-Reader ISBN: 978-0-9996775-3-7
Paperback ISBN 978-0-9996775-2-0

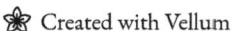 Created with Vellum

Books by Vania Rheault

available from Coffee & Kisses Press

On the Corner of 1700 Hamilton

Summer Secrets Novellas 1-3
Summer Secrets Novellas 4-6

Don't Run Away
Chasing You
Running Scared

Wherever He Goes

All of Nothing

The Years Between Us

His Frozen Heart
His Frozen Dreams
Her Frozen Memories
Her Frozen Promises

Chapter One

T he plane jolted when the wheels touched down onto the tarmac, and Katrina Ford's blood hummed with anticipation as she braced her arm against the seat in front of her.

Swallowing to clear her ears one last time, she smoothed her palms along the comfortable cotton floral skirt she wore to travel and adjusted her thick frames as the plane taxied toward their terminal at LAX.

Even before they stopped moving, passengers began to gather their things, the impatient ones already standing, stretching their cramped legs after the two-and-a-half-hour flight from Dallas/Ft. Worth.

Kat shifted, wanting to stand as well. She hadn't moved since the plane had taken off, and now her butt tingled from sitting for so long.

As she adjusted her bun, pushing in a stray bobby pin or two, a male voice in a smooth baritone asked, "Can I help you with a carry-on?"

Kat looked up, and up. Everyone was tall compared to her five foot, one inch frame, but he towered over her seat. "That would be great, thanks," she said, finally standing and scooting into the tight space in the narrow aisle between him and another passenger.

His hair was jet-black, and a beard of the same color covered the lower half of his face. His icy blue eyes were kind, but framed with lines of fatigue. "Which one?" he asked.

Kat blinked. "What?" His words were lost as his stare mesmerized her.

He raised his eyebrows, dark slashes partially hidden by thick locks of hair falling over his forehead. His lips quirked. "Bag?"

A passenger reaching for her own carry-on stowed in the overhead bin jostled her, and to give her room, she stepped nearer to the man, her shoulder brushing his broad chest. He wore a white button-down dress shirt, a black and silver tie hanging in a loose knot around his neck, and charcoal grey dress pants.

He smelled divine, and she took a deep, heady breath of smoke and earth before answering. "Sorry. The hot pink one."

He shot her a puzzled frown.

"What? It was on sale," Kat defended herself, knowing the outrageous color didn't mesh with her current appearance.

"I didn't say anything," he said, easily pulling her carry-on from the compartment above her head.

"Thanks." She jerked the handle upward to pull it off the plane.

If people would start moving. It always took forever for passengers to deplane.

"You're welcome."

Lost in the excitement of stepping into one of the most famous airports in the United States, she hoped she'd see a celebrity—she *was* in LA, after all. She read the rag mags, perused the pictures of stars coming and going, going on their glamorous vacations or returning home to their mansions after spending months in Europe vacationing or wrapping up movies in exotic locations. Maybe she would catch a glimpse of Julia Roberts or Hugh Jackman. Maybe Angelina Jolie. Nah, she flew her own plane.

Stopping just inside the terminal teeming with people waiting to board their flights, Kat pulled her phone from her purse to let her friend, Nan, know she landed.

Nan had texted her first: *I'm running late! Wait for me!*

Kat laughed. Like she had a choice. *No problem,* she answered. *Landed safely.*

The restaurants were packed with people laughing and drinking, scents from one of the open grills wafting through the air. Her stomach growl. Sitting with a glass of wine and an appetizer while she waited for Nan sounded wonderful, but she promised she wouldn't drink anymore . . . and hopefully lose ten pounds, too.

The gorgeous gentleman who helped her walked by, trailing his own plain black carry-on behind him.

Where was he going? Home to a wife and a couple of kids, probably. A man who looked that good—and who was that nice—was surely taken. She hadn't looked for a ring, but she wasn't in the habit of looking for wedding rings on strangers. Kat fingered her own ring on her left hand, and the bite of the diamond brought her back to the bustling airport. Dodging harried travelers, she shuffled to the escalator, tucking her phone into her purse.

A little girl waved at Kat, distracting her with an angelic smile, and she missed the top step as it disappeared from beneath her foot. She stumbled, losing her grip on her carry-on. Narrowly missing a woman speaking on her phone, the case tumbled to the bottom and hit the floor. Desperately, trying to regain her balance, she followed, her hand sliding along the moving handrail, her summer sandals searching for purchase against the metal stairs.

Her heart jumped into her throat as the floor rushed to meet her.

The man wearing the charcoal grey suit had unwisely decided to check his phone at the bottom of the escalator, and try as she might, she couldn't stop herself from slamming into his back.

Her purse dropped from her shoulder and crashed to the

shining waxed floor, scattering her makeup, hand lotion, phone, and wallet.

"Hey!" he exclaimed in surprise, twisting, and she clung to his chest, gasping. "Be careful."

"Sorry, I tripped," Kat said, pausing a moment to calm her racing heart. Her hands shook against the soft fabric of his shirt.

His look of irritation smoothed, and a slight smile replaced his frown. Leaning close, he spoke into her ear, his beard tickling her cheek. "Breathe. Escalators can be dangerous, you need to pay attention. Better gather up your things. You don't want your wallet and phone stolen."

Kat's blood hummed, but it wasn't from the near-miss.

Not anymore.

Just when she was about to pull away to pick up the mess, a young man holding a camera jumped in front of them, a sparkle in his eyes, a grin lighting his face.

"Gotcha!"

Aiden Price frowned. He didn't like having his picture taken, though he should be goddamned used to it by now. Especially in LA.

"This picture is gonna make me rich!" the kid crowed, snapping more pictures of them, his camera clicking and whizzing at top speed.

People hurrying toward the baggage claim stopped to gawk, and Aiden dropped his arm from the brunette's back. Her shaking hands still rested against his chest, her breath coming out in little gasps.

"Joe and Anna having an affair! This is the scoop of a lifetime!"

"Buzz off." He didn't have time for this. All he wanted to do was grab the shuttle to the rental office and pick up his car. He had a vacation to start.

"I'm sending these to my editor right now," the photographer said, focusing his camera on the woman standing beside him. "You tried to look different with the glasses, but I know it's you."

He clenched his fists.

The kid noticed and scurried off, fiddling with his camera. He looked over his shoulder at Aiden and winked.

The brunette licked her lips. "What was that about?"

"Sounds like he mixed us up with someone else. It happens to me here, sometimes."

She dropped to her haunches and began shoving her things into her purse. "Oh, well, whatever. My friend is picking me up any minute; I have to find out where to wait."

He pointed toward the ceiling at a bright blue sign. "Follow the arrows to the baggage claim. You have a suitcase?"

"Yeah," she said standing, pushing her purse strap over her shoulder.

She was a pretty woman, shiny hair and clear skin, but she dressed too conservatively for his taste: a thin, purplish sweater covered her from neck to hip, and a long skirt decorated in purple flowers skimmed the ground as she walked, hiding every inch of her legs. She was lucky the hem hadn't gotten caught in the escalator stairs.

"The baggage claim is near the shuttle pick-up area outside. That's the best place for your friend to pick you up. Do you want to walk with me? I'm going in that direction, too." Aiden silently groaned. Why in the hell did he offer?

He knew why.

There was something about her golden-brown eyes, a spark she tried to hide, the way she carried herself, that intrigued him, but he should know better.

"Oh, well, I was going to . . ." She cleared her throat, but he barely heard her over the crowd of tired passengers who were disembarking from an arriving flight and the patrons of the restaurants lining the corridor. "I have to go to the bathroom first."

"No problem, so do I. They're down here." He pulled his carry-on down the wide hallway, the excited, but exhausted, chatter fading into a dull murmur.

"You know a lot about the airport," she said, rushing to catch up.

"I fly in all the time," Aiden said. "I'll wait for you."

While he did his business, he wondered if she would give him the slip; he was coming on kind of strong. She didn't need him to show her the baggage claim area. The signs and arrows made it clear enough.

He waited outside the women's bathroom entrance feeling like a stalker, but he relaxed when she appeared and gave him a grateful smile. "I appreciate your help."

"What are you in town for?" he asked, leading her past a restaurant filled to the brim with people drinking tall pilsner glasses of beer and munching on baskets of chips and salsa. It looked good, but he would be at his brother's soon enough—just in time for dinner.

"My friend is throwing me a birthday party. Nan's already been here for a few days, and she's late driving from Santa Barbara to pick me up."

"Traffic can be a bitch, sometimes, but happy birthday. I hope you have a good time."

"Thanks! I'm looking forward to it. I've never been to California before."

He bet she hadn't been many places before.

Her cell rang, and she stopped to pull it out of her purse, waving him on. "I need to answer this," she said, looking at her phone's display. "I can find my way. Thanks again for your help."

He shook her hand, hoping the shock from the contact didn't show on his face. Her skin was so smooth, the bones delicate, as if he squeezed too hard he would crush them. Reluctantly, he released her and in disappointment he said, "You're welcome. Good luck finding your friend."

Dismayed he lost her so soon, he dragged his carry-on down

the hallway toward the baggage area. He was dreading the shuttle and the long lines at the rental car company. His brother, Dylan, offered to pick him up, but since he'd be in California a lot longer than his normal vacation time, he wanted his own vehicle. God, he needed the break, and he was looking forward to lots of pool time and booze.

He stopped at a bright red sign warning him if he went any farther, due to security reasons, he wouldn't be allowed to reenter the airport. Over his shoulder, Aiden searched for the petite woman. He spotted her off to the side of the corridor, speaking on her phone, her hand waving frantically as she paced in a tight circle. Whoever called her wasn't delivering good news, and he felt sorry for her because it was her birthday.

Pulling his own phone out of his pocket to text Dylan he landed safely, he tried to mentally tune her out. Her problem wasn't his problem.

A ferocious screech interrupted their back and forth, his brother telling him to hurry up, cold beer and a hot steak waited for him. "What the—?" he mumbled as the woman in the long skirt stomped toward him, tears streaking her face.

"What's wrong with you?" he asked, concerned, pulling her arm, guiding her along the wall to avoid the throngs of people streaming toward the baggage area.

"My fiancé just dumped me, because of you!"

"What? I don't understand. I don't even know you."

The brunette glared, the lenses of her glasses catching the light, her eyes blazing. "Well, the whole world thinks I know you!" She thrust her cell phone into his face. "That phone call was my fiancé breaking off our engagement because of this."

Aiden took the phone, protected in a plain black case, and studied the picture. It was of him and her, just like she said, her hands braced against his chest, his arm around her. The caption at the bottom made him laugh. "Joe Manganiello and Anna Kendrick Canoodling in LAX!"

Squinting into her face, Aiden searched for a resemblance to the famous actress. In the right light, she looked a little like Anna Kendrick, but maybe he would see it more if her hair was down. With her curls bound, the thick black-framed glasses hiding half her face, and her lips pursed in irritation, she looked more like a hipster in withdrawal from her favorite coffee shop. "Just tell him it was a mistake. It's not a big deal."

It wasn't the first time he'd been told he looked like the famous actor. Every once in a while, he would even sign a coffee cup for a giggly teenager proud she had the courage to ask.

She wiped her eyes. "Of course it's a mistake, but look at the picture, *Joe*. It's not who this article said we look like, it's what we're doing." With her back pressed against the wall, she began sobbing into her hands.

Aiden conceded that, okay, they did appear like lovers. The picture brought him back, what was it, not even fifteen minutes ago, to her in his arms, the vanilla scent of her skin tickling the inside of his nose.

It'd been a while since he had a woman. The case, then that disaster. A mousy little girl shouldn't get him hot and bothered, not like this. He didn't *want* to be hot and bothered. And this one was unavailable.

Whether her fiancé just dumped her or not.

"Can't you call him back and explain you tripped down the escalator stairs?"

"Don't you think I would have done that already?" she cried, swiping her phone from his grasp. "He hung up on me, and now my calls go to his useless voicemail."

"Well, have your birthday vacation, then go home and work it out. I don't see how anyone would—"

"Birthday!" she moaned, covering her mouth with the back of her hand. "I can't stay now. I have to go home and beg him to take me back."

Aiden wanted to wipe the tears off her cheeks, but, of course, refrained. "I'm sorry . . . I don't know your name."

"Katrina."

"Katrina . . . Kat? Do you go by Kat? Or Trina?"

"No! Katrina, that's it."

The fear that shot through Katrina's eyes made Aiden flinch. "All right, calm down. If you really think you need to go home, I can help you find the ticket counter, and you can change your return flight. My name is Aiden; it's going to be all right."

A look of relief replaced the fear, and a smile fluttered over her lips. "Thank you. Yes, I need to get home as quickly as I can. Neil . . . I can't lose him. I just can't."

Biting the inside of his cheek to prevent himself from saying something stupid, like Neil didn't deserve her if he was going to fly off the handle at a simple picture, he led Katrina up the concourse toward a customer service counter.

They were waiting in line when the large monitors reporting arrivals and departures suddenly went black.

Shock rippled through the crowded terminal. People began muttering in low voices, with some more vocal, yelling, "Hey, what's going on?"

Kat echoed their concern. "What happened? A power outage?"

Aiden shook his head. "No, the lights are still on."

Groaning, Kat searched the terminal for answers, though she didn't know what she was looking for. The flight attendants behind the counters punched at their keyboards and anxiously whispered to each other, shielding their mouths with their hands. "I need to get home." She pulled her phone out of her purse; she missed a phone call from Nan. While she stood in line next to Aiden, she returned Nan's call. "Nan—"

"Hey, you're lucky you landed—"

"I'm trying to fly back—"

"Why—" Nan's shriek pierced Kat's eardrum.

"Why am I lucky—" she started to ask.

"Stop, stop, stop," Nan demanded. "I was saying you're lucky you landed . . . all the airline pilots just went on strike—"

"What?" Kat whispered. "You mean I can't fly home?"

"What's wrong?" Aiden asked, rubbing her shoulder.

She lifted a finger to silence him and listened to Nan's response.

"No, you can't. The planes are all grounded. No one is flying. You're lucky you made it here—the pilots are landing at the nearest airport; it doesn't matter where they are. You could have been stranded in Nebraska!"

"Oh, my God."

"What is it?" Aiden asked. He leaned toward her, and she inhaled a lungful of his cologne. "Tell me."

Just then the intercom crackled to life, and Kat looked toward the ceiling. "Attention ladies and gentlemen, we regret to inform you that pilots of American, Midwest, TransValley, Trans-Euro, and Coastal Airlines have voted to strike. Future flights pending successful contract negotiations. There is nothing we can do at this time. We repeat, there is nothing we can do at this time."

"Nan, I need to go. I need to find a way home."

"But why—"

"No, look online. My picture . . . Neil dumped me. I need to go home."

"What do you mean, look online? Kat, you're not flying anywhere. How do you think you're going to get there?"

Her eyes flew to Joe's face. No, not Joe. He said his name was Aiden. "I don't know," she said to Nan, "but Neil was serious. I can't—"

"Do you want me—" Nan attempted to ask.

"There's nothing you can do," she said, her throat thick with tears. Sending her friend away was stupid. She should go with

Nan. Maybe she didn't feel like partying, but what else was she going to do? She couldn't fly home.

Dammit.

"I'll drive you home," Aiden said.

Her mouth dropped open. "What? What did you say?"

Nan replied, "I said, it's stupid for you—"

"No, not you," Kat said to Nan. "I'll call you back when I know what I'm doing. Bye." She hung up on Nan who was making her objections known loud and clear. "What did you say?" she asked Aiden.

Tipping his head back, he screwed his eyes shut, as if what he was going to say would physically hurt. "I said I'll drive you. I feel like I'm responsible for this mess."

Kat wanted to laugh; he sounded like bringing her home would be a trip across town. "I live in Minnesota."

Aiden scraped his fingers through his beard. "Fuck. Come on."

"Where are we going?" Kat scrambled to chase after him, at the last second remembering to pull her carry-on with her.

The terminal was in utter pandemonium. People were crying and yelling. Kat dodged a couple screaming at each other while a toddler sat near the woman's feet, sobbing, her face pressed into her mother's leg.

Kat felt horrible for all these people. If Neil wouldn't have dumped her, she'd be on her way to Santa Barbara with Nan, laughing, planning what to do for her first night in California, selfishly not caring about the strike. Only now she was one of them, desperate to go home, and racing after a man who promised to drive her there.

Her pace slowed as she second-guessed her decision to trust him. She didn't know the man. Maybe she should call Nan back . . . maybe she should call Neil. For as quickly as he saw her photo online, he must have heard flights were grounded until . . . forever, maybe.

People swirled around her, and Kat lost sight of Aiden.

Her mouth dried with fear.

"Hey, come on," Aiden said from behind her. "What are you doing? We have to get out of here."

"I don't know—"

"You're having second thoughts now?" Aiden ran a hand across his forehead in frustration. "I don't want to leave you alone. If you don't want me to help you, fine, but call your friend, or figure something else out. I'll feel like an asshole for the rest of my life if I leave you here like this."

Kat made a quick decision. "Tell me one thing that will make me trust you."

"I'm an attorney."

"That . . . wasn't what I was looking for." She gripped her carry-on and checked that her purse still hung from her shoulder.

"It's all I got right now," he said. "Come on, we're wasting time. Do you know how many people are going to need vehicles?"

"What do you mean? Don't you live here?"

Aiden grasped her hand, his skin connecting with hers with an electric sizzle. She reeled from the contact, his palm fitting hers with surprising perfection.

"No, I don't live here. I'm visiting my brother. But I was going to stay for a while, and I have a rental car booked at Payless. We have to ride the shuttle to the office."

With the bottoms of her sandals slapping against the polished floor, she scampered beside him. She followed him through a set of heavy metal doors, the ominous red sign warning her if she took one more step, she couldn't go back. The point of no return. Kat knew what that meant. It meant she'd gone too far in one direction to turn around. That's what deciding to trust Aiden felt like.

If she left the airport with him, there was no going back.

"What about our luggage?" she asked, eyeing a Starbucks tucked into the wall. A few high-top tables were sprinkled in front of the coffee vendor, some laden with garbage people couldn't be bothered to throw away.

What she wouldn't give for a cup of coffee.

"No." Aiden pushed through a pair of glass doors.

"No what? No luggage or no coffee?"

"Your luggage. We can stop for coffee later. You have some things in your carry-on that will get you through the next couple of days? You don't really need your suitcase, do you?"

People were jammed near the luggage carousel, hoping against hope the conveyor belt would spit out their suitcases. There was no way to know how long it would take, if it happened at all.

Quickly, Kat ran through what she packed. She'd lose all her makeup. Her shampoo and conditioner. Most of her clothes. But if they drove straight through—how long would they need to drive from California to Minnesota?

If they took turns driving . . .

"No. I guess not. What about you?"

Aiden waited on the curb and looked both ways. "A shuttle for the rental offices should be by here any second—all they do is loop around. I have what I need in my carry-on. I don't have a suitcase."

"You don't need to bring clothes to your brother's?" she asked, confused.

"No, I keep clothes there. I spend a lot of time at his place."

Someone bumped her from behind, and Kat slipped off the curb. Her muscles frozen, she stared in horror as a bright yellow taxi bore down on her, his horn blaring.

Aiden pulled her onto the sidewalk just before it crushed her. "Be careful."

Kat stared into his blue eyes. They were framed with lines of fatigue and filled with a hurt she couldn't name. "Thanks." She inhaled a deep, shuddery breath. "You don't have to do this," she said, all at once feeling selfish he was giving up his vacation time to help her. "I can call Nan back or . . ." She didn't know what else she would do. Neil's words echoed in her head, the cruel things he yelled at her.

A large shuttle bus pulled in front of them, stinking of gas fumes, and Aiden grabbed her carry-on along with his. "It's too late."

Kat was afraid of that.

By the time Katrina and Aiden boarded, standing room only remained on the bus. Katrina's body pressed against his while they stood toward the rear. The top of her head barely came to his shoulders, and the scents of vanilla and something musky—Aiden guessed it was her skin mixed with a little sweat—floated to him. *Get it together*, he told himself. The bus hit a bump, and she leaned closer, steadying herself with a hand to his chest. *This isn't something you want to do again.* Damn straight he didn't. He didn't fuck with engaged women.

Not anymore.

Even if her fiancé dumped her. It didn't mean she was any less engaged. She still loved the man.

Keep as far away from her as possible.

"What's in Minnesota? Do you have electricity up there yet?"

Katrina scowled. "Of course we do. You're thinking of North Dakota. They're the ones who don't have electricity and they still use outhouses."

Aiden stifled a smile.

"Where are you from, then, Mr. Trendy Cosmopolitan Man?"

"Miami."

"Bugs."

Over the frantic chatter of the other passengers, he missed what she said. "What?"

"Bugs," she repeated, a bit louder, rising on her toes, a wasted action as she wasn't any taller. "You have bugs down there."

He shook his head. "Ocean."

Tears filled her eyes, and she looked away.

Great. He volunteered to drive a moody woman half way

across the country. Before he could ask her why in the hell the ocean would make her cry, the shuttle stopped in front of the building that housed the car rental companies.

Thank God.

"We're here. Come on."

He spoke too soon, and they had to wait until most of the passengers stepped off the shuttle before shuffling their way to the front.

The driver handed Aiden their carry-ons from the luggage rack behind the driver's seat.

Aiden grabbed both handles. "Thanks."

"You're welcome." The plump man took off his blue cap and scratched his bald head. "You know my wife's a real fan, *True Blood* and all, and she'll never believe me when I tell her that Joe—"

"I'm not him," Aiden said. "And she would be right—he'd never ride a shuttle."

The driver squinted at Katrina through the thick lenses of his glasses. "But isn't she—"

"No." Aiden carried his and Katrina's carry-ons off the bus and set them onto the sidewalk. He waited impatiently while she gave the driver her autograph. "Why did you do that?" he asked as the shuttle pulled away in a cloud of heat and exhaust.

Katrina shrugged. "I've never given anyone my autograph before."

"Did you sign your name or Anna's?" he asked, trailing behind her up the ramp. She went the long way, and he tried to rein in his temper. He could have carried their bags up the steps in five seconds.

"Mine."

"I'm sure he loved that," he said and scoffed.

"I could be rich and famous one day. Then my autograph will be worth millions," she said, following him into the rental building. "Oh, my God," she breathed.

He shared the sentiment. Long lines snaked around the wide

VANIA RHEAULT

room, and the counters were filled to capacity with agents helping customers as quickly as they could.

Aiden planted himself in a line that would eventually meet him up with a Payless agent. "We're fine. I have a reservation, but it's going to be a while." He pulled out his cell phone and skimmed the messages Dylan sent him. Instead of trying to explain through text what he was going to do, he called.

Dylan picked up on the first ring. "Good thing you landed when you did," he said, not bothering to say hello.

"Yeah, I know. I'm at the rental place. The lines are longer than hell."

"Fuck that," Dylan said, "let me pick you up. I'll be there before you can rent a car, and you can grab one tomorrow, maybe. Though by tonight, I bet there won't be a car left in the joint." He laughed.

Aiden turned his back to Katrina to keep her from hearing what he said next. "I can't. I'm helping . . . someone. I told her I would drive her home."

Dylan pounced. "Her? Just what have you gotten yourself mixed up in, little brother? I thought you swore off women."

"Have you been online at all? Apparently, there was something—"

"Yeah, I saw that, actually. But what does that have to do with anything? You get mistaken for him all the time. In fact, how many times did you get asked for your autograph, anyway? I have a bet with Mom it was more than five."

"The woman who was with me—"

"You mean 'Anna?'" Dylan chuckled. "That photographer must've been high. She looks nothing like Anna Kendrick. I met her once at a Whole Foods, you know that?"

Aiden could feel Katrina's eyes boring through his back. He needed to wrap this up. "Well, her name's Katrina, and her fiancé saw the picture and broke off their engagement. I told her I would drive her home so she could explain. It was just an accident."

His brother whistled. "That's mighty nice of you, bro, but it's not your responsibility. What's she in town for? Let her do her thing, and you do yours. You need the break, Aiden. Seriously."

"I feel like it's my fault, that's all," Aiden muttered, his shoulders hunched with tension and guilt.

"Don't. Send her packing. Where in the hell does she live anyway? You don't need this shit."

Aiden blew out a breath. "I know, I know. It's just something I have to do, okay? She lives in Minnesota. It will only take a few days."

Dylan lowered his voice. "Jesus Christ. Minnesota." He sighed. "I know I'm not going to be able to talk you out of this, so . . . just . . . be careful."

"Yeah. Thanks. I'll keep you posted. Sorry about the vacation."

"Not a big deal. Hey, don't get hurt, okay?"

"It'll work out."

Aiden turned to face Katrina, sliding his phone into the pocket of his pants. He nudged her forward a step. "How are you holding up?"

"Neil won't answer my calls." She dragged her purse strap up her shoulder. "How do you think that kid posted our picture online so fast?"

"Probably has a family member connected to the business or something. Better question is how did your fiancé see it the second it posted?"

"He's . . . online a lot."

"Can you move up, please?" an older woman behind Katrina snapped, preventing her from elaborating.

He glared at the woman in frustration. "Sorry, ma'am," he said, nodding, forcing calm into his voice. He scooted into the half inch space in front of him.

Katrina played on her phone, but he was too polite to ask what she was doing. He didn't care anyway, except he grew bored after ten minutes of people watching. He thought about asking her a question, maybe get to know her, but there would be plenty of time for that in the car. If he asked her everything he wanted to know right now, they'd run out of things to talk about before they even cleared the California state line.

Finally, they reached the counter.

Aiden told the rental agent his name and read his reservation number from the confirmation email on his phone, his heart hammering. Neither of those things would ensure he had a car, but he blew out a sigh of relief when she nodded and pulled out a sheaf of papers for him to sign.

"I'm driving to Minnesota. Do you have a location in that state?" he asked, signing his life away. At least, that's what it felt like he was doing. Nothing about this situation gave him a good feeling. What he wanted was to be lying on a lounge chair on the balcony of his brother's condo sipping on a beer while Dylan grilled steaks, the complex's sapphire blue pool shimmering below them.

"We're partnered with Enterprise. Drop it off at any location," the woman said, already done with him and looking around Aiden and Katrina to the impatient woman standing behind them.

"Thank you," he muttered.

He dragged his carry-on down a dirty hallway crowded with people waiting in line for the bathrooms.

Aiden didn't slow, hoping Katrina didn't have to go again, but she stayed in pace with him, following him into the large garage where they could pick up the car.

The enormous area smelled of gasoline, and there were even more people waiting for the attendants to retrieve their vehicles.

"Mr. Price?" a blue-uniformed Latino attendant asked, and Aiden nodded. "We have your car ready, follow me."

The whole process was going smoother than he anticipated, and he relaxed. He reserved a luxury SUV, and he was almost cheered at the thought of driving it across the country. At least he could hook up his phone to the speaker system and listen to an audiobook. Then he wouldn't need to depend on Katrina for entertainment; she looked like all she wanted to do was curl into a ball and cry.

"Here you go, sir," the attendant said, handing him a key ring with two keys dangling from it.

"I . . . don't understand," Aiden said, gaping at the vehicle. What the fuck was he supposed to do with that?

"My apologies, sir, but with the pilots on strike, we did what we could. You're lucky to even have a car, if you want to know the truth."

"I could go to a dealership and buy something better than this." He could, too. Most dealers took an American Express Black Card, didn't they?

"Take it or leave it. We have a waiting room full of people who would be relieved to have any vehicle at all."

That wasn't a lie. If they were resorting to renting a vehicle like this, Payless was more than likely out of cars. If he passed it up, any number of people still waiting would jump at the chance.

Silently, Katrina had watched the exchange, and he turned to her. "What do you think?"

"We can get rid of it somewhere else right? Trade it in at a different rental place? We wouldn't be stuck with it all the way to Minnesota. I guess we better take what we can get. I'm so sorry." She wiped at a tear sliding down her cheek.

Aiden sighed, and he nodded at the attendant. She was right. Trading it in was a good idea.

"Yeah, okay."

"Good choice, man. Drive out those doors," he said, pointing, "and take a right. Tracy will need to see your papers and your driver's license before you can leave the lot. Have a good one."

The attendant hooted in Spanish to a group of Payless staff standing across the room, and they burst into laughter.

"What do you think he said?" Aiden asked, grimacing at the hideous wood-paneled station wagon older than he was.

"He said if we break down, at least you have room to fuck me while we wait for a tow truck," she said, opening the back passenger-side door.

"Really? You know Spanish?"

"A little. There's a large Latino population where I live. Don't you? You should, living in Miami. Aren't there a lot of people who speak Spanish down there?"

"There's a lot of Spanish everywhere, but no. I don't know much." He opened the door with a loud creak that echoed throughout the entire garage. "We should get out of here before they think we've changed our minds."

"Yeah."

Aiden slid behind the wheel and quickly assessed where everything was located. The old FM radio shot his Audible dreams to shit. He'd have to depend on Katrina for his entertainment after all. The prospect wasn't very promising.

He waited until she buckled her seatbelt, then creeped out of the garage, hoping against hope the car wouldn't lose its muffler before he could trade the monstrosity in for something better.

The station wagon was roomy, but that was the best thing she could say about the old, rusted vehicle. How Payless even had it available was anyone's guess, and Kat wouldn't have been surprised if one of the attendants rented out their personal vehicle to earn some extra cash. The radio didn't look like it worked, and there were no charging docks for cell phones. She'd have to be careful with her usage—until they stopped or traded in the ancient wagon, she wouldn't be able to charge hers.

"How do you know where to go?" she asked as he navigated the streets of LA. She should've been interested in the sights, but she couldn't find the energy to care. Katrina twisted in her seat and studied Aiden's profile. Who would have thought her looks —and his—would have gotten her into so much trouble?

"We have to go east, right? That's all I can do right now."

"So, no ocean."

"Nope. Not this time. Unless you want to call your friend back and take your vacation."

Kat thought about that for a moment. It sounded appealing, she couldn't deny it, but she remembered how angry Neil was at her, and it broke her heart he dumped her so fast. It was as if he were waiting for an excuse to get rid of her . . . But no, he wanted to marry her just as much as she wanted to marry him. In the end, she said, "I can't. I need to explain in person what happened. It's the only way he'll see reason."

Aiden tossed a frown her way. "How long have you been engaged, anyway?"

"Six years."

"*Six years*?" Aiden asked, incredulous. "How old are you? You don't even look twenty-five."

"I'm twenty-eight. We've been friends since we were kids. Our mothers were best friends, and a few years ago we realized our friendship had turned into something . . . more."

"Right," Aiden said, squinting into the sun, not sounding like he believed her.

Well, why should he? She barely believed herself. Raising her chin, she said, "What?"

"Nothing. I've never met anyone who's been engaged for six years. Maybe it's a Minnesota thing. Hey, can you reach in the back and pull out my sunglasses? They're in the side pocket of my carry-on."

Grateful for the change of subject, Kat released her seatbelt. "Sure."

She unzipped the side compartment of his bag and shoved her hand inside. Her fingers slid over a paper of some sort, and she pulled at it, revealing a bright pink color and an American flag stamp in the upper corner. An envelope. Quickly, she pushed it toward the bottom and looked over her shoulder. She didn't want him to accuse her of snooping, but his eyes were steady on the road.

The car hit a bump, and she braced herself against the seat.

When she pulled them out of the side compartment completely, a faint smile touched her lips. Wayfarers. Aiden would look hot in these. Yeah, like a real movie star.

"Having trouble back there? I'm sure I put them in the side pocket."

Kat blushed. In her position, he spoke to her butt. "Yeah, I got 'em." She plopped into her seat and handed them over.

"Thanks," he said, slipping them over his eyes.

"No problem. I don't want to be rude, but would you mind if I took a nap? It's been a really long day."

"Yeah, go ahead. We've got a few hours until we make it to the next city."

She should be more interested in this road trip as they'd be driving through places she'd only flown over in the plane, but she didn't care what the next city was. Guilt gnawed at her insides ever since Neil saw her picture with Aiden, and she was worried about Nan. She should text her, but she didn't want a lecture on how irresponsible she was being. Trusting Aiden may be foolish, but he was her best chance, her *only* chance, at getting back to Minnesota in a reasonable amount of time. Twisting her engagement ring around her finger, she turned toward the window and rested her head against the backrest.

With tears running down her cheeks, she drifted to sleep.

Chapter Two

The car slowing woke her, and Kat rubbed her hands over her bun. It would be nice to pull the pins out and scrub her scalp. And wash her hair, too. Traveling made her feel gross.

She felt like she'd been sleeping forever, but when she cracked her eyes open, the sun was still shining; it wasn't as late as it seemed. "Where are we?" she mumbled. "Are we there yet?"

Aiden swore under his breath, guiding the car to a stop alongside the busy interstate. "No. Fuel pump, I think. When I press on the gas, nothing happens. Honestly, I'm surprised we made it this far."

"It doesn't seem that far."

"It's not. We've been on the road maybe two hours, but we're close to a little town called Harmony. We'll have to call for a tow and hope they have a mechanic so we can keep going." Aiden's lips twisted. "But don't worry, I won't fuck you in the back while we wait."

She didn't know if she should be relieved or insulted. "Why not? I'm not fuckable?"

Aiden scoffed. "I wouldn't touch you with a ten-foot pole. You are *so* not my type."

She sniffed. Of course she wasn't. At least she could tell Nan she didn't have to worry about Aiden using her. He might've been crass about it, but she was sure he'd never spoken truer words in his life.

No, she knew his type. Probably on par with the real Joe Manganiello. Women with legs up to their armpits and hair so blonde if the sun hit it just right, the glare would blind a poor unsuspecting soul.

As she waited while he made the phone call, she leaned against the car, stretching her legs. The traffic flew by them, some spitting sand and small rocks at her. She should wait inside, but she was tired of sitting. The weather was wonderful, and she could've been lying on the beach, or at the hotel's pool, a waiter serving her limitless margaritas.

She scowled.

". . . Sounds good. Thanks." Aiden clicked off his phone and threw it onto the front seat. "They're sending someone out. At least I won't have to pay for this wreck; I took all the insurance Payless offered."

"Think we'll be able to trade it for something better in Harmony?"

"Doubtful. My Maps app said Harmony's population is only nine hundred. Even padding that number, it's a long shot they'll have a car dealership or a car rental company. We're stuck in this thing until we reach Vegas." He kicked the rear tire with the tip of his black dress shoe.

A semi-truck hauling a load of timber screamed past them, and Aiden stepped in front of her, protecting her from the wind and debris the truck kicked up as it roared by.

Vegas.

Huh.

"I've never been to Vegas," she said, leaning into him as another semi thundered by them, shaking the station wagon with the force of its speed.

Aiden grinned at her. "Then this is your lucky day after all."

"Nope. It's going to take a day, maybe longer, for the part to come in. Sorry 'bout that, but you know, that's the way it is." The old mechanic shifted a toothpick from the right side of his mouth to the left. "We got a mighty fine motel up the block, though. Vacancies, too."

Aiden couldn't imagine a time when it would be full.

Dammit.

Nothing he shouldn't have expected, not with the way things were going. And he didn't mean just this past twenty-four hours, either.

"Thanks . . . "

"Elmer," the old man supplied, running his thumbs along a pair of rainbow-colored suspenders that were doing a poor job of keeping up his oil-smeared work jeans.

"Elmer." He nodded and stepped onto the sidewalk outside the mechanic's shop. He was tempted to tell Elmer they would just ditch the car and catch a ride with the parts delivery service, who was, ironically, driving from Vegas, but that wouldn't buy them any extra time, and he couldn't leave the stupid car behind, no matter how much he wanted to.

Katrina sat on the sidewalk, her black and purple flowered skirt swirling in a puddle around her legs. She poked at her phone, her lips pushed into an unhappy pout.

"Do you want the good news or the bad news?"

Pushing her glasses up her nose, she said, "What's the good news?"

"The good news is their motel has vacancies." He leaned against the picture window of the building, the peeling red letters proclaiming, "Elmer's Mechanic Shop—the Best in Harmony."

Probably the only in Harmony.

She sighed. "And the bad news?"

"We have to use it. Elmer doesn't have the part in stock, and we have to wait for it to be delivered."

"That's fine," she said, waving a hand in what he took as an "I don't care" gesture. "As long as I can shower and get some sleep. Coffee?" she asked, raising her eyebrows.

"I didn't ask. I doubt the motel has any complimentary, and even if they do, I wouldn't risk it. Come on, you can't get there sitting on your ass." Aiden held out his hand and grasped the smooth skin of her fingers when she took it.

"Bossy," she muttered, adjusting her purse. "Are you a workaholic or something?"

"I'm an attorney. What do you think?"

"Right."

He walked by her side to the motel, exhaustion dragging his feet.

In the lobby, he checked them in, and a short round woman with purple hair that matched Kat's sweater ran his credit card and gave them single keys on large black plastic key rings.

The motel was like any kind of rundown shithole he'd ever seen, each room having its own door, one right after the next. His room and Katrina's were side by side.

She didn't look at him, simply opened her door and shut it quietly behind her.

Even though she felt like she could sleep for a million years, Kat couldn't relax enough to fall asleep. The air conditioner didn't work, and heat permeated the room. Tossing on the bed, sweat trickling down her neck, she berated herself. She'd been rude to Aiden, not thanking him for paying for her room, and her lack of manners embarrassed her. Her mother raised her better, and she had no excuse.

After a moment of arguing with herself, she knocked on his door intending to apologize and thank him for the money he'd spent on her so far. The rental couldn't have been cheap, and even the dumpy rooms he booked them ran sixty a night. Her heart sank when her knocking yielded no result, but now she was up and moving, she didn't want to sit in her room by herself. All she'd end up doing was trying to call Neil, but that was useless.

She wandered to the motel's lobby, and a sparkling pool caught her eye through the glass back door.

She hitched up her skirt and toed off her sandals. The pool looked clean enough, and she sat on the concrete edge and dipped her feet in. As the cool water swirled around her legs, some of the day's tension eased out of her.

Pulling the pins from her hair, she made a small pile on the textured white concrete. She scrubbed her scalp with her fingernails and rolled her head, wincing when her neck popped. Exhausted, she checked her phone—she'd been awake for sixteen hours, and it was barely evening. She stretched her arms over her head and enjoyed the glittering pink of her toenails as she kicked her feet through the water. Against all her objections, Nan had treated them to a pedicure before the trip, but Kat was grateful for it now.

Old chairs and rusted tables littered the pool area, and it looked as if no one stayed at this motel on a regular basis.

Harmony was in a strange location anyway, between two huge cities—Los Angeles and Las Vegas—and the desolate feeling of the empty town brought to mind a setting for a horror movie. But anyway, they were lucky the place had a mechanic. She wouldn't want to know how much a two-hour tow would cost. It should be illegal for Payless to rent out such a piece of crap, even if all the pilots in the United States did go on strike.

She should have gone with Nan and forgotten the rest of it. She held her hand above her face, the diamond glinting in the sun. Aiden was right—six years was a long time to be engaged.

But she had to keep faith.

Her phone rang, and she hoped it was Aiden, searching for her. Nan's name popped white on the black screen, and she remembered she and Aiden hadn't exchanged phone numbers. That was something they should do, just in case. Looking him up online wasn't an option—she didn't know his last name. Without his phone number, if she lost him, she'd never be able to find him again.

"Hey," she answered before her phone could send her friend's call to voicemail. "Where are you?"

"I'm almost to Santa Barbara," Nan shouted.

"What's happening? What's all that noise?"

"I rented a convertible. Didn't I tell you that? It's hard to talk with the traffic, but I wanted to make sure you were all right."

She swallowed against a lump in her throat, picturing Nan driving a convertible to their hotel, a scarf wrapped around her blonde pin curls, sunglasses shielding her eyes, her mouth painted a strawberry red. It should have been Nan mistaken for a celebrity, not her.

"I'm fine. Aiden's a really nice guy."

"That's his name, huh? What else do you know about him?" Nan asked.

"He's an attorney, lives in Miami, and he was in LA to visit his brother."

"I looked up that picture you mentioned. How did you end up with his arms around you? You two looked pretty cozy, and he's crazy hot."

"Don't start," she objected. "I fell down the escalator, and Aiden caught me at the bottom. I was lucky I didn't get hurt. The photographer just happened to be there. If that idiot wouldn't have been around, Aiden and I would've gone our separate ways, and I would be with you right now."

"Ah-huh. Well, you know what they say, everything happens for a reason."

"Right. Maybe after this Neil will see he really does love me, and he should stop putting off our wedding."

"That's not where I was going with that, but okay. I get that you love the guy, Kat—"

"I do love him," she snapped, not liking Nan's doubtful tone.

She jerked when Aiden caught her eye holding two bags and

two large disposable coffee cups, the familiar green mermaid stark against the white.

"Okay, okay," Nan soothed. "I know you do, honey. But there's love, and then there's *love*. Anyway, the traffic is getting bad, and I'm going to hang up. Check in with me. You don't know this guy, and maybe he's only trying to earn your trust."

She sighed. "He's not like that, but I'll keep you posted. Have a good time and say hi to the rest of the girls for me."

"Ask Aiden to take you out on the town for your bir-th-day. Bye, bye, baby," Nan sang, and giggled wildly.

"Bye," Kat whispered, but Nan already hung up.

Aiden hated seeing the dejected slump to Katrina's shoulders. He hated hearing even more that she loved her moron fiancé, though he had no right to feel that way. Scowling, he held out the coffee and bag pretending he hadn't heard a word of the conversation.

"I thought you might be hungry, and earlier you asked for coffee. Thank God for commerce—there's a Starbucks a block away."

"Thank you," she said holding out her hands.

Her ring gleamed on her finger—the same rock he watched her admire before she answered her phone. Aiden bought an engagement ring for a woman once—she hadn't admired it the way Katrina admired hers.

And now it lay at the bottom of the Atlantic Ocean.

"I don't know what you like, so I ordered you a café mocha, and there's a ham and Swiss cheese sandwich in the bag. Unfortunately, there aren't many places to eat around here. Maureen, the woman who checked us in, said if someone wants to eat anywhere fancy, they drive to Vegas. Makes sense, but I wouldn't be happy having to drive two hours every time I wanted a decent meal." He snapped his mouth shut. He was an attorney for God's sake. He knew how to speak efficiently and professionally. He hadn't spent a whole day with this woman and she already turned him into a babbling buffoon.

"That's fine, thanks. I looked for you earlier. I feel bad I haven't said thank you for the rental car and the rooms. You're spending a lot of money on me, and you should let me pay for some stuff. You're doing me a huge favor, and I wouldn't blame you if you left me here." Kat sipped her coffee and let out a shuddery breath.

Aiden kicked off his shoes and sat on the white concrete near her. After rolling his dress pants up to his knees, he dipped his feet into the pool. "I'm not leaving you here." He sipped his coffee. Plain black. Strong. Just the way he liked it. "You have beautiful hair," he said, tempted to run his fingers through it. The waves looked soft and silky, and the strands glistened in the sunlight as bright as her diamond did. "Why do you wear it up?"

"Neil likes it that way."

"I see," he said, but he didn't, not really.

She huffed. "I'm glad someone does. Thanks for the food. I think I'm going to eat in my room, shower, if I dare, and get some sleep. When will the car be done?"

He shrugged, oddly hurt. The minute he sat down, she wanted to leave. He heard plain enough she loved her fiancé, and maybe she didn't want him to get any ideas. She didn't have to worry about that, though what he told her earlier was only partially true. He *wouldn't* touch her with a ten-foot pole. Not knowing what he knew about her, and about what he'd recently learned about himself.

But she was his type.

She was definitely his type.

"Come on, I'll walk you to your room," he offered, standing. He gathered his socks and shoes, and tucked his own sandwich under his arm. "I don't know when the car will be done. Hopefully tomorrow. If the part is delivered in the morning, and Elmer works on it right away, we could be out of here by late afternoon."

"That's if our luck turns around," she said, following him into the motel's lobby.

"We can't have bad luck forever," he said, though that wasn't true. It seemed the last two months of his life were nothing but incidents of bad luck, one taking up where the last one stopped.

"Speak for yourself," she said before pushing her way into her room.

Not having a retort, he only opened his door and shut it behind him.

As far as rooms in a grubby motel went, it was okay. Faded blue wallpaper covered the walls, and the comforter that used to be the same color, or had tried to be, covered the mattress. He turned on the TV, clicked the channels up until he found ESPN to drown out his thoughts, and settled on the bed.

The coffee soothed his soul, and he sipped quickly while the brew remained hot. He'd bought the same sandwich he'd chosen for Katrina, and he devoured it in four bites. He should have asked Maureen if there was someplace they could eat a real breakfast, but he didn't hold out much hope, unless there was a little mom and pop diner that could fry some eggs. Not something he would be opposed to; eggs were difficult to fuck up.

He just hoped this would be the only night they would have to stay here.

Maybe he could convince Katrina to spend the night in Vegas. They could at least have a decent night's sleep and a better shower. They could buy some clothes. He smelled, but he'd much rather wait to shower and change into something clean.

He stripped to his boxers and white under-tank and wondered what Katrina would sleep in. Panties and her bra? Not needing that visual planted in his head, he lowered the volume on the TV and closed the blinds. Even with the sun still shining, it wouldn't take him very long to fall asleep, and he was dead to the world the minute his head hit the pillow.

Until a scream sliced through Katrina's side of the thin wall.

He didn't waste time putting on his clothes, and he bolted to her room, cursing her and praising her at the same time for not locking her door. "What? What is it?" he asked, his chest heaving, his lungs trying to draw in a breath. Panting, half asleep, he wildly searched for an intruder or a thief—or worse, a rapist or a kidnapper.

Katrina stood on her bed, her hand covering her mouth, trying to hold in another scream. "There, on the floor! Oh my God, what is that thing?"

Aiden squinted. The industrial-grade brown carpet hid everything, just like it was meant to do.

Then it moved.

"You're screaming over a scorpion?" He sighed. "Just don't step on it, and you'll be fine."

"'Just don't step on it'? Are you *crazy?*"

"Don't you have scorpions in Minnesota?"

"No!"

He wracked his sleep-fogged brain. While the sight of a scorpion didn't rattle him, he didn't want to touch it to get rid of it, either.

Then he realized what Katrina was wearing, and all thought of *anything* left his brain. She'd taken off her skirt, and while she was short, her legs seemed to go on forever. The apex of her thighs disappeared under the hem of her lilac sweater, but the material didn't quite cover the curve of her ass, revealing lacy pink panties.

His mouth dried.

"Aiden!"

He jerked his gaze away. "What do you want me to do?"

"Kill it or something."

If he was wearing shoes, he could have stepped on it, like any other insect pest he didn't want bothering him, biting him, or maiming or killing him, but he was barefoot as well. "I need to get my shoes."

"Don't leave me alone with that thing."

He scrubbed at his beard. "I can't kill it, and I don't have anything to use to capture it and put it outside."

"Can I go to your room with you?"

He sincerely doubted his room was bug-free, but he wouldn't tell her that. She could have an anxiety attack and want to leave the motel. Only, there wasn't anywhere else to go, especially with no car. "Yeah, I guess so."

He turned to leave.

"Can you, I mean, I don't want to get down."

Giving Stan the Scorpion a large berth, he approached the bed. "Come on then," he muttered.

Kat folded her arms around his neck and wrapped her legs around his hips. "Thank you," she whispered.

Aiden snaked his arms around her, weaving his fingers into her hair. "Yeah," he said, taking just a moment to bury his face into her neck and breathe in her scent.

He hardened, uncomfortably, as her lithe body molded to his, but there was no way he was touching her. He'd lie awake all night if that's what he needed to do to keep his hands off her.

She clung to him for dear life as he walked her back to his room.

"I'll just sleep in the chair," she said into his ear.

"Are you sure? You don't have to." She didn't have to, but it would it would be a lot easier to tolerate her in his room.

"I'll be fine."

"If you say so," he said, setting her into a chair covered in brown Naugahyde.

She drew her feet up, her heels digging into the edge of the seat and pulled her sweater over her knees. "I'll be fine," she repeated, but her voice lacked any conviction.

Smart enough to know when not to argue—this wasn't his first rodeo—Aiden fell into bed. Exhaustion weighed him down, but he wasn't dozing for more than a second when sniffling filtered through the air.

"Katrina?" he mumbled, burrowing into the bed. For a ratty motel, the place had amazing pillows. He hoped they weren't full of bedbugs.

"I'm fine."

He sat up and pulled the comforter over his chest. "No, you're not. What's wrong?" Besides the fact she was suffering from sleep-deprivation.

"I might be a little homesick."

"First time away from home?" He'd believe that. Small town country girl, all alone in the big city for the first time.

"Oh, no. I like to travel. Just, you know. Neil is mad at me, I'm missing my birthday party, and I'm inconveniencing you."

His eyes adjusted to the darkness; Katrina sat with her cheek pressed into her knee. "You're not an inconvenience. True, there are better ways for me to spend my vacation, but look, I get to see some of the country . . . a pretty woman is some nice scenery, too. A road trip isn't that bad, but I would enjoy it more if my travel buddy would stop crying."

She made a sound that was half hiccup and half laugh. "Do you mean it?"

"If we don't make the best of it, we'll both be miserable," he said. "Now, come on, this bed has plenty of room for both of us. Things will look a lot better after some sleep. I promise."

"Okay. I mean, thanks. Watch out."

He slid over just in time.

She jumped from the chair onto the bed, jostling him, his head thumping against the cheap headboard.

"Damn. A little notice would have been nice." He slid under the sheets and comforter and adjusted the pillow.

"Sorry," she said, scrambling into the bedding. "I didn't want to touch the floor."

"Go to sleep. I've been awake just as long as you have."

"Sorry," she said again. "Goodnight, Aiden. Thank you for all you're doing for me."

"No problem."

And it wasn't a problem, not now.

But he was sure it would be.

"You know, you look nothing like her."

Kat took her eyes off the road for a moment to arch an eyebrow at him.

Aiden slouched in the passenger's seat of the old station wagon, his knees propped against the dash. The driver's seat and the passenger's seat were connected, and with her height, or lack thereof, to reach the pedals she'd needed to scoot the seat up as far as it would go. That gave him no leg room, and she told him to spread out in the backseat, but he'd refused.

Now he was twisted like a pretzel, and all she could do was shake her head and try not to tell him, "I told you so." Luckily, Vegas was only half an hour away.

"Whom?" she asked, her eyes on the road again. She was a decent driver, and she wanted to prove to him she wasn't a scared little nobody. Driving the two hours to Vegas from Harmony, giving him a chance to sip his coffee and relax, would hopefully be a good start.

"Anna Kendrick. I don't see it."

"Oh, yeah. What's crazy is I've never been compared to her before, which is good, since I don't usually like her movies. *The Accountant* was pretty cool, but I watched that for Ben Affleck. *Up in the Air*, I guess, but George Clooney made that movie. I liked *Pitch Perfect*. You look a lot like him, though. Joe, I mean."

He groaned. "I've been told. Have you seen *Magic Mike*? I get a lot of grief for that movie. One Christmas, my brother, Dylan, bought me stripper lessons for a present."

She shook her head. "No, it's not my kind of thing."

That movie totally *was* her kind of thing, but she couldn't watch things like that without Neil getting pissy at her. He said it made her seem like an airheaded idiot, and he preferred it when she watched documentaries on Netflix. She didn't mind those, and before her trip, she watched an interesting one about Bigfoot.

"Did you take them?" she asked, pursing her lips together against a grin, picturing Aiden gyrating against a pole.

He scoffed. "No. I'm not into stuff like that. Dylan ended up using them, and he dated the teacher for a while, too."

"That's too bad. I bet the pictures would have been fun to look at." She paused. "Thanks again for letting me sleep with you last night." She kept her eyes on the road, a blush crawling up her neck. She shouldn't have thanked him—all it did was bring up the awkward way he was holding her when she woke up. Spooning her, his morning wood pressed against her butt, his arms wrapped around her.

It'd been strange, lying in bed with a man, but it was lovely waking up in someone's arms. It made her realize . . . well, nothing that mattered anyway.

"You're welcome," he said, looking away. "Good news is," he mumbled toward his window, "there won't be any scorpions in Las Vegas."

"You mean they don't gamble?" She liked teasing him a little; liked the way his cheeks turned just a slight shade of pink.

He slanted his eyes at her. "Oh, they play, but they're too rich for us. They get VIP treatment in the back. Goddamned whales."

She laughed.

"You don't mind we're making another stop, do you?" he asked.

Kat sobered. She should mind. She should mind the extra night. In fact, it would be more than a night. They could make it as far as Utah, maybe even Colorado, if they stayed on the main interstate and drove as far as they could before they needed to stop again to rest. She had a good night's sleep after all, and besides needing a shower, she felt wonderful. Rested. Buzzed. But that could have been the caffeine from the coffee Aiden had been sharing with her since they left Harmony.

Because it definitely wasn't his company.

"I never took a shower last night, and sleeping in a proper room without extra guests won't be so bad," she said, veering toward the exit Aiden said would spit them out in Las Vegas. "And I need clothes, even if I don't want to stop. I can't wear these the whole way there. I want to get home as soon as possible, but we need to be smart. Plus, you're going to trade this car in for something else, right?"

They'd been lucky—with the new fuel pump, they hadn't had any problems. True, they'd been on the road for only an hour and a half, but no point in tempting fate.

"Right. I'm sorry about your suitcase. We should have stayed long enough to pick it up," he said, throwing his empty coffee cup onto the floor in the back.

"The airport will keep it, won't they? For a while? I'll get it back, and you were right. If we hadn't gotten to the car rental place when we did, we might not even have had this car to drive."

Aiden tried to adjust his legs to no avail. "I would have bought something from a dealership. I'll get you home, Katrina, I promise."

"I know. I trust you." And she did. Maybe it was the look in his eyes, or the sincerity in his voice, or the way he hadn't tried anything funny while she was in his bed, but she trusted him.

"Trading in this piece of shit won't take long—we really don't have to stop overnight," he insisted.

"I appreciate it, but it's fine. You need a shower and fresh clothes, too."

"If you're sure—I don't want you pissed at me later."

"It's okay. Stop talking about it. Do you know how to get there?"

Aiden laughed. "Honey, you'll find the way."

She didn't know what he meant until signs began to dot the sides of the interstate.

Kat wiggled in her seat in excitement as they began to pass billboards proclaiming free buffets, the largest payouts of any casino in Vegas, and famous performers. She should have been worried about wasting time, but after she married Neil, she'd never have the chance to do anything like this again. Her blood ran cold at the thought, and she gripped the steering wheel as if she could head off the inevitable.

After handing over their car to the valet, who, to his credit, didn't bat an eyelash at the ugly 1970s station wagon, Aiden led her inside the lobby.

Kat stepped into another world.

The ceiling loomed stories above them, and large, clear plastic balls hung from transparent wires, giving Kat the impression she stood under layers of bubbles.

Decorated in black and silver, the lobby sparkled. The walls were painted black and framed with silver piping. Black tiles covered the floor and glittered with flecks of silver.

She followed Aiden farther into the lobby, dragging her carry-on behind her, and more plastic balls rolled along the floor as she pushed them away with her toes. A silver runner guided them to the bank of reservation desks along the back wall.

Black tables were scattered throughout the lobby, and silver mermaid sculptures gazed at guests with longing.

The intense black should have made the room appear dark, but somehow, it didn't.

While she waited for Aiden, she picked up one of the huge balls. Light, like a beach ball, and made with clear plastic, Kat tossed it into the air, and bouncing, it landed with some others a few feet away.

"What is this place?" Kat asked as Aiden spoke with the reservation agent.

The woman's clothing matched the rest of the décor: black skirt, silver blouse under a black blazer.

"Blackout. My favorite casino," Aiden said, sliding his credit card across the counter. It blended into the sparkling black lacquer.

"You've been to Vegas before?"

"I haven't been lately, too busy at work. Come on," he said, smiling at the woman who gave him a thin stack of paper, "we need clothes."

They walked by a floor-to-ceiling aquarium, and Kat stopped to stare. The back wall of the enormous tank was painted black; silver light illuminated fish that didn't care they were being gawked at. They glided through the water, blank expressions on their flat faces. "What kind of fish are those?" she asked, gently tapping on the glass.

"Piranhas."

"Ew," she said, stepping back.

Aiden chuckled. "They're just for show, but when the staff feeds them it's interesting to watch. Come on."

Kat followed him down a black-carpeted corridor, and they stopped outside the entrance to an elegant boutique.

"This is Luna Noir," Aiden said, nudging her shoulder. "And next door is Sephora. I think that's makeup? Buy your body wash and stuff in there. Here's your keycard. I'll be over there," he tilted his head toward a gentleman's clothing store, "to buy some clothes, too. Can you find your room on your own if we split up?"

Kat nodded. She could handle a casino. Even if her whole neighborhood could fit into the building.

She should take advantage of the situation and ask him for his cell phone number. Not because she thought she'd get into trouble and need to call, but the idea of him . . . disappearing . . . churned her stomach way more than it should have.

"Katrina?" Aiden asked. "Will you be all right, or do you want me to stay with you?"

She wanted him to stay with her, all right. "I'll be fine, but maybe we could swap cell numbers?"

Aiden pulled his phone from his pocket. "That's a good idea. What's yours?"

After they exchanged numbers, he strode down the hallway oozing confidence and disappeared into the luxe gentleman's store that, from the outside, appeared to be more of a club than a boutique.

What he'd wear for the rest of the trip made her curious. He'd traveled wearing a suit. Would he buy more? What did he look like in jeans? Jeans and a tight-fitting t-shirt . . .

Kat fingered her dirty skirt and brushed at her sweater streaked with, she didn't know what. Mustard, maybe, from her sandwich yesterday. It was time to get rid of these crappy clothes.

Neil preferred she wear modest clothing, but he wasn't here now and she could have a little fun. Besides, she'd never get to do this again. They'd get married, have a couple of babies, and settle into domestic bliss.

A saleswoman clearing her throat jerked Kat out of her nightm— *For God's sake.* Domestic bliss with Neil wasn't a nightmare. She felt like throwing up only because she was tired and hungry.

"Miss Ford?"

She blinked, confused the saleswoman knew her name.

"Mercedes at the front desk told me to watch for you? You need new clothes, yes?"

"Yes, yes, I do," Kat said, tossing her greasy hair over her shoulder.

Screw Neil. He wasn't answering her calls, and he wasn't here. She'd do what she liked.

While she still could.

"This wasn't the plan."

"Does anything ever go according to plan?" Aiden mumbled, ruffling through a display of jeans, the hangers squealing on the rack. He hated everything. All he needed was a good old-fashioned pair of jeans.

"Dylan told me you're driving some chick somewhere. Where you headed, anyway?"

He forgot about Nick, his best friend. Nick, whom he planned to meet at Dylan's place for a couple weeks of R & R.

"I'm sorry. I . . . forgot." He positioned his phone away from his mouth. "Do you have anything . . . plain?"

The salesman, a young guy with a neat goatee, dressed in black like everyone who worked at Blackout, nodded. "Two racks behind you."

"Thanks," Aiden said, turning around. He didn't need stones glued to his pockets, or silver thread holding the seams together.

"Is she hot?" Nick asked.

Was Katrina hot? Aiden supposed she was. He remembered her legs wrapped around his waist as he carried her to his room, the length of her body cuddled into his while they slept. "She's gorgeous, but that has nothing to do with it. She's engaged, and I'm not doing that again. I'm helping her because of the pilots' strike, that's all."

"That's not what Dylan said."

The store had two pairs of jeans in his size. He grabbed both of them, a package of boxers, and a package of white ribbed tanks he wore in lieu of an undershirt.

He pulled two dress shirts off a bar hanging from the wall, black, of course, but they'd look okay with the jeans. "And just what did my brother say?" He assessed his pile on the counter by the register. He wasn't thrilled about wearing his dress shoes for the rest of the trip, and he mouthed, "Shoes?" to the sales guy folding his dress shirts.

"Against the back wall."

Aiden nodded his thanks.

"He showed me the picture. You two looked pretty cozy," Nick said. "What are you doing?"

"I'm at Blackout," Aiden said, making a beeline for the small shoe department.

"Without me?" Nick asked, hurt. "You always ask me to go with you."

"Katrina's never been to Vegas."

Shit. He'd need a new suit. He couldn't very well bring Katrina to Vegas and not give her the full treatment. He hoped she would buy a nice dress. And it was her birthday. He needed to make a reservation at Top Hat for dinner. A cake. Katrina should have a cake.

"That's her name? Katrina? She looks like Anna Kendrick. If Anna Kendrick wore ugly glasses."

"She does not," Aiden said, choosing a pair of loafers to wear with his jeans.

"She doesn't what? Look like Anna Kendrick, or wear ugly glasses?"

"Neither," he muttered. "Look, I have to go. We stayed in a slum last night because the car broke down, and there was no way I was going to shower in that pit."

"Wait," Nick said in a rush. "Samantha asked me to call."

Aiden's mouth dried at the mention of his ex's name. Nick's announcement stunned him. He sank onto a bench meant for customers to use to try on shoes, and he waved off a salesman who approached to help.

"Why? Isn't she on her fucking honeymoon? She doesn't give two shits about me."

"She didn't go through with it. Aiden, she wants to talk to you."

"I'll . . . I'll . . . need to think about it," he muttered. He couldn't do this now. He needed a hot shower and a drink.

Not in that order.

"She feels terrible."

"Yeah, well, so do I," he snapped. "Look, have fun at Dylan's, he'll be more than happy to fuck around with you. Natalie dumped him again. I'm sorry I forgot about our plans and I'll make it up to you."

"You can make it up to me by calling Samantha," Nick said. "She's been—"

Aiden hung up.

He didn't need this bullshit.

The hovering salesman eye caught his eye, and he hurried over the sparkling tile. "I need a black suit. Coat, forty-six long. Silver tie. Slacks, thirty-four, thirty-six. Can you charge all that and the rest of my clothes to my room and deliver everything upstairs?"

"Right away, Mr. Price. Don't worry about a thing."

"Thank you." Aiden grabbed his carry-on and pulled it toward the elevator bank.

On the cusp of an anxiety attack, he jabbed at the UP button and bent at the waist, trying to suck in air. He grappled with his tie for a moment, desperately trying to loosen it to give himself room to breathe, but he wasn't wearing one.

The elevator doors opened, and he quickly punched the DOOR CLOSED button to prevent anyone from using the same elevator.

He needed to be alone.

Samantha hadn't gotten married.

406, blessedly, was located only two doors down from the elevator.

Blackout's hallways were decorated in black and silver, accented with one bright color. A sizzling electric blue exploded in this dim corridor, but he didn't appreciate the decorator's efforts, only shoved his keycard into the slot and slammed the door of his room behind him.

He rushed to the mini bar and dumped the contents of the first bottle his fingers met into a lowball crystal-cut glass.

After he knocked it back, the alcohol invaded his system, and he poured another, gulping that one, too, the second after he poured it. Perspiration and anxiety dampened his skin, and he sat on the bench at the end of his king-sized bed and smoothed the sweat from his forehead.

Someone knocked on his door, and Aiden sucked in a breath of filtered hotel air before answering it.

The concierge stood holding his boxes of clothing.

After tipping him, he dropped the boxes, uninterested.

He'd been looking forward to taking Katrina out for her

birthday, but now all he craved was time alone. Time alone to lick wounds he thought had healed—or, at the very least, scabbed over.

He pulled the envelope from the side pocket of his carry-on and sat on his bed. The bed he'd be sleeping in alone.

No scorpions at Blackout.

Just like he promised.

Aiden ran his fingertips over the swirls of his name on the front.

After pulling the scented pages from the pink envelope, he began to read.

The jeans cost more than she made in a month at her job.

Kat left her carry-on near the door and wandered around the store. No one would know by looking at her, but she loved clothes and once, a long time ago, she'd dreamed of opening a boutique like this. Racks and racks of jeans, blouses, dresses. A wall full of purses, jewelry.

And shoes, oh the shoes.

Luna Noir's floor gleamed silver, the walls black, but the clothes were a mix of bright colors. She wandered to the dress section located in the back corner near the fitting rooms. Dresses upon dresses filled the space: silk, chiffon, tulle, and more gems than she could count.

She longed to try on everything, but the prices were astronomical. That was one thing she always said about the boutique she would open. There would be a mix of clothing—she wanted everyone to be able to shop in her store.

Of course, this was Vegas, and on the Strip. Blackout's guests were given the total Vegas experience, and that included designer clothing at Luna Noir.

Kat fingered the smooth silk of an emerald green blouse. She wouldn't be able to replace any of her clothes.

She sighed in dejection and grasped the handle of her carry-on.

"Miss Ford? There's nothing of interest to you? Perhaps the boutique down the corridor?" The saleswoman stopped Kat with a worried frown.

Unless the boutique was a Debbie's Discounts and Thrift Store, she wouldn't be able to afford anything there, either. "No, it's not that. These clothes are beautiful, I just can't afford . . ."

The wrinkles in the woman's forehead smoothed and a smile replaced the unhappy pucker of her lips. "Don't worry about that, Miss Ford. Mr. Price told us to bill his room for your purchases."

Aiden Price.

That was his name. Odd she hadn't known his full name until now.

It fit him.

"Oh, but I really couldn't—"

The saleswoman stared pointedly from Kat's toes to the top of her head. "Excuse me for saying so, Miss Ford, but, yes, you really should."

Because Kat couldn't argue, she did.

The next time she headed toward the door, her arms were laden with bags. She'd chosen two pairs of jeans, three gorgeous blouses, and a dress for the evening. Made from a thick cream Spandex material, small, jagged pieces of mirror covered the entire dress. It sparkled, the bits of reflective glass glinting in the light of the fitting room. Silky spaghetti straps would do little to keep the dress in place, and the hem barely covered her rump. She wanted to dance with joy. She swore she'd seen a celebrity wearing that very dress in an issue of Vogue.

She hoped she'd have a chance to wear it, that Aiden wouldn't want to order room service and stay in all night.

With all the excitement, Kat forgot it was her birthday.

The big two-nine.

Maybe as a gift to herself she'd have a mid-life crisis. Kind of.

Not quite midlife, but it wasn't too difficult to feel panicky when she thought of all she *hadn't* done with her life yet.

In Sephora, though she browsed, she bought the bare minimum, and the saleswoman took pity on her, throwing two handfuls of samples into her bag.

Kat charged shampoo, conditioner, and body wash to her own credit card. She may not be able to afford to shop in Luna Noir, but she could buy the vanilla birthday cake body wash—even if it cost more than she'd ever spend under normal circumstances. She asked about a razor, and as the woman shoved her receipt into the bag, said the rooms were equipped with razors, curling irons, and hairdryers.

Pleased she'd have everything she needed to clean up and dress for the evening, Kat hummed on her way to the fourth floor. Her room number was 408, one down from Aiden's.

She thought better of knocking on his door, wanting to be a bit more presentable the next time he saw her.

Fishing the keycard Aiden gave her out of her purse, she juggled her bags. When she lifted her arms, she caught a whiff of herself.

Ick.

And Aiden had shared a car with her for two hours this morning.

The poor man.

It seemed he was a poor man, too, never quite looking happy. And the pink envelope puzzled her.

Maybe it was a love letter.

She shouldn't be worried about him; it wasn't her business.

When she pushed open the door to her room, she caught her breath.

Holy crap.

Letting the door bump shut behind her, she stepped into the suite, dazed, her ragged sandals sinking into the plush carpeting. The room, decorated, of course, like the rest of the casino, gleamed black and silver, bright teal accents catching her eye.

Determined to enjoy herself despite her guilty conscience when she thought of Aiden's wallet, she fell backward onto the king-sized bed, giggling.

She wouldn't let herself grow too close to him, but she'd have fun, turn the road trip into something to remember. She owed herself that for what she was giving up.

Running hot water into the black sunken tub, Kat placed shampoo, conditioner, and body gel along the rim. As an afterthought, she squeezed some of the vanilla buttercrème scented body wash into the running water and grinned at the bubbles. She couldn't remember the last time she'd taken a bubble bath. Neil always lectured her about wasting water, even if she was the one paying the utility bill.

Sometimes she thought he poked at her to intentionally make her miserable, and it always worked. It was her one promise to always see to his happiness, and she tried like hell, giving up every little bit of hers. It was never enough.

Torn between coffee and pouring herself a glass of wine from the minibar, she made herself a mug of coffee with a teal Keurig sitting on the speckled black counter near a massive flat screen TV.

As the water ran, she sipped her coffee and looked over what she could see of Las Vegas.

She listened to Melissa Etheridge on her phone while she soaked. Maybe she should call Nan. No, she wasn't in the mood for another lecture.

Her cell chimed with a text while she shaved her legs, and she wiped her fingers on a dry washcloth before she looked at it.

Meet me downstairs in the lobby in two hours? Aiden asked.

That gave her plenty of time to finish bathing and dry her hair. *Yes!!!* she replied.

She paused. Perhaps she shouldn't be so excited about spending time with a man she just met.

But, that had been the plan, to have a sinful one-night stand in Santa Barbara. Or maybe more than one.

She wouldn't use Aiden like that, of course, but she could be his friend. There wasn't any harm in being his friend, and it seemed like he needed one.

Cheered by the thought, she ducked her head to finish her bath and dress for her first and only evening out in Las Vegas.

Kat surprised herself by being ready with half an hour to spare. She turned out rather pretty, if she did say so herself, though she'd forgotten what it felt like to dress this way. Sexy dress, high heels. Hair and makeup done. And . . . no ugly glasses. She'd been in the process of shoving them onto her face when she realized she didn't need to, and in a childish act of defiance, she stuck her tongue out at them on her way out of the bathroom.

She decided to wait for Aiden downstairs, and after stepping into the quiet lobby, she pulled her phone out of her purse to call Neil. Just to see if he would answer.

She'd never known him to be angry at her. Full of disdain, yes. Indifference. Annoyance. Irritation. But he'd never ignored her before, and it made her sick to her stomach.

Reaching his full voicemail didn't surprise her, as he didn't do anything for himself—that included any type of cleaning—and she left the message she would have, if there'd been room. "Hey, Neil." She cleared her throat. "It's me. I'm driving to Minnesota, because, you know, of the pilots' strike. I'm going as fast as I can. I know you're angry, but you don't have to be. It's only a picture. I'd fallen down an escalator at the airport—" She choked in distress and tried to keep the misery from seeping into her voice. "He broke my fall. I would think you'd be happy I wasn't hurt. Anyway—"

Someone came up behind her.

"Excuse me, Miss, have you seen a—"

Kat turned toward the voice, still speaking into her phone. "—I love you," she mumbled, meeting Aiden's blue eyes. "Bye," she whispered. She lowered the phone to her side. She didn't press Disconnect; the recording had hung up several moments ago.

"Katrina," he finished, a light dimming in his eyes.

"Aiden, hi." She blushed. Dammit. He heard her stupid message.

"You look fantastic," he said, his gaze sweeping from her head to her toes.

"Thanks. I was just on the phone with—"

"No need to explain. I, ah, made my own phone calls upstairs," he said, scrubbing his beard. "Are you ready to have a little fun?"

Kat squashed her disappointment and forced a smile. It was good he'd heard her. She couldn't start something that in no way she could finish.

"Let's go." Placing her hand in the crook of his arm, she allowed him to escort her across the lobby.

Aiden didn't sit and brood for long.

Nick could beg on his sister's behalf all he wanted, but the fact was, he needed time to process the information.

And there would be plenty of time to think about things. He didn't know how many times they'd stop, but Katrina would want to start making time on the road. While he agreed with her that this stop had been necessary, there wouldn't be any reason to do more than take bathroom and meal breaks the rest of the way. If he were lucky, the strike would end in time for him to fly out of her hometown. Or city. Wherever the hell she lived.

He stood under the hot spray of the shower while he let his mind drift. He hadn't minded letting Katrina share his bed last night—he couldn't lie, scorpions creeped him out, too—but it would be nice to get a decent night's sleep without worrying about what insects were crawling around on his floor.

He dressed in the suit he purchased downstairs and pulled out one of the few pairs of socks he packed in his carry-on. Because of Nick, he forgot to buy a new package.

He shouldn't answer his phone anymore.

Even if Samantha's name popped up on his screen.

Especially if Samantha's name popped up on his screen.

On the way to the lobby, he pictured what Katrina would be wearing. Jeans and a turtleneck? Maybe a dress—the hem dragging on the floor the way she preferred. No cleavage, obviously. Not that he wanted to see it.

If she bound her hair in a bun for her fiancé, she probably dressed like a nun for him, too.

Aiden couldn't understand that. He'd loved going out on the town with Samantha. Her body had more curves than a road snaking up a mountainside, and he'd loved showing her off. It hadn't been her attractiveness that got them into trouble. She'd been faithful in a strange sort of way.

Right on time, he roamed the lobby, kicked at a few clear balls. He circled back to the elevator banks, but there wasn't any sign of Katrina. A short brunette, with her back to him, stood by an elevator, but he dismissed her. The woman was dressed too provocatively to be Katrina.

While he watched the piranhas swim, he let another five minutes go by. Maybe Katrina had come down and decided to explore the casino. She could have gotten lost.

He checked his phone, but the screen remained blank—no texts from her. That could be good or bad. Slipping it into his pocket, he approached the brunette wearing a creamy, sparkly dress, her wavy dark brown hair brushing the curve of her lower back.

Some lucky man would wind the silky strands around his fingers while he—

Whoa.

Samantha hadn't been that long ago. He needed to get it together.

"Excuse me, Miss, have you seen a—"

She turned around, holding a cell phone to her ear. ". . . I love you," she whispered, meeting his eyes. "Bye," she murmured, finishing the call.

He swallowed, unsure if it was the words she was speaking or the way she dressed that made his fingertips numb. "Katrina," he rasped.

Katrina lowered her phone and blushed.

She'd finally gotten a hold of her fiancé then. He was happy for her. "You look fantastic."

Her heels gave her a few more inches, though she was still shorter than the women he normally dated. But they did wonderful things to her legs, and her dress hugged her in all the right places. Her mahogany hair draped, glistening down her back, her makeup impeccable.

She looked delicious, and not at all like the woman he met at the airport.

"Thanks, I was just on the phone with—"

"No need to explain. I, ah, made my own phone calls upstairs," he lied. Let her think he was taken. He could be if he wanted to be, and it would be better for him—help keep some distance between them. "Are you ready to have a little fun?"

Katrina smiled, holding onto his arm, and he looked away to keep her from seeing the strained expression that he was sure was on his face.

"Let's go."

Chapter Three

The restaurant was decorated in an Alice-in-Wonderland-type theme.

Mimicking the lobby and the bubbles, top hats hung from the ceiling, and the tables were made of clear glass cubes with life-like sculptures shining brightly inside them.

The host, dressed to the nines in tails, white gloves, and a top hat (all that was missing was a cane), showed them to a cube where fairies were suspended in mid-flight over a pond filled with waterlilies, frogs, and water sprites.

At least, the fairies looked frozen in flight, but Kat blinked, and it seemed as if the fairies' wings moved and the water rippled.

Each table had its own mini chandelier, and at their table, the lights were pink, casting a watermelon glow over the silverware and plates.

"Champagne?" the waiter asked, and Aiden nodded.

"I've never been in a place like this," Kat said, peering through the glass. She would have bet her new dress one of the frogs slithered out a tongue to capture a fly.

"Top Hat is all magic."

"It looks like it," she agreed, and smiled as a waiter brought a magnum of champagne to their table.

He poured an inch into a flute for Aiden. He sipped and nodded his approval.

The waiter poured them flutes of the bubbly gold liquid, and the production he made fascinated her. She was about as far away from Red Lobster as she could get.

"What are we celebrating?" she asked, after trying a mouthful of the bubbly fizz. The champagne popped on her tongue.

"It's your birthday, isn't it? Today?"

Kat gazed at him over her glass. He looked so handsome in his black suit, his broad shoulders filling out his jacket. He and Neil were nothing alike. Where Neil was on the shorter side for a man, and blond, Aiden topped six feet, his hair darker than coal. And Aiden's beard—yummy. She never dated a man who'd grown out his facial hair. His beard gave him an air of importance, intelligence. It probably helped him win in court. The jury would fall in love with him and believe every word he said.

She blushed. "Yeah. Thank you for remembering."

"You're welcome. You only turn . . ."

"Twenty-nine," she supplied.

". . . Twenty-nine, once. And in Vegas, no less. Might as well enjoy it."

That's what she'd been telling herself. But dammit, she should have been with Nan, partying, screwing a guy she'd never see again.

Screwing a guy she didn't *want* to see again.

She gulped at her champagne to wet her mouth, and her blood began to hum.

Or it could have been the way Aiden was looking at her.

"Right."

"Do you want to tell me a little about yourself?" he asked, handing her a leather-bound menu.

She didn't but being they were virtual strangers, they'd have to talk about themselves eventually, or they'd have a very long trip ahead of them. Maybe the next vehicle Aiden rented would have a working stereo, and they could listen to some music.

It would take the pressure off to force communication neither of them wanted.

She wrinkled her nose. "How about you start?"

"Well," he said, then cleared his throat. "Uh."

He didn't want to talk any more than she did. She felt somewhat better about her own reluctance, but it also made her curious.

She skimmed her menu; she wouldn't press him to talk. Maybe he had a problem getting close to people, or maybe he didn't think it was worth it. It wasn't as if they were going to end the road trip best friends. He'd drop her off, and that would be that.

"The steak here is good," Aiden said, filling in the silence that settled over the table. "You aren't a vegetarian, or a vegan, are you?"

Pressing her eyelids against the tears that suddenly threatened to spill down her cheeks, she shook her head. She wouldn't cry, she wouldn't cry. There was nothing to cry over.

She jumped when he touched her arm. "Are you okay?"

Kat pulled away and swiped at her nose with her napkin. "Yeah, sorry. I know you told me to stop crying. Just emotional, I guess."

"Katrina, I didn't mean—"

Before he could finish, a waiter approached their table, and Aiden glared at him for interrupting. She rattled off her order before Aiden could send him away, the first steak entrée she found on the menu.

A magic show began in the center of the room, saving her from trying to make polite conversation after all. She watched, entranced, as a roly-poly man dressed in a tuxedo elaborately waving a black wand pulled rabbits out of hats and made doves disappear into wads of colorful scarves. The tricks were common, but she had never seen a magic show in person, and they did seem like magic to her.

She caught Aiden's eye and smiled. Things would work out.

They had to. All she had to do was believe in magic. And maybe throw in a little bit of Fate.

After a delicious meal of steak, twice baked potatoes, and some kind of creamed corn that looked like gold and tasted better, Aiden nodded toward the corner of the restaurant. A waiter approached them, holding a large platter with a silver cake placed in the middle, and silver sparklers fizzed from the center.

"Happy birthday, Katrina," Aiden said.

The waiter set the platter in front of her, and the frosting glittered like aluminum foil, the sparklers' fire burned her eyes, the heat warmed her skin.

This was the sweetest thing anyone had ever done for her.

Anyone.

Ever.

The vehicles, the hotel rooms, the clothes. Now this.

Unable to suck air into her lungs, she fisted her hands in her lap.

"Katrina? Do you want to blow out your candles?"

She opened her mouth to speak, but she couldn't force the words out of her mouth. "I . . . I . . ."

There was nothing she could say, nothing she could do.

So she did the only thing she could.

She ran.

"Dammit."

Aiden hadn't meant to make her feel bad. He wouldn't have guessed she hated celebrating her birthday.

But that wasn't it.

The panic was real, the misery in her eyes was real.

Throwing his napkin onto the table, he stood. "I'm sorry about that," he told the waiter who stood by, helpless, watching Katrina's back as she wove around the tables and disappeared through the restaurant's doors. "Women, you know?"

The waiter didn't look like he did, but nodded.

"Bill the meal to my room, please," he said. He didn't wait for the waiter to say anything more, only turned on his heel and headed to find where Katrina had run off to.

"Mr. Price, wait. She left her purse behind."

"Thank you," he said, winding the black straps of her purse around his hand and letting it dangle at his side.

"Good luck."

Aiden nodded, but he'd run out of luck a long time ago.

He couldn't guess where she'd run and hide, didn't know her or her habits. Following his gut, he looked for her outside. If he'd been the one to need air, time to himself, he would go outside and seek refuge in the shadows.

The problem was he could search for hours; there were nooks and crannies everywhere. He couldn't call or text her since her phone was in her purse. She must have really been upset to leave her purse behind. Samantha never—

Aiden ran his hand along the nape of his neck in frustration.

Samantha was the last person he should be thinking about.

Aiden strolled by a small bistro attached to the casino, people spilling onto the terrace, dining alfresco in the mild weather. An excited buzz filled the air—people on vacation, trying their hand at Lady Luck, enjoying a few days away from their nine-to-five jobs.

The way he should be doing. He needed this vacation. Too much.

The case had torn him to shreds, and instead of the R & R he promised himself at Dylan's, he was hunting down a woman who likely didn't want to be found.

Rubbing his face, he debated going upstairs. Katrina was a big girl, and he very well might have let her fend for herself if she had her purse. Her phone and keycard were inside it, and she wouldn't be able to show ID to reception for a new one to get into her room.

Aiden passed the pool where a small wedding reception was

taking place. The bride glowed in a short white dress, a tiara perched on her head. The groom looked happy too, or shit-faced, grinning from ear to ear, accepting congratulations and pats on the back from his friends and family.

That would have been Aiden if Samantha hadn't run off.

He came to the back of the property. A large fountain sat in a luscious garden, and a gigantic mermaid played in the center, her arms raised above her head, displaying her bare breasts, spitting water, lights casting the streams gold.

A figure spun pirouettes on the edge, her long hair flew around her lithe body, her arms outstretched, though not to keep her balance, but only in the graceful positions of a dancer. The short skirt gave her legs the room they needed to move, and she balanced on the tips of her stilettos.

She looked like a ballerina, the lights of the fountain reflecting in the little pieces of mirror sewn onto her dress as she twirled on stone.

Smoking, a lone man sat on a bench near the fountain and watched her dance.

Aiden's hackles rose. He glared, and the man stomped out the cigarette and hurried away, leaving him and Katrina alone.

"I've been looking for you," Aiden said, turning angry he was worried about her when she'd been fine all along, giving some creep a show. And he meant a show. Whenever Katrina raised her leg, she flashed her black lace panties.

Katrina stopped in mid-twirl, stumbling, catching her balance before she tumbled into the fountain. "I'm sorry," she whispered, and he had to move closer to hear her.

"What the hell?" he asked, leaning against the brick, letting her purse fall from his hand where it clattered to the cobblestones that surrounded the fountain.

She sat on the edge, and his arm brushed her leg.

"It wasn't you," she said, rubbing at the tears that wet her cheeks.

"Then what? Jesus Christ, it was a cake." He gripped her chin, his fingers digging into her skin, forcing her to meet his eyes. "Look at me. What happened back there?"

Her light brown irises sparkled with tears in the fountain's light. "It was more than just a cake, Aiden. No one, no one's been that nice to me in a long time."

He could read between the lines easy enough. She didn't mean no one. Her friend would have ordered her a cake for her birthday. A birthday trip to California would warrant drinks and a cake. Dancing. Possibly an ill-thought tattoo.

No, she meant a man. A man hadn't been that nice to her in a long time. Maybe in so long she'd forgotten how a man should treat a woman.

It made him sick.

But his heart wouldn't let him forget that sometimes women forgot how to treat men, too.

He moved his hand from her chin, along her cheek, to her temple, then smoothed her hair. "Where are your glasses?"

Katrina sniffled, a smile tugging at the corners of her mouth. "I don't need them. They're fakes." She covered her hand with his. "Thank you, for the cake. Even if we didn't eat it."

He turned his body toward her, her legs cradling his hips.

Bad idea, his mind screamed. Bad idea. She wasn't available, and he'd already been down this road.

She leaned into him just a millimeter, and there wasn't anything else he could do.

He tilted his head to kiss her.

Kat looked away, and his lips landed on her cheek. His beard scratched her, but rather than hurt, the rough sensation made goosebumps cover her skin.

That wasn't good. Not at all.

"Aiden—"

"I'm sorry, Katrina. I am so sorry." He backed up, his hands out, palms turned toward her in surrender. "I had no business doing that. I know you're engaged, and you . . . love him."

She raised a hand to her cheek, her skin tingling from the touch of his lips. "No, it's okay. I just don't want us to start—"

"You don't have to worry about me, I promise."

Shaking her head in confusion, she said, "I don't understand."

"I don't want you worried about whether or not I'm going to try anything funny while we're on the road—that is, if you're still willing to travel with me. I don't want you scared of me."

She hopped from the fountain's edge, her heels snapping against the cobblestones, the sound echoing through the dark quiet. "The last thing I would be is scared of you—you rescued me from a scorpion," she said, trying to coax him to smile.

She hated that the tired, worried look had come back to his face. It disappeared, for a little bit, during dinner. But now strain marred his features, and he squinted his eyes agains the pain, his mouth turn downward into an unhappy scowl. Exhaustion. Anxiety. He couldn't hide any of it. "You look tired. Maybe we should go upstairs. It'd be nice to be on the road as early as possible—you know, get this over with. I'm taking up so much of your time."

"Yeah, yeah," he mumbled. "Get this over with."

Kat's heart dropped; he agreed so quickly.

"But first . . ."

With hope, she lifted her eyes from the cobblestones that surrounded the fountain.

"We can't visit Vegas without a little gambling."

Secured with a few more hours of company with Aiden tonight, she sagged against the fountain in relief. She'd enjoy him, and tomorrow they would be back to business. She'd treat him like a bus driver, or a stranger who drove for Lyft. And that would be it.

Keep him at arm's length, because she'd wanted him to kiss her.

And that wouldn't be any good for anybody.

"Sounds perfect."

In a daze, she followed him through the casino. She had little memory of how she came to find the fountain. That Aiden had been kind enough to have the foresight to order her a cake shocked her. She hadn't had a cake for her birthday for many years. Since her mother was alive.

He knew his way around the large hotel, and by the time they reached the casino proper, Kat doubted she could have found the fountain again, even with a map.

The main lights of the enormous room were dim, and the bright blinking strobes of the slot machines blinded her. They hurt her eyes, and the whining and bleeping as the screens spun drove icepicks of pain into her skull.

"People sit here for a long time?" she asked, tempted to cover her ears.

"Days," Aiden said, gazing across the room. "What do you want to do first?"

"I don't gamble—do what you want."

He led her to the farthest corner and claimed a seat at a bright green felted table.

The dealer dealt him into the game, and standing near his shoulder, Kat tried to understand the rules and how to play as Aiden won a couple hands.

"You play pretty well," Kat said, impressed, as the dealer pushed a small pile of chips toward him.

"My brother taught me to play. Do you want to try?"

"No, that's okay." The only card game she knew how to play was Go Fish.

Unused to walking in high heels, she shifted from one foot to the other, her feet beginning to hurt, one narrow strap cutting into her little toe. She ran her hands along her arms. Cold air blew from the vents, and her dress didn't cover much.

"Come on. I'll lose this at Craps, then we can go upstairs. Are you cold?"

"A little. I'm fine. Take your time." She wanted to encourage him to have as much fun as he could; she'd never get over him wasting his vacation for her.

"Here, you can wear my coat." Aiden took off his jacket and draped it over her shoulders.

Immediately, she was brought back to the fountain and being held in his arms. Kind of. His body heat was still trapped in the jacket, and the heady scent of his cologne warmed her. She closed her eyes, just for a second, to revel in the pleasure. "Thanks, this is a lot better."

She followed him to the other side of the room, dodging cocktail waitresses delivering drinks, men and women wandering with glassy looks in their eyes, or staring at their phones, not paying attention to where they were going. She bit back a feeling of claustrophobia and concentrated on the eclectic crowd. People were dressed in everything from jeans to ball gowns, and they stood at tables and played games Kat didn't recognize.

Diamonds sparkled, drinks swished in glasses.

A cup of coffee would have been nice. And some ibuprofen.

"What game is this?" she asked as Aiden laid his chips onto a table.

"Craps," he said, an arm around her shoulders, drawing her close.

She leaned in, happy he forgave her for running off like a child, for ruining dinner. She bet none of the women he dated acted like that.

He belonged here, she thought, studying his profile as he watched the dealer throw dice. Handsome, charming, and rich, he'd never have a reason, or a need, or a want, to choose, someone like her.

Yet, he tried to kiss her.

She should have let him.

No, she was right at the fountain. They needed to travel the rest of the trip as friends only. No more crawling half naked into his arms because of a scorpion, no more near-miss kisses.

61

Even if his cologne made her feel drunk, even if the scratchiness of his beard against her skin made her a little wet.

"Well, that's that," Aiden said, rubbing his hands together. "Not very lucky tonight."

"You did all right at cards." She didn't understand why he lost this game, but he didn't seem upset about it.

"Yeah, Blackjack has always been my game. Dylan's good at Craps, I'm crap at it." He smiled. "Come on, I'll walk with you upstairs."

"Okay." Kat limped at Aiden's side, tempted to take off her heels and walk barefoot to her room. She could get away with it. No one was paying them any attention.

She stopped outside the casino's doors. Maybe she should try her luck at just one game. No one went to Las Vegas and didn't gamble at least once. A bank of slot machines sat against the wall, and Kat bit her lip in temptation.

An older woman, leaning on a cane, punched buttons with lightning speed, but Kat judged by the scowl on her face she wasn't having any luck.

"Stupid machine," the elderly woman muttered and slammed the side of the Megabucks machine with her cane. She teetered precariously in her support shoes before righting herself at the last minute. Pulling down the hem of her cream sweatshirt to cover her ample bottom, she hobbled away toward a twenty-four-hour buffet.

Kat's stomach growled. It seemed like forever since dinner. Maybe she could talk Aiden into sharing room service with her before going to bed.

Hmmm.

Aiden in her room didn't sound like a good idea.

No, it sounded like an excellent idea, and that was a huge problem.

"Are you sure you don't want to play?" he asked, his eyes flicking over the Megabucks machine. "It's easy. Let it take your money, you push a button, you lose. It only takes a second."

"Doesn't anybody ever win?"

"House always wins, but you can't visit Vegas without trying at least once. I have ten bucks in my wallet." He reached for his jacket.

Kat reluctantly slipped it off and handed it to him, instantly missing the warmth and his scent. "I'm not wasting any more of your money. Thanks for remembering my purse at the restaurant," she said, digging through it and grabbing her pocketbook. "I can't believe I ran off without it. Will it take a five? I don't want to use a twenty."

"It will take whatever you give it; it's greedy that way. Will you share your winnings?" he teased, leaning against the machine, the purple strobes lighting his distinguished features.

She laughed. "That's why you wanted to give me money. So you could claim my jackpot. Too bad, mister." She fed the machine her five-dollar bill, slammed the button Aiden pointed to, and watched the machine reels spin.

The reels stopped, but nothing happened. Blackout's logo decorated each slide.

Kat's heart sank. She wasn't familiar with slot machines, but in all the movies she ever watched, cherries meant you won. She hadn't stood a chance at winning, but she had a glimmer of hope she'd strike it rich.

"See, I knew I'd lose," she said, pushing away from the machine, five dollars poorer.

She could understand how people became gambling addicts. If the call of coffee hadn't been so strong, she would have wanted to try again.

Just to see.

Before Aiden could respond, the machine started wailing and lights began flashing.

Kat stumbled backward. "What's happening? What did I do wrong?"

"You didn't do anything wrong. You won," Aiden said with a laugh.

Call An Attendant flashed on the screen in bright blue letters, but before Kat could ask Aiden what that meant, the old woman who'd been playing the machine stomped toward her, her cane raised like a Field Commander leading his marching band in a parade.

"That's my machine," she hollered, the pale crepey folds of her cheeks and neck quivering with rage. "You stole it from me!" She swung her cane, and unprepared, Kat didn't move out of the way. The jagged tip of the cane caught her shoulder and scratched her skin as it dragged down her arm. Stunned, the cut burning, she covered the scrape, and her palm came away wet.

"Stop," Aiden said, grabbing the cane as the angry woman reared back to swing again.

"You can't steal my jackpot!" The woman yanked on her cane attempting to free it from Aiden's fist, but he held firm, his eyes narrowed in anger.

"What's going on here?" A Black burly man thundered toward them, a grey security uniform stretched across his massive shoulders. He towered over Aiden; he looked like a football player.

A casino attendant also approached, a slim strawberry-blonde woman dressed in a navy-blue business suit. She reached behind the slot machine and stopped the wailing and the strobe lights.

All Kat wanted to do was sit down. Her shoulder and arm ached, and pain roared through her head, competing with the agony stabbing the soles of her feet. She literally ached from head to toe.

"What happened?" the security guard asked again, folding his arms across the immense expanse of his chest, his dark eyes narrowed.

Aiden explained, not looking the least bit intimidated, and Kat admired him all the more. The attendant glared at the old woman still trying to tug her cane away from Aiden's strong grasp.

"This is ridiculous. I'm suing this casino for everything I can," the woman threatened, letting go of her cane and reaching for a fanny pack buckled around her waist.

"Roscoe, please take this woman into custody," the blonde woman said, tapping her foot, "before she can cause any more trouble."

"But I didn't—" Kat objected.

"She doesn't mean you," Aiden said, transferring the cane to Roscoe.

"We'll need to watch the tapes," the attendant said, ignoring the woman's wails as Roscoe secured her arm, "to make sure, but I can guess what happened here. It's a daily occurrence." She put her arm around Kat. "She walked away, and you won at her machine, right?"

"We can—" Kat started to say it wasn't worth the hassle, that she just wanted to wipe at her shoulder with a tissue and sit in some quiet with a mug of coffee, but Aiden spoke over her, like he knew exactly what she was going to say.

"No," he snapped, "that money is yours. You won fair and square." He directed his piercing gaze to the attendant. "That woman was half way across the casino when Katrina won. Be careful," he added, including the security guard in the conversation, "the cane is all for show, and God knows what she's keeping in her fanny pack."

"Let's get you to first aid," the woman said, squeezing Kat's uninjured shoulder. "We'll take a look at your scrape while you wait for your winnings. We want everyone to have a pleasant experience at Blackout, and we hope this negative incident won't impact your decision to visit us again."

Kat hummed in agreement. The attendant didn't need to know Kat would never visit Las Vegas again.

She and Aiden followed the woman down an empty service corridor intended for Blackout staff and stopped at an unmarked door. "My name is Celina, and I'll be back after I check with security. I know it's not the VIP lounge, but you'll be able to bandage that shoulder and get off your feet. Those heels are beautiful, but I bet you're hurting like crazy."

Celina swiped her identification badge that hung from her neck on a Blackout lanyard and swung the door open. Flipping on the overhead light, she revealed a small room painted taupe, equipped with a gurney and two cushioned chairs. "This is a small first aid room. We've had people come here to sleep off too much alcohol, ice sprained ankles, that kind of thing. I think you'll have everything you need, but if you think you need stitches, use the phone to ask the casino manager to alert me. We really *do* want you to have a pleasant experience here," Celina said, patting Kat on the back. "I'll figure this out as quickly as I can."

With that, Celina stepped into the tiled hallway, closing the door behind her.

"I don't suppose she'd be too happy if we disappeared on her, would she?" Kat asked, sighing. She started to search the room and opened a large metal cabinet full of first aid supplies. In a large mirror attached to the wall, she studied her shoulder. Swollen and turning purple, her skin oozed blood, but the cut didn't look deep enough to need stitches.

She met Aiden's eyes in the mirror. "What?"

With the long scratch on her arm, dark circles under her eyes, and her hair tangled from dancing outside, she looked a mess. The overhead light did nothing for her complexion making her appear sallow, like she suffered from a severe case of Hepatitis C.

He cleared his throat. Digging through the containers of Band-Aids, gauze, and antibiotic ointment, he said, "Nothing. You're fiancé's a lucky guy, that's all."

"Thanks," Kat murmured, turning away from her reflection and hopping onto the gurney. Her skirt slid up her thighs, and she wished she was still wearing Aiden's jacket. She shivered. Her muscles ached, and a headache thrummed through her skull. The small room was slightly warmer than the wide open space of the casino floor, but it didn't help much.

"Do you always lead this exciting of a life?" Aiden asked. He sat next to her and tore open a wound wipe. "I don't know if this will sting or not," he warned, and began dabbing her shoulder.

She moved her hair out of the way, giving him better access. It didn't sting, at least, not that she could feel through the ache already there. "No, not really. Nan gets into her fair share of trouble and she used to bring me with her, but we don't hang out much anymore."

Aiden grunted. "She's the friend who was going to pick you up?"

"Yeah. The trip was her idea."

"Huh." He rested his hand on the nape of her neck and gently blew on her skin.

Her mother used to do this for her whenever she'd gotten hurt as a child. Skinned knees and elbows, bloody palms from running too fast and wiping out on the road or losing her balance on her bike. Tears pricked at her eyelids. She hadn't thought about her mom like that in a long time.

"I'll wipe some antibiotic cream on it. You don't need a bandage. It's just a scratch. The impact probably hurt more than the scrape. For an old lady, she was stronger than she looked."

"Thanks." She met his eyes, his face a mere inch from hers. Her fingers itched to run along his jaw, to feel his beard against her fingertips. She wanted to know what his kisses felt like, not only on her cheek as he had by the fountain, but all over. Down her neck, to her breasts, along her stomach. Lower.

"Aiden," she whispered, her resolved to keep him at arms' length evaporating like dewy mist in the sunrise.

He lowered his head, his lips a hair-breadth from hers.

The door swung open, and she jerked away from him, teetering on the edge of the gurney.

Stepping into the room, Celina crowed, "Good news! Katrina Ford, it's your lucky night! You won twenty-five thousand dollars!"

"How's the road trip?"

Aiden juggled the phone and tried to turn a sharp corner at the same time. "Hold on," he said, grasping the wheel with both hands, running over the curb, steering into the Enterprise parking lot. He needed to get rid of this piece of shit. It was time to take this trip seriously—he was done fucking around. He wanted to get Katrina home and figure out the dung pile his life had turned into.

Jerking the car into Park, he brought his cell back to his ear. "Sorry. Are you still there?" he asked his brother.

"Yeah, where are you? Still in Vegas?"

"I'm trading in the car those bastards stuck us with in LA. It's time to get her home, stop screwing around."

"You don't sound very good," Dylan commented.

Aiden didn't feel very good. His gut had been twisted into knots all night. "This isn't something I thought I would be doing on my vacation."

"Don't, then. Let her rent her own vehicle and tell her to go home. She's a grown woman; she can handle the drive. Then get your ass back here. Samantha—"

"Can we not do this? I haven't even had coffee yet."

After a sleepless night, he rolled out of bed at six. He showered, gotten dressed, and crammed the rest of his new clothes into his carry-on. He was on the way to the rental place by seven-thirty and he'd wake Katrina when he returned to Blackout with a different car.

"But aren't you going to talk to her? You loved her, Aiden, and she didn't get married. Nick said she's been asking for you. She sounds desperate to talk to you."

Aiden scoffed. "Samantha can wait. I'm going to get Katrina home as quickly as possible, because I'm not letting her fend for herself. I just hope we don't run into any more trouble."

"More trouble?" Dylan asked. "What else has been going on besides you breaking down, and I mean in the literal sense."

"Ha. Ha. Funny." He wasn't in the mood for his brother's

jokes. "Katrina played a hot slot machine last night, and the woman who abandoned it attacked her. You know how it is here."

"Is she all right?"

"She's fine, but I'm done messing around. She has a fiancé to get home to, and I have to fucking figure out what I'm going to do about Samantha and work. I can't think straight when I'm around her."

"Is there something going on between—"

"No." He didn't wait for Dylan to finish. Katrina wasn't anything to him, and he would make damn sure she stayed that way.

"Well, you know what you're doing," Dylan said, blowing into the phone.

"I'd like to think so, but unfortunately, that isn't always the case. Listen, I need to get going. I'm hoping to make it to Denver tonight. If we don't make too many stops, we can do it."

"Be careful."

"I always try. I'll keep you posted."

He hung up and traded in the station wagon for the kind of vehicle he reserved in the first place. He nodded in approval when the rental attendant pulled the gigantic luxury SUV in front of the store from the back parking lot. Traveling would be a lot easier, and they could stop worrying about breaking down—in the literal sense. Christ.

His mood lifted as he drove to Blackout to wake Katrina and grab a cup of strong coffee. The rest of the trip would be all right. Great timing, actually, since if he'd been at Dylan's when he heard the news Samantha hadn't gone through with her wedding, he'd be cruising to Miami to be with her, head over heels in love.

And he wasn't sure that was the best thing for him right now. Or ever again.

He wasn't fooling himself. Katrina made his emotions scatter all over the place, and if it hadn't been for the pilots' strike, she would have been just a pretty blip on his radar in the airport and nothing more.

That's all Aiden wanted her to be, because he couldn't afford for her to be anything else.

"You ready to go?"

Kat stepped aside and let Aiden into her room. "I just need to pack my things. I ordered room service, I hope you don't mind."

Aiden laughed. "You're the one who won last night. I figured you'd pay."

She blushed. She wasn't used to having money. When Celina handed her a slim aluminum briefcase stacked with twenty-five thousand dollars, she'd nearly gone into cardiac arrest. Seeing it was surreal, as if she were looking at Monopoly money. She'd run her hand over the bundled stacks of one-hundred-dollar bills, a glimmer of hope sparking in her heart that her life could be different. She'd snuffed out that wish before it could do any damage. It didn't matter how much money she did or didn't have.

Her life couldn't change.

Not like that.

"Of . . . of course. Sure. I'll be ready in a couple minutes."

"Don't worry about it. I was joking. The casino already has my credit card on file. It's not a big deal. It's cool, and I'm happy for you." Aiden flopped onto her bed looking relaxed and fresh in jeans and a black dress shirt.

Kat tore her eyes away before he caught her staring.

"Thanks. Have you won big before?" She'd been excited to dress this morning after her shower. Her soft jeans fit her like a glove, clinging to her rump, giving her a lift she hadn't had since her teens when she'd had dance class six days a week. Her blouse, a mossy green silk with ruffles sewn down the front, hugged her breasts and exposed a healthy amount of cleavage. It'd been years since she'd worn anything so revealing and decadent—if she didn't count last night.

"I don't play the slots. I like Blackjack, sometimes Craps, but I don't come here to gamble. Most of the time my friend, Nick, and I party; there's a gigantic dance club downstairs I didn't show you. Or we lay out in the sun all day. We didn't look at the pool area last night, either. No, I've never known anyone to win as big as you. My brother won five thousand playing Craps, but that was a few years ago. He was drunker than hell, too; the next morning he didn't remember a damn thing."

She laughed. "I think I'll remember last night for the rest of my life. If you don't want me to pay for these rooms, can I at least pay you back for the clothes I bought yesterday? And everything else that we need on this trip? Your time is so valuable, I don't want you wasting your money on me, too."

"If you like, but it's not a waste."

His immediate acquiescence pleased her immensely. She hummed as she gathered her things from the bathroom. "Do you have a route planned for today?" she asked, stepping into the bedroom.

She hauled her carry-on to the bed, and slowly unzipped the zipper. Crap. She didn't want Aiden to see what was in her carry-on. It would be a dead giveaway what she'd been planning to do in Santa Barbara.

Grabbing the clothes she bought at Luna Noir, including her dress and heels, and holding them close to her chest, she eased open the top of the case. Looking at Aiden out of the corner of her eye, she shoved the ball of clothes on top of wisps of lace and satin and tried to zip the carry-on closed.

She was too slow.

"What's all this?" Aiden asked, his arm snaking into her case as quickly as a diamondback struck at unsuspecting prey.

"Nothing," Kat said, swatting his shoulder. "Leave my stuff alone."

Through the small slit the zipper made, Aiden yanked at a piece of black lace. Holding up a teddy she bought from a lingerie store in the mall, he whistled. "Just what kind of birthday party were you going to have?"

Kat yanked it out of his hands and shoved it into her carry-on. With her hands shaking, she jerked the zipper closed. "I don't know what you're talking about."

"Katrina," Aiden said, sitting up and grabbing her wrist, "your carry-on is full of lingerie. You don't need that stuff for a girls' week. What were you going to do?"

He sounded so concerned, she couldn't do anything but spill her guts. "I was going to have a fling, okay? Just one last hurrah before I get married. Plenty of people do it, have a good time before they settle down. I wanted to, too. Go clubbing, get drunk, bring a couple men back to my room, maybe even at the same time." She lifted her chin. "Have some fun for a change. What's the harm in that?"

There. Now he could think what he wanted. She hadn't been very complimentary when it came to her fiancé in the first place, but why she was marrying him was her own business.

"There's a lot of harm in that. You never know who you'd bring to your room, what they'd do to you. You just can't go wild. You could get hurt."

Like she didn't hurt now.

Stiffly, she shrugged. She was through talking about it. "It doesn't matter now, anyway. My trip is ruined, and I'll never have another chance. Things happen for a reason. A one-night stand wasn't meant to be, and like you said, maybe it's for the best. Let's go. I'm ready. I just want to go home."

Her voice cracked.

Not because she was homesick.

Not because she missed Neil.

But because going home was turning into the last thing she wanted to do.

Katrina sat in the front seat and stared out her passenger-side window, her aloofness shielding her better than a brick wall ever could.

Aiden drove, quietly seething, occasionally sneaking a peek at the back of her head, relieved her stupid plan had slammed to a stop by the pilots' strike.

They were already a half an hour out of Las Vegas, and it wasn't even ten o'clock. They'd make good time today. The weather was holding its end of the bargain, the sun shining, not a cloud in the sky. The SUV, while having terrible gas mileage, would at least get them to Minnesota in comfort. His plan to stop in Denver for the night seemed more than doable.

"Do you want me to put some music on? Or do you want to listen to an audiobook?"

"I'm tired of books," she mumbled, staring out the window.

Okay.

"How do you get tired of books?"

Samantha didn't read—she partied. It hadn't mattered to him much when they first started dating, but when he wanted to settle in for the evening with the latest thriller, she roamed restlessly around his condo. He'd grit his teeth until he let her talk him into going out. Samantha, employed as an account executive at a PR firm, loved being out on the town, schmoozing with Miami's elite.

Katrina turned in her seat, finally meeting his gaze.

She'd done something with her makeup, and long eyelashes framed her eyes that glittered like the color of his favorite beer. Her was skin clear and pale, besides the small scratch peeking from the short sleeve of her blouse. She pulled her hair up, a messy bun with strands trailing down her neck. Samantha liked to wear her hair like that as well. She called it "just-fucked damage control" and that's what it looked like on Katrina, too. Like she'd been good and laid, but instead of trying to brush out the knots, she twisted it in an elastic near the crown of her head.

She'd gone back to wearing her glasses.

"I'm a librarian. Neil didn't know Nan was throwing me a party. He thought I was going to a librarian's conference."

That startled a burst of sarcastic laughter out of Aiden. "That's not surprising."

He also wasn't shocked by the fact Katrina had to lie to her fiancé to enjoy a week's vacation. The more he knew about the guy, the less he liked.

Ignoring him, she turned her back and stared out the window.

"You don't like it?" he asked. He hated her bad mood, though he understood her reasoning behind it. The idiot photographer destroyed a fantasy weekend of booze and sex. She'd probably looked forward to her trip for weeks, if not months. Maybe years.

"It's fine," she whispered, her breath fogging the glass. Aiden strained to hear her.

"But not what you would do if you could do something else."

"Does anybody ever do what they want?" she muttered.

He thought he had been. He'd liked his job. "Sure. Lots of people do."

She twisted to face him. "Do you? An attorney? Really?"

"I used to like it. I've just been having a rough time, lately," he said, focusing on the road. Red, brown, orange rock. As far as the eye could see.

"That's why you needed a vacation?"

"Needed one, forced to take one, same difference."

Katrina frowned. "You were forced to take time off?"

"My last case didn't go so well. I was in bad shape, and after a psych eval, they recommended I take a leave of absence. Unwind, get my head on straight. You know."

"I'm sorry."

"It's not so bad. I wouldn't have been able to work anyway. I had other things going on. All this shit kind of dumped on me like an avalanche. I was going to hide out at Dylan's."

"Bringing me back won't use up all your vacation, and hopefully by then the strike will be over and you can fly out."

"Where exactly am I driving you, anyway?" he asked.

"Oh, I live in Rosemont Valley. It's a suburb of Minneapolis."

"That's great. If the pilots are up and going, I won't have to drive far to get to an airport. Have you checked the news?"

Katrina shook her head. "No. I doesn't matter anymore. I'll get home when I get home."

"Have you talked to him lately?" he asked. He didn't have any right to be curious, but it was interesting how a man could be so angry about something so little. If she had to live with that on a daily basis, it was no wonder she acted like a skittish rabbit. "He doesn't hit you, does he?" Horrified, he grabbed her arm. She hadn't so much as flinched when the old woman from last night raised her cane.

She jerked her arm out of his grasp. "Of course not. I may seem like a naïve and inexperienced nobody, but that's not who I am, and I would never put up with that. Not even for my mother."

"Your mother?"

"Never mind. Forget I said anything. Look, I know we haven't been on the road long, but can we stop soon? I drank a lot of coffee while I was getting dressed."

"Yeah, sure."

He had to drive another twenty minutes before a highway sign announcing food and lodging led him to a small town with a population of two thousand. Katrina disappeared the minute he stopped the SUV at a small Starbucks attached to a strip mall containing a daycare and an Irish pub.

He took a moment to breathe, undoing his seatbelt.

The woman was a puzzle, and he wanted to solve it. The way she dressed and the way she acted intrigued him, and his need to put the clues together and solve the mystery made his attorney's mind shift into overdrive.

About to push out of the truck to take his own bathroom break and grab a coffee, the singing ringtone of his phone stopped him.

Surprise, love, dread, and fear all swirled in a tight ball in his stomach.

Samantha.

Chapter Four

She had to lighten up. Holy crap, she couldn't act like that for the rest of the trip. But God, oh, God, she was mortified when he found that teddy. She'd felt like a stupid moron when she explained what she planned to do in Santa Barbara.

Humiliated, she hadn't been able to look him in the eye the whole way to wherever the hell they were now. And him accusing her of letting Neil beat her up? Icing on the birthday cake she didn't eat.

Hoping she rinsed her mortification down the drain with the soap while she washed her hands, she didn't see him when she finally came out of the bathroom.

Thinking he might want a coffee too, she headed out to the SUV to ask him.

He leaned against the driver's side door, hurt radiating off him like a kicked puppy.

"Hey, are you okay?" she asked.

He straightened and rubbed his hands over his face. "Yeah, yeah. Are you set?"

Kat shook her head. "No, I came out to see if you wanted anything? Coffee? Pastry?"

"An Americano, black, would be fine, thanks, but I don't feel like eating anything."

"Did you get bad news while I was—"

"Katrina, it's not a big deal, okay?" he snapped, opening his door. "Just buy your coffee so we can get going. At this rate, it'll take me until next month to get you home where you belong."

His angry blue eyes and the unhappy line of his mouth made her take a step back. "Yeah, sure. It'll just take me a minute."

"Katrina—"

Disappearing into the café, she ignored him and the regret in his voice. Luckily, there wasn't a line and five minutes later, the air of the SUV saturated with the scent of coffee, they were speeding down the interstate in complete silence.

"There's a state park up ahead."

Aiden's voice roused her from a light sleep. She should have been excited at the prospect of seeing this part of the country for the first time, but his silence and the drone of the SUV's wheels against the pavement acted like a sleeping pill.

They hadn't driven far from the Starbucks when she tilted her seat, turned her back on him, and started daydreaming about what Nan was doing in Santa Barbara. Kat should call her soon, tell her that Aiden, while grumpier than all get out, had been a gentleman so far. And she could tease Nan about the money she won in Vegas. Luck like that didn't happen to them often.

"What?" She wet her mouth with a sip of cold café mocha.

"There's a national park coming up in about half an hour. We're driving along the border now. Did you want to stop and look around?"

Her mouth dropped open. "Seriously? All you can talk about is getting my ass home, and now you want to stop?"

"We can keep going. Never mind." Shoulders tense, his hands

tight on the wheel, he stared out the windshield, not meeting her eyes.

"Why do you want to stop?" Kat asked, considering. She shouldn't turn down a potty break. Surely a national park would have a tourist center. Maybe a place to eat.

"I thought you'd like to look around—and I need some air."

He spoke the last almost to himself, and she nibbled her bottom lip with worry. *Something* happened while she was in that Starbucks, but God help her, she couldn't convince him to tell her.

"Yeah, sure. I'll never be out this way again."

"You and Neil don't travel?"

"We don't have the money to travel. The money I won will go toward fixing our house. It needs a new roof; we deal with leaks all the time." Not that it was any of his business, but she was the one who brought it up.

"What does he do for work?" he asked, turning onto the exit toward Red Ravine National Park.

"He doesn't. He can't." That was true before, but it wasn't now. Now, now, he just . . . didn't.

"I'm sorry." He looked at her from the corner of his eyes.

She took another sip of her mocha. She hated cold coffee more than anything. Well, not more than anything. Not more than this conversation. "Don't be. We make it work."

"Not well by the sounds of it," he muttered.

She ignored him and stared out the window, the red and brown rock and smattering of vegetation going on for miles, like a rusty brown and green ocean. "Have you been here before?"

"No. I don't travel, either. I fly back and forth from Miami to LA when I want to visit my brother. That's it."

Aiden navigated them through the park entrance and idled in silence while he waited to pay the entry fee for a day pass. After they were waved through, he followed the line of cars and parked at the tourist center.

"We can grab a map of the park and a drink," he said, turning off the SUV.

And a snack, she thought, jumping out of the truck.

She roamed the tourist center and found the restrooms. While she waited in line to pay for a bag of chips and a bottle of water, she snagged a stuffed ringtail cat. According to the small fact card attached to the shelf, they were an abundant species in the park. Grey and white with large eyes and a long tale, the stuffed animal made Kat laugh, and she purchased it with the rest of her things, turning down a clearance t-shirt the clerk offered her before she paid.

"What took you so long?" Aiden asked when she came out of the center. He leaned against the SUV sipping from a bottle of Diet Coke.

"I bought you a gift, Mr. Grumpy Pants," she said, waving the stuffed animal at him. "You were the one who wanted to take a detour." She climbed into the truck and placed the cat on the dash. It stared at them with huge black plastic eyes.

"That's not creepy at all," Aiden said, backing out of the parking spot, but a smile he tried to hold back puckered his mouth.

She laughed. "Where are we going?"

"There are a lot of sight-seeing opportunities around here, obviously. The park is known for its hiking and rock-climbing, too."

"I'm not up for either of those things," she said. "All I have are my sandals and the heels I wore at Blackout."

"I think some of the trails are okay, even with your sandals, if you wanted to stretch and look around."

As he drove them through the park, the mountain formations and deep valleys made Kat's stomach plunge.

He parked in a small lot across the street from an observation point and the beginning of a switchback that Kat read in the brochure was five miles long.

"This is called Scissor's Edge Switchback," he said. "It's not steep at all, if you want to walk down some of it."

It was tempting, but she didn't want to hurt herself. "No, I'll be fine. It'll be fun to poke around here and take some pictures."

"I'm going to explore a little bit. Will you be okay alone?"

"Yeah, sure. Go." Maybe being alone in the fresh air would give him time to think. After his hike, perhaps he would open up to her.

"Here are the keys to the truck. Don't get lost. Please."

Aiden slid out of the truck and slammed the door behind him before she could promise that would be the last thing she would do.

Forty-five minutes later, Aiden still hadn't finished his hike, and Kat sat bored and a little worried. He told her not to get lost, but she hoped he hadn't, either. Maybe he was on the phone, or texting someone. Even if he was on leave, he could be consulting on a case or answering email.

She opened the back of the SUV and sat, letting her legs dangle over the back bumper. Her aluminum suitcase was hidden under the backseat, and she pulled it out, entering the numbers into the combination the way Celina showed her.

All that money made her head spin. She should share. She wouldn't have been in Vegas if it weren't for Aiden. And the pilots' strike, of course.

How much money would she have won if she would've put in a twenty dollar bill instead of a five? Probably nothing.

She pulled Aiden's carry-on closer and looked around the park. She didn't see him, and she would have to be careful he didn't catch her. He would never accept money from her, and by the looks of it, he didn't need it anyway. The suit he wore when they met at the airport looked like it cost more than what she made in two months at her job.

Unzipping the sides, she searched for a place in his carry-on he maybe forgot about. A plane ticket from five years ago, or a receipt that he hastily shoved into an obscure pocket. If she slipped the money into an area he didn't use on a regular basis, maybe it would be a while before he found it. Then he would think of her, and this stupid, crazy adventure they'd taken.

She stilled when her fingers met the ragged edges of thick paper, and she pulled out the pink envelope she found the other day. Her heart racing, she debated on whether to read what was inside. Were there laws about privacy? Maybe he would sue her. No, he wouldn't sue her, but she had few doubts he'd have no qualms with leaving her alongside the road if she made him angry enough.

Tapping the envelope against her lips, she took another quick look around the park. People spilled from their cars, eager to stretch their legs, children screaming in delight to be free from their vehicular cages. But she didn't see Aiden.

The envelope had already been torn open, and as she lifted the flap, a spicy, amber scent spilled out at her. The earthy fragrance brought to mind a sophisticated woman, tall, blonde. Exciting. Or maybe a curvy Latina woman, all fire and passion, panting in Spanish as they made love.

If she was going to read it, then she'd better hurry up, and with one last quick glance to the start of the switchback trail to check Aiden wasn't doubling back, she pulled out the creamy stationery that looked like it had been handled a thousand times already and began to devour the words on the page.

"My Dearest A—
When you read this, I'll be on my way to be married . . ."

Oh, my God! That's what made Aiden so grouchy. He was heartbroken. She should have known the whole thing was about a woman. Kat sighed in sympathy.

". . . I'm sorry things ended the way they did between us. I can only say that I'm trying to do the right thing. For you, for me, for Max . . ."

Who was Max? The man this woman ran off with? Their child? Did Aiden have a son? Kat's stomach churned with the idea.

"Please know this had nothing to do with you. Sometimes, Aiden, sometimes the decisions we make are not ours. I did my very best. I love you, and I always will.

Yours always and forever,
Samantha."

Kat checked the stamp on the envelope. It had been mailed to him only weeks ago.

Aiden's figure trudging up the trail caught her eye, and quickly, her hands shaking, she folded the paper along the crease already pressed into the stationery and scrambled to slide it into the envelope.

As she pushed the pink envelope into his carry-on, Aiden waited to cross the street. Luckily for her, he had to let a car go by, giving Kat precious seconds to zip the side pocket and shove his carry-on to where it had been on the floor.

When he rounded the truck's back panel, she held her brief-case in her lap, resting her chin on the cold aluminum like she'd been sitting, ruminating on life the whole time he was gone.

"Guarding it?" he asked, amused.

She squinted into the sun, promising herself she wouldn't be bitchy the rest of the way. It couldn't be easy for him, knowing the love of his life was now married to another man. Maybe his son calling another man Daddy.

The truth explained his bad moods, and she wanted to reach out, touch him, try to soothe away the hurt. Gripping the case until her hands ached, she forced a smile. "No, not really. Just daydreaming. How was the trail?"

"Good. You could handle it, if you wanted to see a little bit of the park."

"No, that's okay. I took some pictures," she lied, hoping he wouldn't ask to see them later and pushing the briefcase alongside her carry-on. "We should get on the road. I looked up Denver—you said you wanted us to get there by tonight? We'll be driving until midnight if you still want to get that far."

"I don't mind if you don't," he said, running his hand through his hair, ruffling the black strands.

"No, I'm okay with that. I can even drive for a while if you want?"

He looked like he needed a nap, lines of worry and stress framing his eyes, creasing his forehead.

She bit her lip. The more she found out about the man, the more she wanted to know. She could spend the rest of her life unearthing little facts about him, and it wouldn't be enough.

"That'd be great, thanks. Come on, let's get going then." He held out his hand, and she took it, sliding out of the truck.

As she started the SUV, she brought the seat up closer, wiggled her butt to get comfortable, and thought of ways to persuade Aiden to talk to her. They had a long leg of the trip ahead.

"Let's play two truths and a lie."

Aiden twisted in his seat and rested the back of his head against the window. Katrina looked good behind the wheel of the luxury SUV, like she belonged there. Soccer mom. No, she lived in Minnesota. Hockey mom. Two kids fighting in the back, a dog barking out the window at the passing traffic.

"How about twenty questions?" he asked. Maybe he could draw some information out of her. Like, why was she marrying an asshole who didn't work. On the other hand, she would ask him questions in return, and there was no way in hell he felt like answering anything she might ask.

She grinned, revealing slightly crooked teeth. Aiden didn't

have middle-class friends, and since he'd grown up with money, it was an odd concept her family couldn't afford to have her teeth straightened.

His grandfather had made his fortune in development and real estate, and his father easily took up where Aiden's grandfather left off.

His mother was a real estate attorney coming from a family of attorneys, and he'd followed the tradition. He'd gone to Harvard, as did his brother who worked in LA at a prestigious architectural firm.

Nick and Samantha's families were full of politicians and came from old money, like the Kennedys. Samantha didn't work to pay bills. She enjoyed her job—her high salary and prestige only a bonus.

"All right," she agreed, lifting her eyebrows, like she couldn't believe he agreed to play. "I'll start. Favorite color?"

Wanting to blow out a sigh of relief she didn't jump into anything personal, he answered, "Black. Yours?"

She hesitated.

"Come on," he admonished—he wasn't going to let her lie her way through the game. "Tell the truth."

"I like pink. Teal. Sparkles."

"Sparkles isn't a color. What were you going to say?"

"Black. I want black to be my favorite color. Boring. Predictable."

"Thanks a lot." He checked his phone, hoping Samantha hadn't called again. He set his phone on silent after spending an hour at the park agonizing over whether or not to call her back.

She'd been so quick to run off. His love for her hadn't stopped her from running away to marry Max, and he couldn't come to terms with it. After she left, nightmares woke him out of a sound sleep, sweat pouring down his back, and only booze had been able to numb the pain.

He loved her, and she'd chosen another man.

"I didn't mean it that way. Sometimes I'm too wild, and I need to tone it down."

Aiden glanced up from his screen. Someone hammered that into her head, and it rattled off her tongue as if by rote, as if she believed it. "Ah-huh."

"Anyway, favorite food?" she asked, steering the SUV around a slower car.

"Steak. Pizza. The usual foods everyone likes, I guess. Yours?"

"Tapioca pudding with whipped cream."

"That's weird."

Katrina swatted his leg. "I love it. When I was a kid, my mom used to make it for me all the time. I make it for myself, now, but it holds a lot of good memories."

"What does your mom think of your six-year engagement?"

"It's my turn to ask a question, thank you," she said. "Have you ever been out of the country?"

He let her deflect his question. It was best if they didn't get too personal, anyway. It would be easier to say goodbye. "Actually, no. Miami has everything I need. You?"

She pouted. "You don't have to ask me the same questions I ask you."

"Okay, how did you lose your virginity?"

With her mouth open in shock, she stared at him.

"You're not a virgin, are you?"

"No!" A horn blared, and Katrina jerked her eyes back to the interstate, grabbing at the steering wheel, lurching the SUV into the correct lane.

"Jesus, woman, keep your eyes on the road." He adjusted in his seat, grateful the seatbelt kept him from flying through the windshield. "You can answer the question, then." He liked the shocked look on her face. Her pink cheeks, the way her lips sparkled when she licked them self-consciously, the sheen of her cleavage. The question made her sweat.

"It was very sweet—in high school, a guy I'd dated on and off took me to an apple orchard, you know, pick your own apples? I lost my virginity under an apple tree. I was nervous about being intimate for the first time with someone who wasn't Neil, but he understood. He had a better time than I did, but I think that's common in most cases, anyway. How did you?"

He played with a water bottle, running his fingers over the ridges of the plastic cap to give himself a few moments. It wasn't his business, but he was happy Katrina hadn't given her virginity to Neil. It didn't sound like that jerk deserved anything Katrina had to give him. "That's a nice story—a lot nicer than losing it in the back of a car and the guy not talking to you anymore."

"Is that what happened to you?"

"Did I lose mine in the back of a car to some guy who never spoke to me again?" Aiden enjoyed teasing her. Their banter was a lot better than the sexual tension that had been sizzling between them since he helped her escape that scorpion in her hotel room in Harmony. The thought of her legs wrapped around his waist still made him hard—when he let himself think about it.

"No. Well, not the guy part." Katrina laughed. "Okay, well, maybe the guy part, too."

"My junior year in high school, my brother paid a senior girl he knew to ask me out on a date. I lost mine on a beach, and yeah, after that night, she never talked to me again." It had been a long time since he thought about it.

"That's terrible!"

He threw the empty bottle onto the back seat and grabbed the ringtail cat still sleeping on the dash. "He thought he was doing me a favor—I was a tall, gangly kid back then. If girls looked at me, it was only to laugh."

"Who's laughing now?" Katrina asked.

He tilted is head in acknowledgment of her compliment. "Thanks. Got another question?"

"Dating anyone? Married? Engaged?"

"That's more than one question, Katrina," he said, hoping to deflect the question as skillfully as she had his earlier.

"I know, but they're all kind of related, so I thought I could get away with it."

He debated telling her he was in a relationship. He didn't feel single, so it would be a partial truth. Katrina wasn't fishing—she was far from available herself—but it'd be better to have her think he was in a committed relationship. That way if that sexual tension ever found its way between them again, they would both know the boundaries. "I've been dating a woman for a couple years. She works PR in Miami." As an attorney, he knew the best lies were steeped in truth.

"Oh, that sounds exciting." Her eyes didn't match her voice, and the dark amber lost some of the sparkle.

"It can be a bit exhausting. She loves to go out, and a lot of the time it's part of her job. But when I've already put in a seventy-hour work week, going clubbing or to a benefit or gala isn't the first thing on my mind. What do you do for fun? When you're not being a librarian?"

Her shoulders hunched, she said, "I don't do too much. There's a lot in Minneapolis, they have a strong art scene—galleries, plays, ballet, things like that. But I'm a homebody. I'd rather stay home with a good book."

"You know where to find them," he said, hoping to bring the smile back to her face.

"I do, and Minneapolis is a popular stop for authors to do book signings or whatnot. I've gone to a few poetry readings. Being a librarian isn't what I wanted to do with my life, though there are worse things. Nan is a receptionist for a large insurance agency. She gets a great discount for her car insurance, but I can't think of anything more boring."

"At least she's not the one selling it."

"Not for long. She's studying to take the exams. Our trip to Santa Barbara was her last fling before she takes them—when she passes, she's going to open her own agency. I'm happy for her. In fact, I was tossing around the idea of giving her a little of the money I won at Blackout, to help with startup costs."

"That's nice of you."

"She's been a good friend."

"Yeah. I've figured that out."

"You being an attorney must take up a lot of your time. What kind are you, anyway?" she asked, pushing her glasses up her nose.

"Is that your question?"

Katrina scowled. "Yeah. It has to be, so you'll answer it."

"I'm an assistant district attorney." He crammed the cat's nose into its face, and its features scrunched up.

"I only know what they do from watching TV. They're always working really hard cases."

"It's not as glamorous as those shows make it look. I do a lot of grunt work, and it's easy to get burnt out."

"I'm sorry. Why did you want to be one, then? Do you eventually want to be a district attorney?"

"Don't know if that'll play out after this last case," he mumbled. "Anyway, we've been driving for a while. Hungry? There's a small town up ahead. We can top off the tank and find some food, if that sounds good?" The conversation had gotten too personal for his taste. He didn't mind offering some information about his work, but he didn't want to talk about the case that had gone to shit right before his eyes, and in front of the jury's.

She looked at him for a moment, and the tension he managed to ward off came back in full force. If she still wanted to drive after their stop, maybe he would stretch out in the back and sleep. Put some space between them—literally and figuratively.

Katrina nodded, swinging her gaze back to the road. "Sure. Sounds good. The snacks from the park didn't go very far."

"Because you were too busy picking up strays," he teased, making the cat's face tickle her cheek.

Laughing, trying to block him by shoving her cheek against her shoulder, she said, "At least it's not real. I had a habit of that as a kid."

"I bet," Aiden said, shifting in his seat and sliding the cat back onto its sleeping place on the dash. Her laugh did all sorts of things to his body.

The town off the interstate was farther away than he realized, and Aiden regretted the suggestion as the miles raced by. Miles and miles of flat, grassy terrain filled the windshield, a mountain range shadowy on the horizon, and the road empty except for them.

"What's going on up there?" she asked, slowing.

"What?" Aiden groaned as the flashing lights of a roadblock ahead became clear. "I don't know. I guess turning around to avoid it would look pretty damn suspicious." He wished they could, though. A roadblock couldn't mean anything good.

"We've got nothing to hide," she said, sliding down the window to speak to the young officer staring at them as they approached.

His police cruiser sat crosswise, blocking traffic each way. Lights flashed, blue and red fighting with the sun beginning its slow decent into the horizon.

"What can I do for you folks?" the officer asked, taking off his hat and running his fingers through his dirty-dishwater blond hair.

"We were hoping to drive through and find a place to gas up and eat. We're on our way to Denver," Katrina said, her tone friendly.

"Town's on lockdown, ma'am," the officer said, adjusting his cap with both hands. "We've a little boy missing since this morning. You won't mind a quick search of your vehicle, would you?"

Aiden sighed. Cops always asked, sounding like a person had a choice, but they never did. He was already unfastening his seat belt when Katrina answered.

"Of course not." She shifted into Park. "That's terrible."

"It sure is," the officer said. "Wolverton's a quiet town. Not much happens 'round here."

Aiden slid out of the truck and stretched. The temperature

was mild; the air smelled crisp and clean, unlike the dense, salty air he always breathed in Miami.

The SUV clicked as Katrina unlocked the doors. "You can look all you like," she invited. "What do you do in cases like this?"

"The last missing child we had in this town was before my time, ma'am," the officer said, opening the back driver's side door. He peered under the seats with a flashlight he'd taken from his utility belt. "Where you all driving from?"

Aiden rested his elbows on the hood of the SUV and enjoyed watching Katrina speak with the cop. She'd pulled her hair out of her bun as they drove, and it tumbled down her back, flitting in the gentle breeze blowing off the plain, her jeans molded to her butt and thighs, the tips of her toes peeking from the hems.

"We're coming from LA. Aiden's bringing me home to Minnesota. Because of the pilots' strike."

"Helluva thing," the officer said. He slammed the SUV's door shut. "You're clean."

Aiden resisted rolling his eyes. The boy's disappearance could have been the most exciting thing that had happened to the kid cop, and he was milking the situation for all it was worth.

"I'd advise you to turn around and make your pit stop elsewhere," the cop said, shoving his flashlight into his belt. "If I let you by, there's no telling when you could leave. Town's on lockdown 'til Jack is found."

"How old is he?" Katrina asked.

Aiden opened his door, hoping to signal to Katrina they should get back on the road. This detour cost them a whole hour already, and it had been for nothing.

"Jack's ten. Never disappeared before. Of course, his parents are worried sick."

"I can't imagine," Katrina murmured.

Aiden climbed into his seat. "Katrina." Getting sucked into this town's problems was the last thing he needed or wanted, but it was as if Katrina heard his thoughts.

"We'd love to help find Jack, wouldn't we, Aiden?" she asked through the open driver's side door.

The pleading in her eyes shot straight to the center of his heart. A woman who would pick up strays as a child, a woman who, with the money she won, planned to help her friend start a business. Of course she'd want to help find a missing child. Even knowing this would set them back another day, maybe more depending on when the kid turned up, he couldn't bear to tell her no.

Resting his forehead in defeat on the dash, he muttered, "Love to."

Chapter Five

"I did a bad thing, didn't I?" Kat asked as she drove them down the highway that turned into a narrow two-lane road. A sign announced, Wolverton, Pop. 900, and as they drove by, she winced. "I'm sorry."

Aiden hadn't spoken since they said goodbye to Officer Holbrooke. The officer was pleased she volunteered their services, radioing to his chief he was allowing in two people who offered to help in the search.

He blew out a breath. "No, it's fine. But we're going to be stuck in this town for God knows how long, Katrina."

"Kat."

"What?"

She twisted her mouth in annoyance. Hearing Aiden say her full name all the time grated on her nerves. No one used her full name except Neil and his mother. "You can call me Kat. At the airport I told you to call me Katrina, because . . ." She swallowed past the guilt turning her throat a scratchy sandpaper. She hadn't given Neil as much as a single thought for the past several hours.

"Because why?"

"Because Kat is a silly nickname. Katrina sounds more mature, and I need to get used to using it."

"Ah-huh," he said, not sounding like he believed it for one minute. "Well, I think it's cute, and it fits."

"Thanks." She appreciated him being on her side, but he wasn't the one she would be spending the rest of her life with. Relationships were full of compromise; she just didn't dwell on the fact it seemed she did most of it.

She drove them into Wolverton, the town milling with people holding flashlights, searching closed stores through dirty windows for the lost boy. As they inched down Main Street, several people stared suspiciously at the unfamiliar black truck.

Cars were parked in the VFW parking lot, the building Officer Holbrooke said the townspeople were using as search headquarters. Kat found an empty space a block away, grateful she didn't have to parallel park. She didn't want to admit to Aiden she didn't know how.

"I'm sorry," she whispered and turned off the truck. Aiden was right—if the town stayed on lockdown until Jack was found, it could be days until they were allowed to leave. "You're right. I'm wasting your vacation."

"Hey," Aiden said, releasing his seatbelt. Smoothing her hair behind her ear, he said, "It's nice you want to help. There's a little boy out there, lost, maybe hurt, and you want to help find him. There's nothing to be sorry for."

She wanted to lean in, let him cup her neck in his hand. She felt like she could curl into his lap and sleep for weeks. "That's nice of you to say."

"And true." He pulled his hand away, and she fought disappointment. "Let's go see what's what."

Kat followed Aiden into the VFW. Lights blazed, and tables were full of people somberly discussing the next place they would look. A corkboard on wheels with a large map attached to it sat at the front of the room, red pins dotting the areas, that, she guessed, had already been searched.

A woman with short brown hair and as wide as she was tall,

approached them, a sad smile lighting her face. "You two must be the city folk Billy said was comin'."

Kat held out her hand. "Billy? You mean Officer Holbrooke?"

The woman laughed. "Little Billy's been a cop for close to a year, and it still tickles me to hear him called that. He radioed in," the woman said, holding Kat's hand. "I'm Sandy. I live next door to the Peterson's—Jack's family."

"We'd like to help," Kat said, grasping the woman's thick fingers. She admired the way the woman tried to remain cheerful, even in light of the serious circumstances.

"And we appreciate it . . ." Sandy trailed off, her thick brown eyebrows lifting in question.

"Oh, I'm sorry. My name is Katrina, and this is Aiden."

Sandy blinked at Aiden. "My, my, you're a tall drink of water."

"Yes, ma'am," Aiden said, offering his hand, sounding as if he'd heard the line a million times before.

Kat stifled a smile. She'd gotten used to his towering size. In fact, she enjoyed it. Being with Aiden made her feel safe. He had a take-charge presence about him that told her he could handle anything.

"Two search parties are being put together now," Sandy said, leading them to a table full of people. "They just came back to use the bath—I mean, restrooms—and put new batteries in their flashlights."

Grim faces looked at each other over the table littered with Styrofoam containers of stale food and cold to-go cups of coffee. They'd been at this for a long time, and Kat's heart ached for Jack's mother. "How long has Jack been missing?"

"Since eight this morning. His mom said he ran off to do his chores around their farm and didn't come in for breakfast." This came from an older man dressed in denim overalls and wearing a dirty ball cap that covered a head full of white hair.

"That's my Marlon," Sandy whispered in her ear.

"He's quite a catch," Kat murmured.

Sandy beamed. "I know." She clapped her hands, and the people at the table gave her their attention. "This here's Katrina and Aiden. They were going to pass through town on their way to Denver, but when Billy pulled them over at the checkpoint, they offered to help. We have two groups going out. Do we have room for them?"

"I can take the big fella," Marlon said around a toothpick sticking out of his mouth. "We're going back over to the coal mine. Ain't fit for women."

Alarmed, Kat jerked around to meet Aiden's eyes. "I don't think—"

He rested his hands on her shoulders and squeezed. "It's fine. It'll be fine. I've never been in a coal mine before."

"If you say so." She didn't like the thought of Aiden in a dark mine. But he wouldn't be alone, and this had been her idea. She'd look like a coward if she backed out now.

"I know so." He pushed a kiss to the top of her head, and her nerves tingled.

He followed the group of men into the street, and Kat swallowed a lump in her throat as he walked away.

Sandy squeezed her arm. "He'll be okay, sugar. The mines are safe, just a bunch of hidey-holes that need to be checked again, in case Jack doubled back."

Kat tried to smile.

"Now, you're coming with us. Here's a flyer so you'll know him if you see him. Us women are going to search the fairgrounds. We hold a teeny-tiny fair every spring, and the benefits go to the 4-H club. Lots of buildings to hide in."

Kat studied the boy—the headshot looked like his school photo. The flyer stated he was dressed in jeans, a red t-shirt, and a blue, red, and white Captain America hoodie.

"We checked earlier in the day, but now we're going through town again. Wolverton is small; Jack must be on the move."

If the little boy was still in town. Sandy didn't say it, but the words hung over the women sitting at the table, and Kat stared her sandals to give them a moment to pull themselves together. "Where are his parents?" she asked when the silence became too much to bear.

"At home, waiting, in case Jack goes back on his own." Tears sprang to Sandy's eyes. Sniffling, she led Kat and three others to a minivan parked in front of the building.

She squeezed into the back beside a teenaged girl who was trying not to cry. "I'm Kat," she said, holding out her hand.

"Poppy," the blonde girl said, wiping her cheeks with a crumpled tissue.

"Do you know Jack well?" Kat asked, as the van lurched onto the street.

"I babysit him, sometimes," Poppy whispered.

"Can you tell me about him?" Kat wanted Poppy to focus on finding Jack, not the fact he was missing. And it would help her to know a little about the boy she'd be looking for.

Poppy sniffed. "He loves dogs and cats—he'd get a kick out of your name," she said. "Likes all animals, really. He's into superheroes, and his dad drives him into Silver Bullet whenever he can. That's a town about a half hour from here, and they have a movie theater. Me and my friends drive there sometimes. I got my driver's license two months ago."

"That's fun," Kat said, encouraging Poppy to keep talking. "Sandy said something about chores?"

Poppy nodded, a streetlight catching the golden spirals of her hair. Once the sun decided to go down, it had dropped like a lead ball. They'd be searching for Jack in the dark. "Yeah. His parents raise horses, and they take in rescues. He probably had to muck out the stalls or something."

"He's an only child?"

"For now; his mom's pregnant."

"And he's a happy boy?"

Poppy lifted her chin. "Yeah. For sure. I don't believe the nasty people who're saying he ran away."

Kat's heart dropped. If he hadn't run away . . . the other options were much worse.

"You got a pretty little wife," Marlon commented, flicking his flashlight over the crushed gravel floor of the mine.

On the drive, Marlon explained the mine was small compared to some, but when Rocky Mountain Power shut it down, the town died. "We're struggling, no doubt about it," he said, and the two burly men who'd squished into the back of Marlon's extended cab agreed.

Though the fence had been cut away in places by kids and vandals who wanted to explore the mine, Marlon had a key for the gate, saving them from having to struggle through one of the many jagged holes.

Dressed in work clothes Marlon kept in the bed of his pickup truck, Aiden stank of motor oil and gasoline. He was thankful for the steel-toed boots, even if they were a half size too small. Walking over the crushed rock would be easier . . . and, thinking of Kat's worry, safer.

His stomach rumbled, and the sound echoed through the tunnel. It saved him from having to explain that Kat wasn't his wife.

"Billy said you were using Wolverton as a pit stop. Sorry little Jack cut into your plans."

"It's fine," Aiden mumbled, not wanting to sound like an asshole about the whole thing. It was sweet of Kat to volunteer their time. Samantha . . . wouldn't have taken the time to help find a lost boy. Her way of giving back was by writing a fat check, sitting on the board of a charity, or snapping at florists when they set the tables with the wrong floral arrangements at high-priced benefits.

"When we find Jack, I'll treat ya to a big steak. You're not one of those weird vegetarians, are ya?"

"No, a steak sounds pretty damned perfect. With a tall glass of beer."

Marlon slapped him on the back. "Thatta boy."

"You married, Marlon?" Aiden liked the old man. He wouldn't mind sitting down and playing a couple hands of poker with him and his friends. When Kat volunteered their time, he'd been annoyed, but now he didn't mind being out in the cool air, breathing in air tainted with age and dust.

He hadn't acknowledged Marlon's comment about Kat, and now the old man believed they were married.

Shit.

Too late now. He'd been too caught up in looking around the mine. He'd never been in one before, had never taken sight-seeing trips with his family. Didn't have pictures of his gawky teenage self standing proudly with his brother and parents in front of cheesy destination places like Yosemite National Park, or in caves with stalactites and stalagmites longer than his body.

"Yep. My Sandy took your girl with her. Been married going on forty years. Would do it all over again."

"Jesus, Marlon, you marry her when you were twelve or what?"

Marlon hacked out a laugh. "Kind of you to say, boy, but I'm going on sixty-five." He pounded his chest and belched, the crude sound bouncing off the stone walls. "Feel thirty, though."

"How'd you manage to stay married to the same woman for so long?" he asked.

"That'd be a question for her, no doubt about it. She's stuck by me, not the other way 'round. When I had a heart attack two years ago, she didn't leave my side for a second. Cotton-pickin' woman."

Aiden hid a smile, though Marlon wouldn't have been able to see it anyway, not unless the old coot shone his flashlight into his face. Though Marlon was a talker, he exuded a concentration Aiden admired. Not for one second had he stopped looking for Jack.

Aiden waved his own flashlight around the tunnel. He didn't know what he should be looking for. Candy wrappers? Maybe the kid himself sleeping in a corner, oblivious to the fear and panic he was causing.

"That's what you gotta do—find a woman who'll stick by ya."

Aiden stifled a scoff. Samantha left him for another man, and he was delivering Kat to her fiancé.

He didn't have a good woman in his life right now. No, that wasn't true.

His mother had never let him down.

"Did you?"

Marlon's question brought him back to the dark, dank, tunnel.

"Did I what?" Aiden asked.

"Find a woman who'll do right by ya?"

He played along. "It's a little late for that."

Marlon hooted. "Got that right. Either you're gonna be happier than a pig in shit, or down right miserable." He slapped Aiden on the back. "Little luck, maybe both. Can't be happy without a little sadness. Learned that the hard way."

Aiden swung his flashlight around. They were wandering deeper into the mine, and he doubted Jack would have ventured this far. But maybe the kid knew the tunnels like the back of his hand, and this was only the beginning of their search.

A sparkle caught the flashlight's beam, and Aiden almost missed it. He was more adept at looking for clues on paper. "How'd that happen?"

"Me and Sandy broke up once. That woman wouldn't know compromise even if it bit her in the butt. For a Christian woman, she's got a temper on her."

Aiden caught the sparkle again and started toward it. "Yeah, you gotta watch those church ladies."

"No doubt about it. I only lasted a week before I was at her door, hat in my hands. Told her I was a fool. Almost cried when she took me back without a single word. Married her that weekend and haven't spent a night apart since."

Hunkering down to his haunches, Aiden shifted the gravel and unearthed a red metal Iron Man. He bet Tony Stark hadn't gotten down here by himself.

Can't be happy without a little sadness.

"Marlon," he said, holding out the action figure. "You may be right."

The next time he had an hour to himself, he'd give Samantha a call. He couldn't know happiness without pain, and he couldn't have happiness if he couldn't compromise. He could at least do the latter and see if it earned him the former.

But first they had a little boy to find.

Kat wrapped an old hoodie that smelled of cinnamon closer around her. After the sun sank under the horizon, the air turned cool, and her blouse and jeans weren't enough to keep her warm. When she stepped out of the van, Sandy caught her shivering and gave it to her to wear. Six sizes too big, the fleece hoodie decorated with the Girl Scout logo acted more as a blanket, but she accepted it gratefully. As it was, the dew-soaked grass wet her feet, and she tried to hide how it creeped her out when the wet blades brushed the tops of her toes.

"The large building yonder belongs to our 4-H organization. There're animals in there, so don't go traipsing in if you're scared of cows and such," Sandy said, aiming the flashlight at Kat, though being kind enough not to blind her.

She didn't mind animals, though in her sandals she would prefer not to step into a big pile of poop. "What's over there?" She pointed to another cluster of buildings.

"Those are the buildings we use to sell things. Jewelry, jam, other homemades like quilts. The grassy clearing is where the fair folk set up the rides. Are you going to stay with Poppy?"

Kat looked at the girl; she'd finally gotten her crying under control.

Poppy nodded.

"Good," Sandy said. "Poppy's a good girl and knows the area. She's got my phone number in her cell, so if you find something, let me know ASAP. I got a text while we were on the road. Jack's mother is having contractions. Doc said it's stress, but it's not looking good. Maude and Thelma will go with me this way, you go that way. Don't split up. If we don't find him here, we'll go back to the VFW to regroup. Good luck, girls."

Kat and Poppy shuffled with their flashlights, drifting the bright lights over the rundown buildings. She didn't know what to say, and she scrambled to make small talk. "Jack's mother is pretty far along?"

Poppy shrugged. "I guess so. Thirty-six weeks, I think. Our school isn't big on sex ed. A girl in our high school got knocked up last year, and she was only fifteen. Her parents sent her off to live with her dad's sister. Don't know what came of it."

"Do you have a boyfriend?" Kat asked, glad Poppy couldn't see the horror the thought of a pregnant fifteen-year-old girl, and her parents giving her away, brought to her face. Poppy led her to the huge 4-H building. Kat could already smell the manure and hay.

"Nope."

"Good. You're too young for it anyway. Men aren't worth the trouble they cause."

"I don't have a boyfriend, I have a girlfriend." Poppy laughed.

"Oh," Kat said, taken aback. She hadn't expected Poppy to say that, and with so much mischief, too. "Good for you."

Poppy elbowed her. "Come on. Of all the places in Wolverton Jack could end up, this would be the place. I bet he's already been here a couple times already. Once he entered a foal in the 4-H competition and won second prize." She paused. "You have a hot husband."

"Thank you, but he's not—"

"Jack!" Poppy called out, cutting her off.

She let Poppy's comment go. There wasn't much harm in letting Poppy think Kat and Aiden were married, and she didn't want to start up any questions about why they were traveling together. "Jack!" Kat joined in over the ruckus their shouting made in the barn. "The animals don't like us yelling."

"Won't do anything anyway," Poppy said, and sighed. "If he doesn't want to be found, all we did was warn him off."

"You'd think he would be hungry or thirsty or something by now." Kat's own stomach rumbled. Her measly bag of chips was too long ago, and the thought of the food at the VFW, no matter how old it was, made her mouth water.

"I bet that kid has stashes all over the place."

They walked through the barn, and Kat covered her nose. Stalls and pens of cows, goats, and horses lined the walls, and at the end of the building, a pig pen took up the last twenty feet. "Who feeds these animals?"

"The 4-H girls learn animal care. Don't feel sorry for them out here all alone—it's the only peace they get. They hate we're in here. Let's go."

Poppy led her out the back of the barn, and she gulped a breath of fresh air. Even if the animals were regularly attended to, they still stank.

Country girl she was not.

"What's out that way?" Kat asked, shining her light toward a grouping of trees.

Poppy shook her head, and her hair swished against the red nylon vest she wore over a white long-sleeved shirt. "Nothing. Wolverton Creek. There's a rickety old bridge, and some old shack thing that my mom said someone used to live in, like in the 1800s, that hasn't fallen down yet. She said not to go in there because any minute it's going to collapse. Mom keeps begging Marlon to have the city tear it down, that someone's gonna get hurt."

"Who's Marlon?" Kat asked, studying the border of trees, trying to find the shape of a small boy in the shadows.

"Sandy's husband. He's our mayor. He keeps saying Wolverton doesn't have the money, and it pisses Mom off something terrible. Sorry," she mumbled. "I shouldn't swear."

"I won't tell. Listen, I think we should at least check it out."

Poppy pulled on Kat's sleeve. "No. Jack knows not to go in there. He's smarter than that."

"But—"

"I'm going to find Sandy," Poppy said, "and tell her the barn is clear. Are you comin'?"

"Let me just check the shack," Kat said, taking a step. "I'll meet you at the van."

"All right, if you really want to. Be careful. I would go with you, but my mom said no. And he's not over there anyway. It's really late—I bet if we talk to Sandy she'll tell us he finally went home."

"I'll be right there."

Kat tried to pick up her feet as she stepped, but it didn't do much to keep the grass from creepily brushing along the sides of her feet. The hems of her pants were damp, and they slapped at her ankles as she walked. She wondered how Aiden was doing. She really did feel guilty about sucking them into this, and now they were going to have to find a place to spend the night. Wolverton may not have a decent motel, and instead of scorpions, she'd be cowering from cockroaches.

Playing Twenty Questions with him had been fun, and she'd learned a little bit about him, too. He obviously got back together with Samantha or he would have told her he was single. He must love her a lot to take her back after she ran off to marry another man. She was a lucky woman he gave her a second chance.

No wonder why he was so angry with her for volunteering their time; he planned to spend the rest of his vacation with her.

Kat couldn't volunteer to drive back to Minnesota alone or tell him he could take the truck and let her find her own way home because she would have to admit she read his letter. He had no idea she knew about his problem with Samantha.

The shack came into view as Kat picked her way over the decrepit bridge. The planks creaked under her feet, but they held steady. Still, she hurried over it, only stopping to breathe after she reached the other side.

The building looked as Poppy described, the roof missing shingles, the wood weathered and rotting. The whole thing sloped to the side, as though it could indeed fall to the ground at any moment. A gigantic hole punctured the porch, and the front door hung on one hinge.

The young girl was right, there was no way she was going in there.

She turned around, ready to find Sandy and the others, when she heard the sniffling.

"Jack?" she asked, her voice sounding too loud in the darkness.

The sniffling stopped.

"Jack," she tried again, "are you in there?"

She should get help instead of checking things out for herself, and against her better judgment, she carefully placed her foot on the porch step and tested her weight against the wood. Though the planks of the bridge held, the entire porch felt like it would not, bowing under the pressure of her foot. She prayed it would hold, and again, she tested the next step, until she reached the top. Those three steps felt like a million. God, she didn't want to break through the wood. Rats probably lived under there.

"Jack, I'm not going to hurt you. The whole town's been looking for you," she said, inching her way across the rotted wood. She peered into the cabin, keeping her light on the ground, as much to look for critters as to keep from blinding the little boy.

Her light struck a gold pile on the floor, and she realized it was a yellow lab nursing a litter of puppies.

A skinny boy sat next to them, tears running down his cheeks, rubbing the mother dog on her muzzle.

"Jack." Relief filled Kat's heart, and she pushed back her own tears. "Are you okay? Are you hurt?"

Jack shook his head.

"What are you—" Kat stopped. It was evident what he was doing. The dog just birthed puppies, and he didn't want to leave them alone. But . . . "Is this your dog? Why didn't you go home and let someone know?"

She slowly slid her way across the floor. The boards looked more intact than the porch, but they groaned under her feet like they could give away any second.

The yellow lab looked at her curiously but went back to her puppies as Jack stroked her neck.

"Can I sit?" she asked when the boy didn't say anything.

Jack looked surprised by the question, but nodded. "I guess you're going to tell everyone where I am," he said bitterly, wiping his cheeks on a sleeve of his Captain America hoodie.

"Yeah." She had to be honest. "Sandy and some of her friends are here searching the fairgrounds for you. I was with Poppy, but she said you were too smart to hide in here. I guess not, huh?" She sat on the floor in front of Jack, near the dog. She let the dog smell her hand before she ran her fingers through the soft fur.

"I wouldn't've, but I found Portia in here."

"That's the dog's name?" Kat cradled the flashlight in her lap, and they used the light to look at each other.

"Yeah. She used to be my dog. Mom and Dad gave her away— said we couldn't afford to keep her. But she loves me, knows where she lives—" Jack started crying. "She runs home, and Dad brings her back, and she runs home."

"Oh, God, Jack," she murmured, covering her mouth.

"She doesn't want to live there, and today, this morning, I went to find her, cuz Ted and Amanda said she ran away again, but I knew she was gonna have her puppies soon. I looked for her all day. Looked everywhere, and finally I found her here. It was too late to bring her somewhere better."

"It's too cold, Jack. She can't spend the night here."

Jack leaned into Portia's body. "She's my dog."

Kat sighed. "Yeah, she is."

"Don't tell them, please, lady."

"My name is Kat, but we have to tell them. Think of Portia and her babies. She needs a vet to look her over, and food. She just had puppies, and she's probably hungry and thirsty. It will be too cold overnight. She and her puppies need to be indoors, warm."

"I'll never get her back," Jack whispered.

"Sometimes we have to do things we don't want to do," she said. "It's part of growing up."

"You're just saying that because you're a grownup, and you can do whatever you want."

Kat laughed, but there was no joy in the sound. "Is that what you think? Do you think your parents wanted to give Portia away when they knew how much it would hurt you? I do things every day I don't want to do, and I've *promised* to do a lot of those things. I know you want to take care of her, and I'll do my best to try to make your parents understand." Kat doubted they could afford Portia's litter if they had trouble feeding Portia alone. "Ted and Amanda, they're nice?"

"Yeah," Jack said, pulling away from the dog.

"Then you should be thankful for that."

"I guess," he muttered.

"You're in a lot of trouble, you know," she warned him.

"I know."

"And your mom isn't doing too good. She's going to have a baby, like Portia? She's worried sick about you. I don't know them, but it sounds like your parents are good people, and doing the best they can, even though they're going through hard times. Life's not easy." *Something you're finding out,* she thought, wanting to hug Jack to her.

Closing his eyes, Jack leaned against the shack's wall, and Kat shone her light around the cabin. Windows with the glass broken out of the panes let in the chilly spring air. Old furniture looked just as it had two hundred years ago, but for a thick layer of dust. The old boards of the floor moaned under her butt when she shifted.

Portia perked her ears at the sound and whined.

"I need to let them know you're here. Poppy's going to look for me when I don't go back."

Jack pressed his nose to the side of Portia's head. "Okay. Even if I can't keep her, I just want her taken care of."

"I know you do. Here, I'm sure Sandy won't mind if we let Portia use her hoodie. She won't be out here much longer." Kat slipped off the huge hoodie and gently laid it over Portia and her pups. "This will help a little bit—until someone can come for her."

Sniffling, and swatting at his jeans, Jack stood. "Who are you, anyway? I know everybody in town."

Kat ruffled the boy's hair; he stood almost as tall as she. "I was going to pass through town, but you disappearing kind of put a stop to that. Rather than turn around, I said I would help find you."

When Portia whimpered, Jack cast a worried look at the dog. "Turn around?"

Kat aimed the flashlight at the floor; she didn't want to trip over anything. "The town's on lockdown, kid."

"Cool!"

She hid her smile. While she could appreciate Jack's enthusiasm, now wasn't the time, and she didn't want to encourage it. "Not everyone thinks it's cool, especially your mom and dad. Portia will be okay here for a little bit longer. Come on, it's time to face the music."

When Kat stepped into the VFW behind Jack, the whole room cheered. Jack's parents, a tall blond man and a woman who looked ready to pop at any moment, rushed to them. The woman hugged Jack and started crying. The man embraced his wife and son, pressing his lips to the woman's head, tears dripping from his eyes.

VANIA RHEAULT

Kat received many pats on the back, handshakes, and promises of help if there was anything she needed, any time she needed it.

She didn't hear any of the thanks, her eyes searching the crowded room for Aiden.

He sat in a dark corner, brooding over a beer with Marlon and his gang, who were talking a mile a minute, but he wasn't listening, as far as Kat could tell.

She let out a breath, relieved he was okay; she hadn't liked the thought of him in the old mine.

Chilled to the bone after giving up Sandy's hoodie to Portia, exhausted, and starving to death, she pushed through the crowd to tell him they could find a hotel.

He met her gaze as she walked toward him, his blue eyes chilled, steaming like a block of dry ice as he watched her.

"Are you okay?" she asked, her voice quavering as she reached out, the diamond of her engagement ring sparkling in the yellowish-green light of the old fluorescent bulbs.

"I'm fine."

She nodded because there wasn't anything else she could do, but she didn't believe him. "We can get on the road now. I know you want to get home as soon as possible."

"Yeah," he said, shoving his beer away, almost tipping the glass over.

"You'll do no such thing!"

Around her huge belly, Jack's mother pulled Kat into an awkward hug. The woman squeezed so hard, her ribs felt like they would crack.

"What?" she gasped as the woman let go, her lungs filling with air.

"You'll come home with us. It's too late to drive anywhere, and we have a perfectly fine guest room you can sleep in. It's the least we can do. I'm May, by the way." May looked over her shoulder at her husband, who nodded gravely, his hands gripping

Jack's shoulders, like he would never let the boy out of his sight again.

"Oh, but we really couldn't—" Kat began, not wanting to delay any longer. Though the whole thing turned out fine, Aiden would stop being so patient. He was doing her a favor, seeing her home, and she had to stop imposing on his kindness.

"We're not going to take no for an answer. We want time to properly thank you."

"It would mean a lot to us," Jack's father said.

"That's my husband, Danny. Please," May asked, her imploring eyes filling with tears.

Aiden sat sullenly in his chair, looking as if he'd rather be anywhere else. "We appreciate it," he said, standing from his seat.

"Good, it's settled," May said, rubbing her belly. "We're all exhausted, and we couldn't leave you to fend for yourselves. Come on."

Kat followed them out of the VFW, well-wishers slowing them down, and it felt like an hour passed before they reached the door.

Through a chilly night speckled with stars and a bright moon cutting the darkness, May led them to a grey truck with an extended cab and full box.

"We have our own truck—we'll follow you," Aiden said, continuing down the sidewalk, his hands shoved deep into his pockets, a heavy gait to his step.

May tilted her head toward him. "Is he okay? Your husband doesn't look happy."

"He'll be okay. He's just tired—we were up early to get ahead start." Shivering, goosebumps covering her skin, Kat trotted to the SUV and settled into the seat, grateful for the warmer temperature inside the vehicle.

The door to the VFW opened, and a joyful sound spilled into the air. There would be a lot of partying tonight. Years from now she would look back at this road trip and smile. Tonight, she became part of this small town's history.

Aiden didn't offer any conversation as he followed the Peterson's truck down a gravel road.

Giving him space, she squished herself against her door, her forehead pressed against the cool glass.

He turned the SUV into a long driveway and parked behind Danny. He sat for a moment, and she thought he would offer some explanation, maybe congratulate her for finding Jack, but all he said was, "Bring in your bag," and he slammed out of the truck before she could reply.

May ushered them into the house, a drafty monstrosity Kat thought would be expensive to heat in the winter. She had some experience with trying to stay warm as the snow fell.

The walls creaked, and the floorboards groaned as they followed May to a bedroom at the top of the stairs. "There's a bathroom attached. You're welcome to clean up, but be warned the water heater isn't very big and doesn't work that fast. In the morning, we'll make you a big breakfast to see you off. Goodnight, and again, thank you so much." May kissed Kat's cheek before making her way down the hall and disappearing into a different bedroom.

Kat used the bathroom to change and came out, her arms crossed over her breasts. All she had for pajamas were sexy negligees and teddies, sheer nightgowns and lace panties. "I'm sorry they think we're married," she said, scrambling into the king-sized bed. At least there would be enough room they wouldn't have to touch each other while they slept. Squishing into a double bed, or even a queen, while he was mad at her, would have been absolute sheer torture.

Aiden didn't say anything, only stripped off his clothes.

She tried not to stare, but she couldn't help it. The man's body was a work of art: broad chest, flat stomach, narrow hips, strong thighs. She squeezed her eyes shut, and Aiden flipped off the light.

The mattress squeaked as he slid into bed, and Kat rolled onto her side, putting as much space between them as she could.

An uneasy silence settled in the room, and many hours passed by before Kat finally drifted off to sleep.

Aiden woke up in an empty bed. He shielded his eyes with his arm, sunlight streaming into the room through a window decorated with white curtains billowing in the slight breeze. He'd been an absolute dick last night, and he didn't blame Kat for hightailing it out of there. He pictured her on the shoulder of a dusty road dragging her carry-on as she hitched a ride because the last thing she wanted to do was spend another second with him.

He couldn't blame her, and he didn't know what he'd tell her if she asked for an explanation. One minute he'd been happy he decided to give Samantha a chance to explain, taking Marlon's advice seriously, and the next he'd been so pissed about the whole mess, he wished he had the balls to tell Samantha to go to hell.

Seeing Kat last night in some sexy little number, pure silver, like the mercury in a thermometer, slithering down her body, hugging her curves like his hands wanted to do, didn't help the way he felt.

He wondered how hurt she'd be if he asked her to take that stupid ring off her finger.

He was tired of people thinking they were married.

Aiden took a quick shower and dressed in the only clean clothes he had left: a black pair of jeans and a black dress shirt. The expensive clothes didn't fit in with this part of the country, and as he trotted down the stairs toward the mouth-watering aromas of bacon and coffee, he felt like a pimp, or a movie star trying too hard.

"Hey, good morning," Danny said, sitting at the table, holding a newspaper. "You're just in time, everything is still hot."

"Black coffee is fine," Aiden said, though his stomach rumbled. He and Kat hadn't ended up eating anything last night.

"Doesn't sound fine," Danny said, amused. "Let me get you a

plate. I owe you more than breakfast for what you and your wife did for us last night."

"It was her idea," he said, then stopped, pursing his lips as Danny handed him a large mug filled to the brim.

Danny let the implication slide. "Then we appreciate it all the more that she was able to convince you to help."

"Where is the scamp?" Aiden asked, looking around the room, as if Jack would materialize right before his eyes.

"Been and gone already," Danny said, sliding into his seat at the table. "Even though it was late, Ted brought Portia and her pups home last night, figured Jack wouldn't be able to sleep until he knew they were okay and home where they belonged. I can't believe this was all about a dog, but I should've. He's had Portia since she was a puppy. I should've known there was no way we could give her away. I should've made it work somehow." He rubbed his eyes.

Aiden had no idea what the man was talking about, and said so, filling is plate from a platter of eggs and bacon placed in the middle of the table.

"Kat didn't tell you?" Danny raised an eyebrow.

"We didn't talk last night," he said and had to hold back a growl when Danny mistook his words.

"Oooooh, I see. Well, then, let me tell you what happened."

Aiden listened to the story, Danny and May trying to make ends meet, paying, or not paying, the bills for the horse farm, giving away Portia, trying to cut down some costs. Jack running away to look for the dog. "I didn't know she was pregnant. Had puppies in an old shack off the fairgrounds. It's where Kat found him. No one thought to look in the cabin because we've told Jack never to go in there. It's going to fall down any minute, but of course, he'd keep that dog company, no matter what. We owe your wife a debt we'll never be able to repay. You're a lucky man, Aiden."

Some man would be, but it wouldn't be him.

The coffee curdled in is stomach, and the scrambled eggs turned to ash in his mouth. "Where is she, anyway?"

Danny nodded toward the front door. "She's outside with May. Showing her the farm. You're not interested in adopting a horse, by chance?"

Aiden pointed his gaze outside where Katrina, off into the distance, leaned against a weathered fence chatting with May. She left her hair down again, and it whipped in the wind. The white of her blouse sparkled in the sun. He compared the two women, May, taller than Kat by a few inches, round with child, her skin glowing with the joy of knowing her little boy was safe. And Kat, his little Kat, petite, thin, and in a flash of wish in his eye, he pictured her heavy with his child. What would it be like to live in a huge house, children underfoot, land as far as he could see? Land he owned.

Resisting the urge to run his hands over his eyes in misery and fatigue, Aiden said, "I think you're the lucky one."

"It's gorgeous out here," Kat said and breathed in a deep lungful of fresh air. Well, it wasn't entirely fresh. Notes of manure, hay, and dust lingered, but it smelled better than the exhaust she had to inhale every day on her way to work.

"We're going to lose it," May said, staring across the corral at three horses sniffing at the grass along the edge of the fence.

"What do you mean?" Kat asked, resting her arms on top of the fence, her chin on her hands. The horses were beautiful, but she didn't know what kind they were. She hadn't had any exposure to horses; she only knew they were expensive pets.

"We raise horses to sell, and board them for neighbors and such, but we take them in too, and there's not a month goes by that someone doesn't drop off a horse." May sighed. "Last month we found a half-starved stallion tied to our mailbox at the end of the drive. We had the vet out here, thinking we'd have to put the poor thing down. Doing okay now, but he's skittish, scared."

"That's terrible," Kat murmured, sympathizing with May. While growing up, she'd been known to bring home a cat or a dog, even a bird, but her mother, bless her, wouldn't have let Kat bring home a horse.

"It is, and it costs money, you know. Vet bills, food. Horses need exercise, and if they've been abused, we get someone out here to work with them. I used to do it, but Danny doesn't want me around the horses that way, not now." May rubbed her belly. "I agree with him, but leaving them in a stall hurts them just as much as what their owners were doing before dumping them on us. We have to get horse whisperers out here, and they cost."

"May, why did Jack run away?" Kat asked tentatively, not wanting to stick her nose in where it didn't belong but wanting to help in some way. "Was it just about Portia? You're worried about paying the bills—did he pick up on that?"

May leaned against the fence. "Yeah. Danny and I, we fight a lot. He thinks we should give up the farm, sell it. Hell, the bank threatens to take it from us on a daily basis, anyway, so let them, you know? Move to Silver Bullet where Danny runs a mechanic shop. But who would take the horses if we stop? See that white one?" She pointed across the corral to a whitish-grey horse, sniffing at the grass like she didn't have a care in the world.

"She's beautiful."

"About two years ago, the Humane Society in Silver Bullet rescued her from a farm about an hour away. They were beating on her something fierce." May whistled, and the horse looked straight at her, trotted to them, and offered her neck for a rub. "Wouldn't let anyone touch her, but look at her now."

"You can't adopt out the horses you take in?" Kat asked.

"Some of the horses aren't mistreated at all, and we adopt those out as quick as we can, but sometimes finding the right family can take a lot of time. We've got a reputation now, for taking horses, no questions asked. I would be afraid of what would happen to those horses if we weren't here. Like Milkshake. If we hadn't been able to take her, she would have been put down. She's one of the ones we can't adopt out. She trusts us, and that's it. Even trusting us comes and goes depending on her mood. She won't let us saddle her. If no one can ride her, she's just a pretty horse that needs food and constant exercise. Who wants a horse like that? No one but me." A tear dripped down May's cheek.

Kat bit her lip. "Can I ask how much you owe?"

"The farm isn't paid off, and most months we have to decide if we pay the mortgage or buy food for us and the horses. Food wins out, but it won't matter if we don't have anywhere to eat it."

Running a hand over May's arm she said, "That didn't answer my question."

"We're behind by seven thousand dollars," May whispered. "We'll never catch up. I don't know why Danny and I fight. There's nothing to fight over. When the little one comes, I'll get a job. We'll make it work. Somehow."

There was no way Kat was going to let Danny and May lose their farm. "Wait here."

She ran across the grass and hollered through the screen door, "Aiden, can you unlock the truck, please?"

"Yeah, just a second," he replied, but she was already off and running, listening for the locks to click open.

She opened the back and grabbed her aluminum case from under the backseat. Quickly, her heart pounding, she counted five bundles of two thousand dollars apiece. It seemed surreal so much money took up so little space.

When Kat reached a bewildered May, all she could do was smile. "Here. I want you to have this. It's ten thousand dollars."

May clasped her hands behind her back as if she were afraid to touch it. "What for? I can't take your money. Where did you get it?"

Holding out the stacks of bills, Kat said, "Aiden and I are driving from Vegas. I won a little at a slot machine. It's okay," she encouraged, pushing the cash toward her. "Take it."

May stepped back. "No. I can't do that. That's too much, and you don't even know us."

"I know enough. Listen, I want to sponsor a horse, or more than one. Milkshake, or the next horse you find tied to your mailbox. I want to help. If you take the money, you can do something for me in return."

A flicker of movement caught her eye. Aiden stood on the porch with Danny, watching her, a scowl turning down his mouth.

Uncertainly, May took the money, holding it like it was a bomb that could go off any moment. "Anything."

"If you ever get a chance to name a horse, will you name it KitKat? When I was a little girl, my mother would call me that. She's been gone for a while now, and it would mean a lot to me to have that passed down in some way."

"Of course. I don't know what to say." May started crying.

Kat gathered the pregnant woman in her arms the best she could and met Aiden's eyes. "You don't have to say anything."

Chapter Six

"That was a nice thing you did back there," Aiden said later, driving them toward Denver.

The goodbyes had been a teary affair, Jack giving Kat a long, hard hug.

Aiden was taken with how the boy had attached himself to her, though he didn't blame the kid at all.

"I hope they can make it work," Kat said, her eyes closed, her head resting against the seat. "It's easy to fall behind."

She sounded like she spoke from experience, and Aiden admired her even more. Not everyone would be willing to give away part of their nest egg.

They drove in silence, an uneasy truce linking them together. He wished they could go back to talking and laughing like they had before they pulled into Wolverton, before the decision to talk to Samantha turned him into an asshole.

He asked Kat to find a hotel she'd like to stay in and make the reservations.

Without saying a word, she scrolled through a list of hotels on her phone and reserved two rooms at a Hilton across the street from a large shopping center.

She hadn't spoken, hadn't looked his way, and the silence wiggled under his skin, irritating him like a stinging bug bite.

At the hotel, he pulled his carry-on from the back. The tense drive made his shoulders and neck ache, the pain shooting into his head, and his temples throbbed. He craved a drink.

It didn't matter if she liked him or not. There wasn't any point remaining friends. She'd marry Neil, and maybe . . . he didn't know what the future held for him.

They checked into their rooms, and Aiden let a determined Kat pay for them to ward off a fight.

"Do you want to meet for dinner?" he asked as they rode the elevator to the third floor. The Hilton was pleasant as far as hotels went, and he wondered if Kat chose it to please him or if she was splurging for herself.

"I think I'll just take a long bath and order room service, if that's all right."

"Yeah, sure." Aiden stood outside her door as she unlocked it with her keycard, let herself in with a bleak smile his way before the door shut with a soft click.

Aiden dragged his carry-on into his room, the suite more space than he needed. It wasn't equipped with a minibar, and he called room service to request a couple lowballs of scotch.

After they were delivered, he downed one in a smooth gulp.

Slowly, he lowered himself onto the bed, his joints creaking like an old man's. He stared at his phone in dread, Samantha's number mocking him. Before he could connect the call, his phone buzzed. Nick's number glowed white text on black screen, and he answered, relieved he could put off his phone call to Samantha a while longer.

"Nick," he said, standing from the bed. He stared across the city, the mountain range sitting in the background like a pretty painting.

"Hey, how's the trip?"

"Could be worse," he said, then took a sip of the other glass of scotch. He should have ordered three instead of two. "We searched for a missing boy yesterday."

"What?" Nick asked. "What are you talking about?"

Aiden explained what happened down to the last when he promised Jack he'd send him a letter from Miami, and told Danny he'd look into making their horse rescue a nonprofit to help them out money- and tax-wise.

"Well, your little adventure is over, you can breathe easy," Nick said.

"What do you mean?" His adventure, as Nick so politely phrased it, would take at least a few more days. In fact, he should map out the next leg of their trip, make reservations for tomorrow night's stop.

"Haven't you seen the news? Strike's over. Get your ass to the nearest airport, buy a ticket for the next available flight, and get back here."

Aiden's mouth dried up.

The strike was over.

He could drive Kat to the airport right now, and he could be at his brother's place by midnight.

"Aiden? Samantha's here, in LA, staying at the Beverly Hills. She's been here the whole time, but she was scared to tell you. She wants to see you, but she's afraid you don't want to talk to her because you're not answering her calls. I said that was ridiculous. Come back and finish your vacation in LA while you work this out. Maybe relaxing at the hotel with her for a few days will help. You can get everything out into the open."

Aiden lifted the drink to his face, the glass cooling his skin. When he didn't say anything, Nick continued, "She loves you. She had her reasons for doing what she did, but you need to talk to her and let her explain. You'll forgive her the minute you know, but it's nothing that should be spoken about over the phone. Especially by me."

"I take part of the blame," he said, staring across the city. "We shouldn't have been together. It's no wonder she turned down my proposal—I shouldn't have asked."

"None of that matters now. You can start fresh, put this all behind—"

He hung up, exhaustion and pain weighing heavy on his heart.

The strike was over, and Samantha was waiting for him.

He should be ecstatic.

But all he could think about was his reluctance to say goodbye to Kat.

Selfishly, he wanted to keep her with him.

She had choices now. She could finish her own vacation, have her fling in Santa Barbara. Aiden's blood ran cold picturing her in bed with some drunk stranger. Or maybe she'd go home and repair her relationship with her fiancé.

He didn't like the thought of that, either.

It was dawning on him he wouldn't like the thought of Kat with anyone, and he had absolutely no business thinking that way.

He knocked back the rest of his drink hoping the alcohol would numb him enough to do what needed to be done—tell her he could drop her off at the airport.

That after tonight she'd never have to see him again.

Aiden rapped his knuckles against her door, sending little shocks through his hand into his wrist.

When Kat answered, dressed in a satin robe, a matching pink negligee peeking from the opening, she peered at him with suspicion. Sounds of water running into the bathtub drifted into the hallway, the vanilla scent wafting through the steam. He inhaled, daydreaming just for a second she would invite him in to bathe with her.

When he stood silent and tongue-tied, she walked away,

leaving the door open, giving him the choice to step inside . . . or not.

Only a fool wouldn't, and he was no fool. At least, he wasn't tonight.

"Can we talk?" he asked, letting the door swing shut.

"Sure, whatever," she said, hurt radiating off her. She poured a glass of champagne she ordered from room service along with what looked like an appetizer platter.

"Can I have some of that?" he asked, drying his palms on his jeans. He shouldn't be nervous; he had good news to tell her. He wouldn't let what she was wearing affect him. He'd seen her in less and managed, barely, not to let her clothes, or lack thereof, bother him.

Too much.

Silently, she poured the champagne into a plastic water cup. "Sorry. They brought up only one flute."

"It's fine, thanks." He sat in a floral wingback chair near a window that framed the same view his did.

"Listen, I found out some news—" he started.

"Aiden, are you okay?" she interrupted, stepping in front of him. "Wait, let me turn the water off in the bathroom."

She came back into the bedroom smelling of vanilla, her cheeks flushed from the heat. She pulled the meshed desk chair close to him and sat, cradling the delicate flute in her hands. Her brown eyes sparkled, her hair draped over her shoulder in a thick braid. She looked at him expectantly, concern turning the corners of her mouth into a sympathetic smile.

Her scent, her compassion, and the scotch and the champagne made him want to do things he shouldn't do, but he did them anyway.

He smoothed her hair, his thumb sliding over the soft skin of her cheek.

She pressed the curve of her jaw into his hand. "I hate it when we fight," she whispered.

"So do I, and last night . . . this morning, it's my fault. Can I tell you something?" He slid toward the edge of the chair; their knees touched.

"Of course. You can tell me anything, just don't be mad at me anymore."

"Sweetheart, I'm not mad at you, and I'm sorry you've been thinking that." He pulled his hand from her face and cupped his champagne with both palms, choosing his words carefully. "I haven't been completely honest with you."

"We're strangers, Aiden. You don't owe me the truth—about anything."

"I feel in this case, I do."

She nodded. "Okay."

"I told you I'm in a relationship with someone—that I had a girlfriend. I used to. Her name is Samantha, and we dated for a couple years." He set his cup on the little table near his chair, next to a lamp covered with a thin layer of dust. He took Kat's left hand and twisted the engagement ring on her finger. The diamond was on the smaller side, set in a plain silver band. "We dated while she was engaged to another man. We were in love, and she promised she'd leave him for me. I asked her to marry me."

"But she didn't say yes," Kat filled in, turning her hand to hold his.

"No, she didn't. She left me a few weeks ago to marry him."

"I'm sorry," she said, squeezing his hand.

"Samantha didn't marry him, Kat, she didn't marry Max, and now she wants me back. She ruined our future, what could have been. It's been difficult for me to come to terms with that, and now I have to decide if I want to try again." He took a deep breath. "That's why I'm angry all the time; it has nothing to do with you." He turned away. That wasn't completely true, and he didn't want Kat to see the lie on his face. "I don't do a very good job of hiding it."

He drank the rest of his champagne in one swallow.

Needing to be alone, he stepped into the hallway, planning to drown his sorrows for the rest of the evening. "I'm sorry I've been an ass. I'll try to do better. And— Goodnight, Kat." Aiden stopped. He wouldn't tell her the strike was over. Not yet.

Besides, the airports would be crammed with people waiting to make up their flights. It would be faster to keep driving, and he wouldn't feel right not knowing if she made it home safely.

He lay awake all night, his heart full of lies and half-truths, praying Kat heard the news about the strike on her own and make the decision for him.

Trapped in a dream, or some kind of nightmare from which there was no escape, she called Nan, her throat raw, the touch of Aiden's fingers on her cheek still burning her skin.

"Gooooood newwwwws!" Nan crowed, a deep thump of bass in the background, vibrating through Kat's phone.

"What? You found a man?" She asked, hoping Nan could hear her over the music.

"Nooooo, but yyyooouuuu can! Get your asssssssss back to LA. Strike's oooooover!"

Kat frowned in concern. Nan was obviously drunk, and she hoped she was being careful—that she and their friends were looking out for each other. Oh, who was she kidding? If she were there, she'd be right there with Nan, tipsy, looking for a hot guy and a good lay.

Wait.

"What did you say?"

"The striiiiiiike's over! Have Mr. Hunk drop you at an airport, any airport! You still have five days of your vacation left. Who gives a shit if Neil's mad at you? He's always mad about something. Come back and have some fffffuuuuuu-unnnnn. We'll eat cake and get drunk . . . er. Where are you, anyway?"

Because she wanted to spend all the time she could with Aiden, there was no way she was going to admit to Nan she was in

Denver, that an airport was ten minutes away. Nan would pressure her to fly back to LA.

But Aiden had his own girlfriend to get back to.

Kat sank onto the bed. What was she going to do? Hope Aiden didn't find out the strike was over? Hope that even if he knew, he'd still want to bring her home?

Hope that on the way there, he'd fall in love with her?

All of the above.

"I still need to go home," she whispered, but Nan had forgotten about her, and she heard nothing but music and people hollering, trying to hold conversations over the noise.

She disconnected the call and dropped her cell onto the green and pink floral comforter that covered the mattress.

Maybe tomorrow Nan would call her back—sober.

Kat covered her face with her hands.

God would send her to hell for her lies, but she wouldn't tell Aiden the strike was over, and she'd pray he wouldn't find out.

She wanted these last few days with him.

They were all she was going to get.

As he settled into the driver's seat, Aiden refused to meet Kat's eyes, knowing the guilt would be crystal clear. He stared straight ahead while Kat adjusted her seatbelt and threw her purse onto the backseat. "If we don't make any stops and take turns driving, we can make it to Minneapolis by midnight," he said.

"Really? That soon?"

"It'd make for a long day, but it's doable."

They'd already eaten breakfast. He asked her if she wanted to meet him in the hotel's restaurant, and she accepted this time, her hair swinging in thick waves down her back, wearing the same clothes she'd been wearing yesterday. With Nick's news, he forgot he wanted new clothes, and he too, wore the same thing he'd worn yesterday, smelling vaguely of dirt and horse.

"Oh, well. That's . . . great," Kat muttered.

He grunted. It sounded anything but great.

"Unless you're up for a little sightseeing on the way," he suggested, feigning nonchalance, keeping his eyes on the road.

"What did you have in mind?"

Grateful she seemed more interested in taking in the sights of Denver as they drove through the city rather than making eye contact, he followed his Maps app that would direct him to I-25 if she wanted to sight-see, or I-80 if she didn't. "I've never been to Mount Rushmore. It's six hours away."

She turned toward him with a smile lighting her face. "That would be great! I haven't been since I was a little kid when my mom took me there in fourth grade. You'll love it."

Aiden rolled his shoulders in relief and handed her his phone. "Can you find Mount Rushmore and pull up the directions? The traffic's crazy—people must be on their way to work." He paused, shifting his eyes off the road for a moment to look at her. "You don't talk about your dad."

She she poked at his phone she said, "My dad died when I was little. He worked for 3M as a maintenance technician, and he was just going off shift when he had a massive heart attack. He took care of himself, but heart disease runs on his side of the family. My aunt, my dad's sister, died from a heart attack in her 30s."

"I'm sorry."

"That's okay. My mom and I were close. Here, your phone says we have six hours and twenty-five minutes. I'm guessing closer to seven though, since we'll need to make at least one stop. The coffee I had at breakfast wasn't enough."

As she handed his phone to him, it rang, playing the sexy song from *Fifty Shades of Grey* Samantha assigned to her number. He winced as Beyoncé's voice filled the truck.

"Sorry," he mumbled. "I usually have my phone on silent."

"I can see why. You can answer it. You should talk to her."

If Aiden had to choose between swimming with starving

sharks or talking to Samantha in front of Kat, he'd choose the sharks. "No, thanks. Now isn't a good time."

"Are you sure? I can't imagine what she's feeling."

Heading out of Denver, Aiden set the cruise control and turned the radio on low. "Yeah?"

"Yeah. She left her fiancé, hoping you would take her back. If you don't, she'll be alone. That's scary."

Aiden met her eyes and asked, "Is that why you're marrying Neil? Because you don't want to be alone?"

She frowned and turned in her seat.

"No, don't shut me out. Talk to me. You're engaged to a guy who doesn't work, who spends all his time online, probably watching porn, yeah, I remember what you said," he added when she shot him a look of surprise, "and who, by the sounds of it, doesn't even like you, so why are you doing it?"

"Of course he likes me," she snapped. "Why would he ask me to marry him if he didn't?"

He didn't want to push; he could make her so mad she wouldn't speak to him all the way to Minnesota . . . or ever again, but he couldn't let this slide.

"He hasn't married you, Kat. You've been engaged for six years. *Talk to me.*"

She lifted her chin. "Then you tell me why you were involved with a woman who was engaged to someone else. Did you even want her to say yes to your proposal?"

"Yeah, I did. I wanted to have a life with her. I've loved her for a long time," he murmured, staring at the car's license plate in front of him. Oklahoma. "She's my friend Nick's sister, and we were always hanging out, or if I was with him, I'd see her. I've always been taken with her spark, her drive. She's never still, she can never sit."

"Then why won't you talk to her? She canceled her wedding to be with you, why aren't you on your way to . . . wherever she is? Miami? Is she waiting for you at home? Aiden, I can get myself to Minnesota. I really can."

"I have no doubt you can. I just need time to think things through."

"Yeah, but isn't the sooner you know her reasons the better? Why waste time with me?"

He rolled his eyes. "Helping someone isn't wasting time. Besides, I need space. Isn't that what you women say? I need space, and after what she's put me through, she owes me that."

"I don't suppose she'd like it if she knew you were driving another woman across the country."

"*Half-way* across the country, and I'd like to think she's secure enough she'd see it as a gallant effort and not be pissy about it."

"I'd be pissy if I knew the man I loved was driving some woman *half-way* across the country in a vehicle where all there is to do is talk."

"Then if you care so much for her feelings, stop talking."

"Fine."

"Fine."

He let two mile markers go by before he said, "You are some piece of work."

Kat grabbed the ring-tailed cat off the dashboard and hugged it to her. "I don't know what you mean."

"Pushing me toward Samantha when you were going to have an affair."

"It's not an affair if you're not married yet."

"Ah-huh."

"Pfft. I bet it's what you told yourself every time you and Samantha . . . you know what. I don't think you should be judging me."

"At least we knew each other, loved each other." He gripped the steering wheel. "She wasn't just banging some guy to get it out of her system."

"You don't understand."

Biting back a sigh, he said, "That's why I asked."

Kat twisted and rested her cheek on the back of her seat. "My mother has been gone for a while. Day after day I sat by her side in hospice waiting for her to go. But she fought, she fought so hard."

Aiden reached for her hand. He hated hearing her cry. She'd been good about it, except crying with May over the horses, but this was a different sort of sorrow.

She gripped his hand and continued. "The doctors couldn't figure out why she was fighting. It wore her out, and finally one day I was so tired, so tired of watching her struggle, and I said, 'Mom, just let go. I'll be okay.' And that's when she told me. She told me she didn't want me to be alone, and she knew that Neil and I were a good match. She made me promise we would marry so he could look after me. I promised, and she died twenty minutes later."

"I'm sorry, Katrina," he murmured. Not adding it sounded like she took care of him, instead of the other way around. Not adding it sounded as if she changed herself to be with him—wearing clothes a nun would dress in, binding her hair into buns, wearing glasses she didn't need. She wasn't wearing them now, the ugly things with thick black frames.

Her eyes shone with unshed tears.

He was just as bad as Neil, telling her all the time to stop crying. He wondered who she'd be if she were free to be herself.

She probably didn't know, trying for years to mold herself into a woman Neil would marry, to fulfill a promise to a woman who wouldn't know the difference.

Kat gave him a watery smile. "Thank you. She's been gone for a while now, but I miss her a lot."

"Do you have any other family?"

"I already told you my dad's sister passed away, and she was his only sibling. My mother has a sister, who had a falling out with my grandma. My grandma passed away, and I haven't heard from my aunt. She didn't come to Mom's funeral, so yeah, besides Neil, I'm alone. But I don't feel like I am. I'm close to Neil's mother, and I have a lot of friends."

He should tell her. He should tell her the strike was over and he could drive her to the next airport. Somewhere in South Dakota, her flight wouldn't be more than two hours long. She could be home tonight, working things out with Neil.

He was all she had.

Aiden drew in a breath to confess, but before he could get the words out, Kat asked, "There's a little town up ahead. Can we stop for coffee?"

After. After they gassed up and bought drinks, he would tell her. Spending the next twenty-four hours with her wouldn't do him any good. She was right. He needed to get back to Samantha. Their relationship could still be salvaged.

"Yeah. That sounds good."

The town looked like any other they'd stopped in. A Main Street, empty this time of day, seemed to be the primary road containing a post office, bank, little shops. A gas station belonging to a chain he never heard of sat on the corner, empty. "If they don't have a coffee machine in here, we'll find a Starbucks or something," he said pulling into the lot and parking at a gas pump.

"Okay." She released her seatbelt, grabbed her purse from the back, and scooted out of the truck.

After filling up at the pump, he went inside. He needed to use the bathroom and get a drink. He wasn't in the mood for coffee, but maybe a soda and a bag of chips. He'd ask Kat if she could drive for a bit; maybe he could think of a different game they could play.

When he came out of the men's restroom, Kat was studying the cappuccino selections across the store. The gas station sold a huge variety of Monster energy drinks, and as he opened the door to grab his usual, a low-carb flavor, the bell over the door rang.

"Nobody move!"

In the round fish-lens mirror attached to the wall above the restrooms, Aiden watched a tall figure dressed in black aim a handgun at the older lady stocking a glass case full of cigarette cartons behind the counter.

Aiden rested his forehead against the chilled glass of the cooler. "Shit."

After their conversation, Kat felt better. She was feeling so guilty she hadn't said anything about the pilots' strike, but when he said he was taking these few days to think things out, she convinced herself she was doing him a favor by not telling him.

She *did* feel bad for Samantha, though, and she wondered what made her call off her wedding.

Kat huffed. It wasn't like she'd ever find out. Just like she'd never know what would happen with May, Danny, and Jack, or their horse farm, though she promised to stay in touch. Once Aiden dropped her home, she would pick up where she left off, and she'd fall back into her old life.

She hadn't intended to tell Aiden the story about her mom, but she wanted him to understand why she was doing what she was doing. Everyone had a reason, a good reason, for doing what they did. She hoped Aiden gave Samantha a chance to explain.

If she could put her own selfishness aside, she admitted it would be nice to know he was happy with someone. Maybe Samantha could give him some balance. He worked way too hard, and when he went back, he'd have to deal with the fallout of that mysterious case.

Maybe, once they said goodbye, she'd search for it online.

Just out of curiosity, of course.

The bell over the door tinkled happily, and the sound jolted Kat out of her daydream. She didn't want Aiden to give her a hard time for being slow. She hadn't chosen a coffee yet, and he was already grabbing a soda out of the cooler.

"Nobody move!"

Kat twirled, and her heart skittered with fear when a man dressed in black, wearing a black ski mask, started waving a gun around, his hand shaking so violently she was afraid he'd shoot without meaning to.

Trying to swallow a huge lump of dread in her throat, she scanned the store; the only people inside were her, Aiden, and the clerk, an older woman wearing a red work vest, shoving cigarette cartons into a glass case behind the register.

The woman straightened, dropped a carton of cigarettes onto the counter, and shoved her hands onto her wide hips. "TJ Morgan, you put that gun away this very instant or I'm gonna tell your momma, and she'll kick you out of her basement faster than you can spit."

"Just empty out the register, Mrs. F, and I'll leave you alone."

"I'll do no such thing, young man. I've already pressed the panic button for the cops, and you better get your sorry ass out of here before they come, if you know what's good for ya. Second time this month. You ain't learned your lesson."

"I need that money. I got plans. Me and Angie, we're gonna go to Hollywood and be movie stars, but we need cash first."

"Movie stars my ass," Mrs. F said, glaring at TJ, not fazed in the least at the gun aimed at her face. "Angie couldn't act her way out of a paper bag. I saw her in *West Side Story* last year, and she almost ruined the whole thing. Gnats have better memories than she does."

"That's not true! You take that back, and gimme all the money you got, or I'll shoot."

Kat swallowed the bile rising in her throat and met Aiden's gaze across the short shelves holding everything from candy to toothpaste. He shook his head, and Kat bristled. She wouldn't do anything stupid. She was too scared to do anything at all.

"You will not," Mrs. F said, wagging her finger at TJ. "Last time you came in here you had a Nerf gun you bought for twenty-five cents at Mrs. Policki's rummage sale. Don't think I don't know. A rock has more brains than you, and Judge Tyler's not gonna be so forgiving this time around."

"You think this gun is a fake, huh, huh?" TJ sputtered. He

aimed at the case of cold drinks not five feet from Aiden and pulled the trigger.

Kat had never heard a gun fired before, not in real life, and the sharp blast that filled the gas station almost made her wet her jeans.

The lights in the cooler blinked out, a plastic shelf cracked, and bottles of orange juice fell to the floor shattering on the beige tile.

Aiden calmly turned away, shielding his face with his arm as the glass shattered, shards flying everywhere. "Hey! You trying to kill someone?"

TJ look around, his eyes twitching in their sockets. "You!" He waved his gun at Aiden, "and you!" He aimed at Kat.

She stepped back, biting the inside of her cheek until she tasted blood.

"You two, get over here."

Aiden put his hands up, palms toward TJ, and Kat met him in the middle of the store. "It'll be okay," he said, pulling her toward him.

Grateful for the support, she leaned in, trusting him to protect her.

"Sit!" TJ pointed his gun to the floor in front of a candy display, and with Aiden's arm around her, they shuffled to the front counter. Settling on the dirty tile, Kat cowered against Aiden's chest.

"It'll be okay," he whispered again.

"No talking!" TJ ordered. He pulled the ski mask off his face revealing gaunt features, bloodshot brown eyes, and blond whiskers. He looked younger than Kat, angry, and sad. "Never had hostages before."

Squeezing her eyes shut in dismay, Kat realized that's exactly what they were.

Ear-splitting sirens filled the air, and TJ peered through the glass door. "Just give me what I want, Mrs. F, and I'll get out of here."

"No," she said, lifting her chin. "You can't get away, no matter how fast you run. Give up, TJ. There're cops everywhere."

"Nope. I promised my Angie I'd get us out of this shit town, and that's what I'm gonna do."

"TJ Morgan, come out with your hands up!"

Echoed through the loudspeaker, the officer's words sounded tinny and far away.

Kat couldn't see much. There were windows but sitting on the floor, coolers of ice cream blocked her view, and the only thing she could see between TJ's legs were the wheels of cop cars parked near the building.

Aiden's breath feathered over her cheek. "Are you okay?"

Kat nodded, her face turned into his side. "Are you? All that glass . . ."

"Yeah, I'm fine. Not the first time I've been around something like that."

"Stop talking," TJ commanded, pointing his gun at them, his arm quivering with nerves and desperation. "I need to think."

Kat pulled away and looked into Aiden's eyes. He already had so much to worry about, and now this. "I'm sorry," she mouthed, hoping he would understand how horrible she felt about the whole thing. It had been her idea to stop.

Aiden smoothed his thumb over her lips. "Don't be," he murmured.

As the minutes ticked by, TJ became more agitated, pacing the floor and mumbling incoherently to himself.

The store's landline phone rang, the shrill trill piercing the tense silence.

Mrs. F answered, listened for a moment, and held the handset out to TJ.

TJ looked around the small shop, a blank look in his eyes, sweat beading on his forehead, dripping down his temples. He wiped his face using the hem of his black shirt and took the phone with a shaking hand. "Yeah?"

Kat took advantage of TJ's distraction to hug Aiden, pressing her cheek against his chest. His heart beat a steady rhythm, and she breathed in the same scent of cologne that had intoxicated her in the airport.

Though it didn't feel possible because he was already holding on so strongly, Aiden tightened his arm around her and pressed a kiss to the top of her head. He cradled her cheek in his warm palm, moving his thumb back and forth over her cheekbone. His calm touch comforted her. If she were to die right there, at TJ's hand, there would be no other place she'd want to be.

There wasn't any use denying how she felt about him now.

Sparks of love lit her heart, glowing emotions she'd never felt for any man, as she'd always been attached to Neil in some way, their mothers pushing them together, whether they wanted to be or not.

"What do I want?" TJ barked into the phone. "I want money, twenty thousand dollars, and a truck to get me and Angie to California. That's what I want."

Kat breathed a sigh of relief. Hopefully, TJ was talking to a negotiator, or someone, at least, who could give him what he demanded.

"I can't wait five hours, I need it now!" TJ hung up, his complexion grey, like putty.

There wasn't any way to know how much time had gone by before the landline phone rang again. It could have been hours, it could have been minutes. Kat didn't have easy access to her purse to look at her phone as it was wedged between hers and Aiden's bodies. She didn't dare try for it, fearful she would rouse TJ's suspicion and make him do something out of anger or despair. To keep herself calm, she focused only on Aiden's breathing and the warmth of his hand on her back through her blouse.

TJ picked up the phone and stood frozen, listening.

She hoped this time they were offering TJ something he would accept, but her hopes were dashed when he kicked the front of the counter, rattling a display of keychains and a jar of pens.

"I'm not waiting that long," TJ shrieked into the phone, and Mrs. F flinched. She'd been steady this whole time, but now her face lost what little color it had. She stepped away from TJ as far as she could, her back pressed against the open case full of cigarettes.

He slammed the phone onto the counter, and it cracked, the black plastic splintering, two double A batteries flying onto the floor.

"You!" TJ grabbed a hold of her arm and yanked her from the floor.

Kat cried out in pain, but his grasp was nothing compared to the arm he cinched around her neck to hold her in place, his forearm pressing against her throat, cutting off her air supply, or the bite of the handgun's muzzle as he pressed it to her temple.

Desperate to see Aiden one last time, she forced her eyes open to memorize his features: his shaggy black hair shining under the artificial lights of the store, his blue eyes framed with lines of anguish and shock, his pinched mouth, his beard he hadn't trimmed since they'd been on the road. He looked so handsome, so worried, she forgot for a moment the precarious position she was in, wanting him to get out of this alive and unhurt.

With both hands, Kat gripped TJ's arm as he dragged her out of the store and onto the sidewalk, leaving Mrs. F and Aiden behind.

Aiden rushed to the door the moment it shut, the remnants of the bell fading in TJ's wake.

Four police cruisers, lights flashing, were strewn about the parking lot, and he counted six officers aiming at TJ. With Kat's body shielding the bastard, he doubted any of them had a clear shot, or the skills to try without killing her in the process.

Inch by inch, Aiden opened the door and Mrs. F followed

him outside. No one paid attention to them as they stood on the sidewalk near a locked metal bin of small propane canisters.

"TJ, let her go. You're making this worse for yourself," one police officer yelled.

TJ ignored the cop, pulling Kat with him toward Aiden's truck.

Fear twisted in Aiden's gut, and his heart pounded.

The punk had already proven he wasn't afraid to use his gun, and a dripping bottle of orange juice could turn into Kat's body, her life draining out of her on the filthy concrete, by the time this was over.

TJ looked up and down the sidewalk, stared at the people who stopped their cars dead center in the road to watch.

Without warning, he suddenly pushed Kat to the ground and ran. Two police officers immediately gave chase.

Aiden rushed to her, not caring about anything but having her in his arms.

She trembled against him, her face pushed into his shirt.

Two blocks away, one of the officers tackled TJ, shoving him to the ground. A shot rang out, and Kat's body lurched against his, her moan vibrating through his heart.

"Don't watch," he mumbled into her hair.

That could have been her. Two minutes earlier, and it could have been her.

The officer stood, but TJ lay motionless on the ground.

His partner, who had also run after TJ, knelt and felt for a pulse. He shook his head, and they took off their caps.

Mrs. F had followed him onto the city sidewalk, and Aiden pinned her with a glare. With his hands fisted in Kat's hair as if he would never let her go again, he said, "You should have given him the money."

Chapter Seven

For what felt like most of the afternoon, they sat answering questions in a small police station attached to a building that contained a social services department and a courthouse. Aiden never took his arm from around Kat's shoulders.

Her demeanor impressed him, and she answered their questions with a calm he definitely hadn't felt since TJ pressed a gun to her head.

"We have a Motel 6 down the street if you don't feel like driving anywhere tonight," said the officer who was interviewing them. Aiden didn't remember his name, didn't remember much of the afternoon after TJ released Kat. Everything was a blur, but he knew for certain there was no way they were staying in this godforsaken town a minute longer than they needed to.

Kat seemed to share that sentiment when she shook her head. "Oh, no, we have—"

"We'd like to get going, if that's okay," Aiden said, standing from the black plastic chair.

Sounds of typing, shuffled paper, and people talking on phones filled the station, and they brought him back to the days he spent at the law library at school. The familiar noises somewhat comforted him, and he was able to say goodbye and shake the cop's hand before leading Kat out of the two-story building and to the SUV.

He kept his cool all the way to the truck, had even reached out to open the door for her, when he pulled her to him instead, and pressed his lips to her hair. "My God, that scared the shit out of me."

"Me, too," she whispered.

He sighed and reluctantly released her. Holding her, double and triple checking she was okay fought with the need to drive out of town as quickly as he could. "Are you hungry?"

"I couldn't eat anything," she said, pressing a hand to her stomach. "The thought of food makes me heave. Let's just go, okay? I want to get out of here."

"Sounds good to me." He opened the door and helped Kat inside. Something made him run his hands down her arms, something made him study her face, mascara smearing under her eyes, her lips swollen and chapped because she'd been biting them all afternoon.

He wanted to kiss her more than he'd ever wanted anything. More than he wanted his law degree, more than he wanted to pass the bar, more than he wanted his penthouse condo on the beach.

More than he wanted Samantha.

He pulled away and shut the door. She belonged to someone else and the only thing he was doing was bringing her home because the last time he wanted another man's fiancée, that hadn't worked out so well.

He pulled off the interstate when he spotted a Holiday Inn, two hours before they would have made it to Mount Rushmore. The detour to see the historical monument seemed frivolous now—he should be concentrating on getting Kat home as quickly as possible—but Kat hadn't looked good after they drove away from the police station. With every mile that sped by, her color grew paler and paler, and he didn't think she'd last two more hours on the road. She needed a drink. A hot bath. A meal. Anything to erase the blank look in her eyes.

"I hope you don't mind we're stopping," he said, pulling their carry-ons out of the back.

Kat placed a hand on his arm, and he tensed.

"You went through it too," she whispered, meeting his eyes. "You went through it too, and you need the break. A decent night's sleep will help. I don't know about you, but I didn't sleep very well at May and Danny's. Their house was too noisey."

"Right," he said, though he didn't agree. In the convenience store, he hadn't been concerned for his own welfare. Through the entire afternoon, his thoughts had centered around Kat and nothing, *nobody*, else.

He hadn't slept well the night before, either, not because of the things that went bump in the night, but because it had taken all his energy to keep as far away from her as possible.

The young kid working the front desk asked Aiden how many rooms he wanted, and he looked to Kat, hoping she would say two. He needed to keep his distance. After that afternoon, he needed the space, the physical space. He was starting to feel things for her he had no business feeling. But he wanted her to say one. The desire to keep an eye on her, to protect her, were feelings on a level he'd never felt before, the picture of her in TJ's grasp a vision that would never fade as long as he lived.

He admitted that was some fucked up thing, and he struggled between a sigh of relief and a moan of dismay when she said one would be fine.

Aiden scrambled for things to say while they rode in the elevator to the fifth floor, but every subject he came up with sounded unimportant and mundane. The weather? Mount Rushmore? That he thought they should eat, but every time he thought of food, he pictured the barrel of TJ's gun pushed into Kat's temple?

"Do you want the bathroom first? I need to shower." Kat stood in the middle of the room, looking at everything from the cheesy artwork to the sleek flat screen TV bolted to the dresser, as if she'd never been in a hotel room before.

Shock. She was in shock.

"No, you go. Take a hot one, and I'll order some room service; we should eat whether we feel like it or not."

"Yeah, I guess." She gathered her toiletries out of her carry-on, leaving it open on the floor, and hurried into the bathroom.

As he searched the desk drawers for a room service menu, his phone rang, and he hoped it wasn't Samantha trying to speak with him. He wasn't in the right frame of mind. But the phone call was from his brother, and he answered, giving up on the menu and sinking into an uncomfortable chair placed in the corner of the room.

"Hey, what airport are you in? Let me know your flight number, and I'll pick you up this time."

"I'm not at an airport. We're about two hours from Mount Rushmore."

"Mount Rushmore? Isn't that in the middle of nowhere? Why aren't you at an airport for God's sake?"

"Mount Rushmore's in South Dakota, not *technically* in the middle of nowhere," Aiden said, rubbing his eyes.

"Whatever. What is it with you and this chick? First the picture at the airport, then this road trip, and now you have a chance to get rid of her, and you won't."

"Earlier today we stopped at a gas station to use the bathroom and pick up some coffee, and while we were in there, some guy tried to rob the place." Aiden explained what happened to Kat, the hours they spent at the police station giving their statements. "We need a little time. I think she's in shock, and I am bone tired."

"Jesus Christ, and you helped search for some kid yesterday? That case blew your brains out," Dylan muttered.

"Don't you fucking say something like that after what I just saw," Aiden said, standing, pissed his brother could be so callous.

"I watched Kat almost get shot today, okay? What's happened to you? You've never been so insensitive."

There was a moment of silence and then, "You're in love with her, aren't you? You've fallen in love with this girl, and you don't want to put her on a plane, you *want* to drive to Minnesota. Hell. Screw Minnesota, just drive her to Florida."

"Would that be so bad?" Aiden murmured.

"Do you want a list of the reasons why that would be bad?" Dylan's voice dropped, and in the background, a door shut. "Samantha's here. She's here, in my apartment, waiting for you to pull your head out of your ass. You don't seem to get that. And this girl, this Anna Kendrick look-a-like, do you even know who she is? She could be playing you, this could be some scheme to make a quick buck, or make a play on your emotional state. She probably knows all about the case that exploded in your face and is taking the opportunity to con you. Don't let her."

Aiden thought of Kat handing May the stack of bills. "You're wrong. She's the one with money—remember she won at slots? She gave some of that away. She's not what you think."

"I don't know what to think. All I know is when Samantha ran out on you, you went on a week-long bender, and I had to call Mom to scrape you off the floor. Couldn't even tell her why. I had to blame it on the case."

"Mom wouldn't have understood what we were doing; she never would have approved of me seeing an engaged woman. And she wouldn't understand this, either. Kat's engaged, just like Samantha was, and it will turn out the same, too, so, it doesn't matter" —the water shut off in the bathroom and Aiden lowered his voice— "it doesn't matter what I feel. I'm bringing her home, and after what happened today, I'm not just going to shove her on a plane. You and Nick can stop hounding me about it. Tell Samantha if she wants to wait, now that the strike is over, she can wait in Miami. I need to go."

"Think about what you're doing, Aiden."

That was the last thing Dylan was able to say before Aiden

disconnected the call. When Kat stepped out of the bathroom, he was lying on the bed, an arm over his eyes, like he'd been doing it the whole time, except now his heart was thumping with fury.

"The bathroom's yours. The water pressure is fantastic."

Aiden grunted. "Good to know." He moved his arm a half inch and peered at her. "Christ, how many men were you going to go through in Santa Barbara?"

Dressed in a black satin negligee, she stood by the squat dresser, playing with the tiny white ribbon sewn between her breasts. She pinned her hair up, and some strands fell from the knot, framing her face.

Her cheeks pinked, and she stared at the floor. "I'm sorry, this is all I brought for pajamas. If you can take me—"

Aiden choked, sure she was going to say "the closest airport."

"—to a Walmart or something, I'll buy some sweats. I don't wear this stuff at home."

"Not even for Neil?" Aiden taunted in jealousy.

"Are you going to take a shower or not?"

"Yeah, yeah. Can you order something for us? I guess I fell asleep." There wasn't any reason to bring up Dylan's phone call, and besides, there was nothing he could tell her about it, anyway. Despite what his brother said, he still thought it was better for him to make sure Kat made it home safely. That meant dropping her off at her door, watching her go inside.

Saying goodbye.

She shrugged, still standing near the bathroom, like she was afraid to move any closer. "I guess so."

Aiden rolled off the bed and grabbed his carry-on. "Thanks."

He stood under the hot stream for over half an hour, working the kinks out of his back and neck lodged there from the stress and strain of the day.

When he came out of the bathroom, the aroma of chicken noodle soup met his nose. Kat crawled into bed and had fallen asleep, a small lump on the huge mattress.

He slipped between the sheets, and too exhausted and strung

out to fall asleep, he dozed, thinking about Samantha. Maybe the sound of her voice would take all his indecision away. They hadn't spoken for weeks, but he hadn't missed her. Not since Kat fell into him at the base of the escalator in LAX.

Kat's whimpering roused him out of his light sleep, and he rolled over onto his side to pull her close. "Hey, hey, you're okay."

She moved onto her back, and her eyes fluttered open. "Aiden?"

"Yeah, you're safe." In the bluish-white glow of the parking lot lights that drifted through the generic white curtains, her eyes sparkled with unshed tears.

Aiden lowered his head. God, he needed to kiss her. He ached with it. His heart, a bloody, mangled mess torn to shreds when Samantha left, throbbed with need.

With a sob, she threw her arms around his neck and covered his mouth with hers, and he sank into the kiss, relieved, finally, that he was touching her, kissing her, that after what happened today, she was safe in his arms.

He ran his hand along her side, down her rib cage, her hip, his fingers whispering over the tops of her thighs. She shaved in the shower, and her skin was sweet, smooth, scented with vanilla. Aiden devoured her, slipping his tongue into her mouth, feasting.

She lifted her hips in invitation, and he played with the waistband of her panties, before sliding his fingers inside, past a small patch of silky hair, finding her hot and wet.

"Kat," he whispered against her lips.

"Please," she said. "Please."

She wasn't ready for sex. He had enough wits about him to know that, and he wouldn't take advantage of her vulnerability. She wasn't ready for the intimacy sex would create between them, and if he could find reason through his foggy mind, he would admit he wasn't either.

But she needed the release.

And he wanted to give it to her.

He filled her with two fingers, gliding them in and out of her slick heat. She was so tight, he didn't want to hurt her, but she whispered, "More, I need more, Aiden."

Aiden added a third finger, praying he wasn't hurting her, and rubbed her with his thumb. He nibbled Kat's neck, the sensitive area between her ear and shoulder, and as she clutched him, she came with a cry.

She trembled, and he held her close. After her tremors subsided, he slowly pulled his fingers from her, freed his hand from her panties, and wrapped his arms around her. "Shh, shh, it's okay. Feel better?"

As she sobbed into his neck, he held her, his skin hot with her tears.

Aiden rested on his back, and she followed, lying half on top of him, her cheek pressed against his bare chest, her tears slicking his skin. "Sleep now. I'm right here, it's okay." He smoothed her hair, and with her fingers digging into his flesh, as if he were a raft in a churning rapids, her breathing evened out, her weight becoming heavy in sleep.

He was happy to help her, hoped the release made her rest easier, helped her forget the horror of the day's events. But it hadn't done anything for him, and he eased out of bed trying his best not to rouse her. In the dark bathroom, he leaned against the cold wall, and with her scent on his fingers, got himself off. It didn't take long, imagining how it would feel to sink deep inside her, her arms wrapped around his neck, his lips on hers.

With his heart pounding from his own orgasm, he cleaned himself using one of the stiff white hand towels hanging over the toilet.

After checking to make sure Kat was still sleeping, he pressed a kiss to her cheek, pulled on his clothes, and went downstairs to sit in the bar.

He needed a drink.

Kat shifted, somehow knowing through her sleepy haze she was alone in bed. Her body ached, but it was a delicious feeling, and she licked her lips, wanting more.

"Good morning."

Kat sat up at the sound of his voice.

Aiden sat at the small table shoved into the corner near the dresser, a plate of toast in front of him with a cup of coffee, reading a newspaper.

With a crash, it all came back what he'd done for her, and *to* her, and she wanted to fall backward onto her pillow and hide her face with the comforter in humiliation. Not that he touched her, no, she'd wanted that, would want it again, if she were being honest with herself. No, it was the very minor fact she'd fallen asleep afterward, and she hadn't helped him in return.

"Aiden. I'm, ah . . ."

"We don't have to talk about it," he said, turning a page of the newspaper, "unless you want me to apologize for crossing a line. I just thought after what had happened, it would help you to . . . you know, forget about it, at least enough to get some sleep." He offered a smile, but the corners of his mouth barely lifted. "I think it helped—it's almost eleven o'clock."

"Oh my God, you should have woken me up." Kat threw the comforter off her body and scrambled from the bed. She slept half the day away—they could have been hours on the road by now, or . . . "Are we, did you still want to see Mount Rushmore?"

Aiden laid the newspaper aside, rested his elbows on his knees, and steepled his fingers. "The question is, do you? We're eleven hours away from Minneapolis. How badly do you want to get home, Kat?"

That wasn't the question. That wasn't the question at all. The real question was, how quickly did she want him to be able to get on with his life? He had a woman waiting for him. A brother, a friend. A career he needed to salvage. He was wasting time helping her. He'd objected when she said that, but he was. She could insist she drive herself home; she didn't need his help.

Eleven hours was nothing, wasn't it?

Not to her heart.

To her heart, eleven hours was everything.

"I'd like to see it," she whispered, standing in front of him in nothing but a black silk negligee, her vulnerability showing as clearly as the need and want she was sure were in her eyes.

"Then we'll go see it, but it will mean spending one more night on the road."

"That's fine, Aiden, I . . ." She wanted to apologize, apologize for taking, last night, and not giving something in return.

"It's okay, Katrina. I'm glad you were able to get some sleep. You needed it."

She nodded, accepting the gift. "Yeah, it felt good. Let's go then. I'll drive."

"What's with you being a librarian?"

Kat flexed her hands on the wheel. She felt different, embarrassed. Aiden had touched her, touched her as intimately as a man could physically touch a woman. Turned the nightmare she'd been having into a lovely dream. And she kissed him, oh, God, she kissed him, poured everything she felt for him from her mouth to his.

She wondered if he felt it—all that emotion—or if to him it had just been a kiss.

He treated her like always while they checked out, loaded their carry-ons into the truck.

But she was achy, alive, her blood fizzed. He'd been rough with her, but she'd needed it, wanted it. The pain grounded her, pulled her back from the convenience store, from the gun TJ pressed against her head.

Sitting next to Aiden in the truck, his presence comforted her, and driving on the interstate toward Mount Rushmore made yesterday feel like it hadn't truly happened in real life, but like a chapter in a book she read long ago.

"What about it?" These were the moments Kat liked best. When they sat alone, talking, as the miles rolled by.

"It doesn't seem like you. Did you want to be a dancer?"

Kat lifted a shoulder. "Not really. I took dance in high school —tried to keep it up, mainly to stay in shape. Even if I had thought about it professionally, when the girls came, that put an end to it, so I'm lucky I wasn't invested."

Aiden pursed his lips and looked away.

"What?" she asked. "What'd I say?"

Aiden whipped around to face her. "I can't believe you've been gallivanting all over when you have children. Why aren't you home? Who's taking care of them? Neil's mother? Because by the sounds of it, it sure as hell isn't Neil."

"What are you *talking* about? Who brought up kids?"

"You did, when you said the girls came along, and you couldn't dance anymore. You know, we should go straight to the nearest airport. You should be home."

Kat gaped. "First of all, just because a woman has children doesn't mean she can't do things. As long as they are being taken care of, I think a woman, a mother, is allowed a break now and then. Is that why Samantha left you? Because she thought if she married you she'd be chained to the kitchen stove barefoot and pregnant?"

"Of course not," Aiden scoffed. "She has a career. She wouldn't stop working to have children, she'd figure out a way to have both."

"Then why is it okay for her, but not for me?"

"I just don't like the thought of you sleeping your way through California when you have kids at home waiting for you to come back."

Kat sat in silence.

She'd disappointed him. He didn't want her to be the type of person who would leave her children behind to party.

He wanted her to be more.

It was sweet, in a way, he held her to such high standards. What did it say about her that she wanted to meet them?

"I don't have children, Aiden. When I said 'the girls' I meant these." She took her hands off the wheel, cupped her breasts, and squeezed. "Have you ever seen a ballerina with boobs? The only work I could get with the figure I have is as a showgirl, and even then, I'm too short."

"You don't have kids?"

"No. Do you?"

"No." He paused. "I'm sorry for losing my temper."

"You didn't lose your temper, but you should think about the kind of role you want your wife to play in your marriage if you had such a strong reaction to the thought of me having kids and taking a vacation. A woman deserves a break. A woman can't be a good mother if she's burnt out. And if you're working all the time, how will you help her? If you're working seventy hour weeks, when will you spend time with your kids?"

Kat's skin prickle with discomfort. She didn't want to talk about kids because being married to Neil, she'd resigned herself to the fact she may not have any. A girl can't get knocked up if she wasn't having sex.

"That's true," he murmured.

"Anyway," she said, directing them to his original question, "librarian was my second choice. I like it. I have no complaints, but I would have liked to open my own clothing store. You wouldn't know it by looking at me and how I dress, but I love clothes. Shopping in Luna Noir was pretty awesome."

"Then why don't you?"

Kat waved a hand. "It's not practical, for one thing, and I have a degree in Library Science, not business. I worked a lot of retail in school, so I know a bit about it, but being a librarian is a steady paycheck, and I get a lot of holidays off, paid, too."

The conversation faded after that, and she focused on the

road. She was tempted to ask what he was thinking about, but she didn't want to start another heated debate.

They were twenty miles away from Mount Rushmore when Kat passed an old car on the shoulder of the interstate, its hazard lights flashing.

An older couple was waving as cars passed, and Kat looked into the rear view mirror. No one stopped.

"Do you think—"

"No. They'll get help. We need to keep going."

Aiden's voice was sharp, and Kat bit her lip. She didn't want to make him angry, but she didn't want to turn someone away if she could help.

She took her foot off the gas, lightly braked, and steered onto the shoulder of the road. The car was less than a quarter mile behind them.

"But look—no one is stopping. We could at least call a tow truck."

"We can do that without stopping, Kat. I'll call nine-one-one and tell them they need assistance. I bet someone already has."

"Wouldn't it be nice to make sure?" Kat asked, looking at the couple.

The older gentleman, dressed in khaki pants and a black and tan polo shirt, stood at the side of the road, waving a newsboy cap at the passing vehicles.

The woman, probably his wife, leaned against the car, the front bumper dented, from what Kat could tell that far away.

Aiden sighed. "Fine. We'll talk to them for a second and call."

"Thank you," Kat said, touching his knee. "Hold on." She shifted into Reverse and slowly backed up, twisting in her seat, staring out the tinted window.

"I'm beginning to think you don't want to go home."

"Of course I want to go home." Kat clamped her mouth shut. She'd go home, after eking out every possible second she could spend with Aiden.

Turning the steering wheel back and forth, over-correcting,

she tried not to drift onto the interstate or into the ditch. She didn't want to cause any more trouble than she already had, and she was sure getting into an accident would be Aiden's last straw.

To say this road trip wasn't going well would have been an understatement.

Kat braked and shoved the truck into Park. "This will only take a second," she said, smiling, hoping to downplay the inconvenience.

"I'm not letting you confront strangers alone," Aiden said, opening his door. "The last little old lady you saw attacked you with a cane—how easily we forget."

"Not everyone is a liar or a cheat, or a violent psychopath," Kat muttered, rubbing the scratch on her shoulder and grabbing her phone to call a tow truck.

She left the driver's side door open—Aiden was right, calling would only take a moment.

"Hi," she said over the rush of cars as she approached the couple, "do you need a tow truck?"

"Hi, thanks for stopping," the man said. "I'm Tony, this is Mary, my wife. I think we ran over a nail. One of our tires is flat."

Kat smiled up at Aiden. "You can fix a flat, can't you?"

Aiden scowled.

"No, we couldn't ask that of you," Tony said, adjusting his hat.

"No, of course not," Mary agreed.

"It's no trouble, is it, Aiden?" She'd never changed a flat tire before, but she didn't think it would be that difficult.

"No, not at all," Aiden mumbled, and Kat could barely hear him as a large semi truck chose that moment to zoom past them, spitting rocks and making her hair fly into her eyes.

"Great!" Tony said, rubbing his hands together. "I have a bad back, and I just don't have the upper body strength to lift off the old tire."

"Triple A could have someone out here in ten minutes," Aiden grumbled, following Tony to the back of the old sedan.

"We don't have cell phones," Tony said. "Mary has a camera we use to snap pictures, but we do it the old-fashioned way and have Walgreens develop them. Then we send them through snail mail to our daughter who lives in Connecticut."

Kat covered her mouth to hide a grin. Tony was adorable in a grandfatherly kind of way.

As she followed Tony and Aiden to the trunk, Mary eased away from her side.

Backing away, Tony pointed to the car jack, and while Aiden bent into the trunk to reach for the metal contraption, Mary took off toward the SUV.

"Hey, what are you doing?" Kat yelled in disbelief as Tony and Mary flung themselves into their rental truck.

Aiden slammed the trunk shut with such force the impact shook the entire car. "See? Do you see what happens when you trust people?"

Kat ignored him as Tony and Mary drove away, tires squealing in their haste to get as far away from them as fast as they possibly could.

Aiden gritted his teeth in an effort to keep his mouth shut. He *told* her not to stop, but no, she had to be a good Samaritan.

He still had his wallet and phone, but Kat had lost her purse and her . . .

"Your money is gone," he said as their SUV merged into traffic and disappeared with the line of cars racing toward the famous monument.

"I'm sorry, Aiden," Kat said, covering her face with her hands.

He pulled out his cell phone and dialed nine-one-one. He wrapped his arm around Kat's shaking body and drew her close.

"Nine-one-one, what's your emergency?"

Aiden explained what happened. He didn't remember the license plate of the rental, but he described the vehicle and the items inside it. Kat could kiss her money goodbye. Once those two found it, it would be long gone. The briefcase was shoved under the seat in the back, but he would bet his beachside condo they'd search the truck top to bottom before dumping it somewhere.

"Help is on the way," the emergency operator droned. "Please stay on the line."

Sirens were already wailing toward them, and Aiden disconnected the call.

"Are you okay?" he murmured into Kat's ear.

It was dangerous to be on the road like this, and he was relieved help arrived so quickly.

"Yeah."

"You'll have to call your banks as soon as you can. At least you have your phone."

"I will," Kat said, staring at the ground, pulling away from him.

It occurred to him she was completely dependent on him. She didn't have any money or identification. She couldn't fly home even if she wanted to; she'd never be able to clear security without her driver's license. It made him sick how much that pleased him.

He wanted to take care of her, and now she had to let him.

Two black and white police SUVs skidded to a stop along the road, one behind Tony's and Mary's car, and one in front, sandwiching them between the vehicles, their lights flashing, the sirens emitting eardrum-piercing shrieks. One of the trucks fishtailed on the gravel, the back tires coming to a stop in the grassy ditch.

"Put your hands up!"

"What?" Kat asked, her mouth dropping open in shock at the violent, angry, and defensive look on one officer's face.

Aiden didn't like it any more than she did, and he took a step away from her, his palms in the air.

One officer released two German Shepherds from the backseat of a K-9 unit, and they immediately began to growl and claw at the beat up sedan.

"We called in that our vehicle—"

"Shut up," one officer snapped at Aiden, shoving him against a police cruiser, pulling cuffs from his belt. The burly policeman matched Aiden's height but outmatched him in rage, and Aiden complied, not wanting to cause any more trouble or earn an undeserved punch to the jaw.

Dealing with the police could be unpleasant, and these guys were after something.

An officer had Kat spread eagle against the cruiser parked half way into the ditch and was patting her down. Her hands were pressed against the windows; the cop confiscated her phone.

The two dogs and their handlers were tearing Mary and Tony's car apart.

Beaming with pride of discovery, an officer crawled out of the car holding thick white bricks.

Aiden knew very well what those were. In Miami, that kind of snow was just as prevalent as the real kind in Minnesota.

Reciting words of warning Aiden knew by heart, the officer began, "You're under arrest for possession of an illegal substance with the intent to sell. You have the right . . ."

They took Kat and him away in separate vehicles, and Aiden sat in the back seat, his hands cuffed behind him, hoping they would treat her all right. She didn't have any ID on her, and Aiden doubted they'd believe anything she said until they matched her with her photo registered with the DMV.

The truth was on their side. Enterprise listed him as renting the truck, and he was glad he managed to call nine-one-one to report it stolen before they were arrested.

The cops drove them to a town that contained very little, surprising Aiden they had a police station to begin with. They escorted him into the building, pushing him through the doorway with unnecessary roughness.

He didn't see Kat.

A plain-clothes detective met him in an interrogation room that stank of sweat and stale coffee. They could at least uncuff him, but the detective only stared him down, trying to intimidate him.

He fought a smirk. He dealt with this bullshit all the time. No matter he was usually on the other side of the table.

"Had a good tip," the detective said, snapping gum between his teeth.

"I want a lawyer," Aiden said.

"Don't need one. Your wife's spilling her guts."

If it had been anyone but Kat, Aiden would have suspected the cops were playing both of them, tricking one of them into a confession against the other in exchange for a plea bargain.

At times, he employed the same technique, interviewing lowlifes to squeeze out information he needed for multitudes of cases.

He had no doubts that Kat, knowing they were innocent, would tell the cop everything, maybe even from the minute she'd met him in LA.

Flexing his arms against the cuffs, he shrugged and didn't say another word, but inwardly, he sighed.

Let Kat talk. His story would be no different.

It had become apparent to the plain-clothes detective, who hadn't introduced himself either, that he had little to say, and after an hour of staring at each other, the detective buckled.

Denied his one phone call—and he could sue this little crap police department for that—Aiden settled onto a bench in an empty holding cell.

He leaned against the wire cage, his eyes adjusting to the dim space.

Dylan would get a kick out of this. He loved ribbing Aiden for the stupid things he did.

He should have called Samantha last night. But God, it had been a hellish day. Sitting in the hotel bar, sipping a G & T, Kat's scent lingering on his fingertips, picturing her trapped against TJ as he dragged her out of the convenience store . . . Samantha had been the last thing on his mind, and that didn't mean good things for them.

Nick seemed sure Aiden would forgive his sister after she told him why she'd run off. Maybe when he returned to Miami knowing he'd never see Kat again, that might sway him into listening to her explanation.

God, he was tired, and he bet it wasn't even dinnertime yet. They'd barely been on the road when Kat had pulled over.

A rustling sound roused him, and Aiden straightened as a female officer escorted Kat down the hallway.

Thinking they'd put her in the cell with him, he shifted on the bench. But the officer unlocked the cell next to his, and after releasing her cuffs, pushed her inside without a word, locked the door, and left as quietly as she'd come.

"I tried to call Neil," Kat whispered, sitting on her bench.

A spark of jealousy flamed inside Aiden's heart. It shouldn't have, but it did. She needed to call someone, and Neil was all she had, but just for one stupid moment he thought she wouldn't need to make a phone call at all because he was right here.

How full of himself he'd become; how important he'd made himself in Kat's life.

"Is he driving down to bail you out?"

"He didn't answer."

"I'm sorry. You've been in touch with him though, right? He knows what's going on?"

"I've tried. I've never gotten a hold of him, and his voicemail is full. I spoke to him at the airport that one time, and that's it."

"But at Blackout, weren't you . . .?" Aiden trailed off, confused.

"I was pretending. I just wanted . . . I just wanted to say something . . ."

Aiden rubbed his eyes. He stood from the bench and sat on the floor near her cell wall, and she did the same.

They were as close as they could be with the plastic-covered wire fencing between them.

Aiden touched her fingers with his, and they sat like that for hours, their fingers wrapped around each other's, his eyes meeting hers, and he swore that was the most intimate he'd been with another human being in all his life.

Chapter Eight

"You're free to go." A brawny officer, whom Kat hadn't seen before, jiggled a thick set of keys.

"What?" she mumbled, her eyes gritty from sleep and tears. She rubbed at her eyelids while moving her tongue around her crusted mouth. She needed a toothbrush and a shower. Sleeping on the floor made her body stiff and sore, and she gingerly stretched, moving her head as little as possible as a headache had taken residence behind her eyes.

"Your story checks out—you're free to go," the cop repeated, opening her door and then Aiden's, the clanking against the wire mesh echoing through the quiet.

"Did you find our truck?" Aiden asked, already on his feet, rubbing his fingers through his beard. Kat envied him his energy, though she suspected by the glint in his eyes it was a product of rage at being kept overnight.

The cop shook his head. "Nope. But we dusted the other car, and your prints weren't inside."

"No shit," Aiden grumbled, and she shot him a warning look. Yes, they needed showers and breakfast—coffee. But they wouldn't be free to find any of that if the cop decided to keep them a while longer out of spite.

Glaring at Aiden, the cop said, "The couple who stole your SUV has done time on and off for possession and dealing. They must have known we were onto them and dumped their car as fast as they could." He gave her a sympathetic smile and patted her shoulder. "I'm sorry. You thought you were doing something nice."

"Yeah," she said, running her fingers through the tangles in her hair. "I had no idea an old couple would do that."

"They've been selling drugs and running scams off and on for decades. This time though, they'll be locked up for years."

"If you can find them," Aiden said as he stepped into the hallway next to her.

She resisted the urge to lean into him.

"We have a BOLO on your truck; we'll let you know when we find it. It might take a while, but vehicles usually turn up on a dirt road somewhere."

"What do we do in the meantime?" Aiden asked.

Kat was glad he was asking all the questions—her mind was still stuck on the fact she'd been *arrested*. That had never happened to her before, and she was torn between feeling proud and horrified.

Nan would be delighted.

"Where're you folks headed?" the cop asked, leading them to the main section of the police station. The scent of donuts and coffee permeated the air, and Kat's stomach rumbled. She had to go to the bathroom, too, but she didn't want to slow them down. The farther away from the police station, the better.

"We're driving to Minneapolis, but we were going to stop by Mount Rushmore. That doesn't seem like a necessity now, does it, Kat?"

"No," she whispered, disappointed.

Aiden must be tired of all this bad luck, and he would be in a hurry to bring her home now. No more pit stops for them.

"There's a car rental in the town over—it's about forty-five minutes from here. Brian, I mean, Officer Morris, offered to drive you out there, if you'd like."

"Don't have much of a choice," Aiden said. "If we can have our things, we'll be on our way."

Kat shivered. His voice was low and gravelly from sleep and lack of coffee.

"Sure thing," the officer said. "Are you two on a road trip? A lovers' getaway? Honeymoon?"

"Oh, well, we're driving from California. We were at LAX when the pilots went on strike," she said.

"Good thing that's over. Could take a rental to Sioux Falls and catch a flight, if you all were tired of driving," he said, leading them to a metal desk where a cardboard box sat among a pile of papers.

Kat stole a quick look at Aiden. The lie was out in the open, now.

"We'll take that into consideration," he said. "But you'll let me know if our truck is found? We had personal belongings in there, naturally, and Kat's small winnings from a slot machine in Vegas."

"Of course. From the paperwork you filled out yesterday, I have your contact information and a list of items stolen with your vehicle. Although, I doubt your personal belongings will be returned. Especially all that cash. We're sorry for the inconvenience, and we'll keep you in the loop if we catch these guys. But miss, don't stop for any more breakdowns, huh? It isn't safe. Something much worse than this could have happened to you."

"Thanks," Kat mumbled, blushing, embarrassed to be chastised in front of Aiden for doing the exact thing he had told her not to do.

"Take care now," the officer said, handing them their cell phones and Aiden's wallet. "Sign these out, and you're free to go. Officer Morris is waiting in front for you."

After a round of handshakes and more promises to be careful, she watched the scenery go by as she sat in the back of another police cruiser. At least this time her hands weren't secured behind her back. Her wrists still stung from the tight metal digging into her skin.

Officer Morris and Aiden talked about what kind of crime plagued this sleepy little part of America. She wasn't interested in talk like that, and tuning them out, she checked the time on her cell. The police had taken their sweet time letting them go, and it was almost three in the afternoon. She'd need to buy a charger for her phone—the battery was almost dead.

Kat groaned and banged her head against the soft seat. She didn't have any money, and she hadn't been able to call her bank, either.

The forty-five minutes sped by, and before Kat knew it, Officer Morris pulled up alongside a building that housed a car rental office attached to a dealership.

"Good luck to you both," the officer said, releasing the locks. "You'll have to open the door for your woman back there. No handles, you know."

"Yeah, got it. Thanks for the lift," Aiden said, unfolding his tall frame from the passenger's side of the cruiser. "We appreciate it."

"Be safe," the cop said, and tore out of the parking lot, sirens wailing and lights blazing, before Kat had barely shut the door.

"I guess he's in a hurry to get back," she murmured, shoving her cell phone into the back pocket of her jeans. She was sick of wearing the same clothes.

"Probably doesn't want to miss out on any more donuts," Aiden said, nudging her arm. "Hey, it's okay. We'll just rent another car and keep going, right?"

"Right." She didn't want to agree, but there wasn't any choice. It wasn't like they'd had an easy time of it, but being with Aiden canceled out everything bad that happened so far. The long hours of sitting on the floor in her cell, her fingers wrapped around his, as she listened to his breathing in the quiet, empty cell, gave her one of her happiest memories. She felt like she belonged, like she found home. A feeling she hadn't had since her mom died.

"Unless . . . you want to spend the night here? It's already late. We could shower, grab dinner?"

"Shop?" she asked hopefully. She hated having to spend his money, but she needed new clothes, and a charger for her phone. If her money was ever found, she'd pay him back.

"Yeah, I guess we need to do that, too."

She followed him into the rental place, and fifteen minutes later Aiden drove a cute little navy blue Rav4 out of the large parking lot.

He asked for a hotel recommendation from the woman behind the counter, and she directed them to a Days Inn that wasn't fancy, but from the outside looked clean enough. A small shopping mall was located down the street attached to a decent-sized Target.

"I need to make a couple phone calls," Aiden said, after he checked them in.

He hadn't asked her if she wanted two rooms, and Kat assumed it was to keep costs down. There wasn't any point in them staying in separate rooms—they were too close for that—but it disappointed her when he flung the door open, revealing two queens. She wouldn't get to sleep with him tonight.

"Yeah, I guess I do, too," she said. "But my phone is almost dead. I need to buy a charger while we're shopping."

"You can make your calls on mine. I'm going down to the lobby to grab a soda. Do you want something?"

"No, I'm fine. I'll wait to eat dinner."

"Okay."

Aiden pressed a kiss to her temple, and Kat's insides glowed. He handed her his phone, and with a tired smile, left her alone in the room.

Kat was in the middle of calling all her banks—she had a Victoria's Secret, JC Penney, and an assortment of other department store credit cards she needed to cancel, as well as her main bank card—when Aiden's phone rang, and a pretty blonde's picture came up, the sexy *Fifty Shades of Grey* song playing.

Samantha.

She let the call play out.

She had to admire Samantha's tenacity. If she thought Aiden's love was on the line, she'd be that persistent, too. He was special, any woman could see that. To lose him, after having had him, would equal undeniable heartbreak. She didn't have a math degree, but she could add.

When it was time for her to say goodbye, she wouldn't feel anything less, but he belonged to Samantha, whether he believed it or not. He loved her; he said so.

It wasn't her place to interfere.

That would be like him trying to tell her Neil was wrong for her, that she shouldn't marry him. And while she hadn't cast Neil in a very kind light, Aiden hadn't so much as hinted she should leave him. Much less for Aiden himself.

They were two strangers who'd been tossed together, and after he brought her home, there wouldn't be any reason to see him again. Their lives were worlds apart.

She thought of the old saying, "When two worlds collide . . ." Yeah. When things collided, all they did was explode.

When Aiden went back to their room after downing a Pepsi he wished was doused with rum, he found Kat curled on one of the beds, fast asleep. She left his phone laying on the nightstand between the two beds, the screen indicating he missed a call.

At least Kat hadn't answered. The last thing he needed was Kat and Samantha having a heart to heart about him.

He eased out of the room and closed the door with a soft click. She needed the rest. He did too—he hadn't had a good night's sleep in he didn't know how long—but he was used to the fatigue that weighed on him.

Aiden found the pool and sat on an unstable white patio chair, the chlorine filling the air and stinging his nose. The pool looked worse for wear, the bottom cracked and the water murky, and he mentally crossed swim trunks off the list of clothes he needed from the store.

He found Nick's number in his phone and connected the call.

As he waited for Nick to answer, he flapped his arms. He was sweating in the the humid air of the pool area, but he didn't want to find a different place to talk where he wouldn't be bothered.

"Hey, are you flying home yet?" Nick answered.

"No, I'm still stuck on the road. We got arrested yesterday."

Nick laughed. "For fuck's sake. What happened now?"

Aiden explained how Kat had wanted to help an older couple, and that it turned into a shitstorm of a problem. "We're spending tonight in some crap town in South Dakota to get our bearings, then I'll be bringing her home tomorrow, no excuses." He paused and swallowed around a scratchiness in his throat. "I know I'm not being fair to Samantha, and I'm sorry." Avoiding her was rude, but he felt he deserved the time to think.

"She's not here. With the strike over, she went home. You're not going to drop Kat off at an airport? You can't be far from one, even in South Dakota," Nick said, then cleared his throat. "Dylan said you're in love with her."

"Kat can't fly. She doesn't have a driver's license; her purse was stolen with the truck. And I'm not in love with her. I'm just trying to do the right thing," he defended himself.

"Hey, listen," Nick said, his voice dropping to a soothing murmur, "if you are, it's okay. Even if she is my sister, I'm not blind to the way Sam treated you. These last few months have been hard—and if Samantha had been giving you what you needed, maybe the whole thing wouldn't have been so tough. The truth is, Samantha can be . . . self-involved. You know that. Even though I love her dearly, I can admit it, and I was relieved when you two started seeing each other. You grounded her. But, if this

Kat, if she's what you need, if she can be more to you than Samantha was, then you need to pursue it."

"She's engaged, Nick."

"Doesn't mean married, my friend," Nick said, "doesn't mean married."

No, it didn't, but Samantha hadn't been married, either, only engaged, and he hadn't ended up with the girl.

Samantha's abandonment shredded his heart, and he needed to keep his emotions in check, or it would happen to him all over again.

Rinsing the sleep out of her eyes and trying to wake up, Kat was in the bathroom when Aiden came back to their room. He smelled of chlorine and carried two cups of coffee. The steam from the sip slots in the tops made her mouth water.

"Thank you," she murmured appreciatively when he handed her one.

"You're welcome. Not a fan of the police department not feeding us. I'm starving. How about you?"

Kat grimaced. She *was* hungry, but she felt grimy and looked forward to new clothes more than she did a meal. She might burn the panties she wore—if she could peel them off.

"I want new clothes more," she said, then sipped the coffee Aiden had liberally doused with Irish cream.

"Then let's get going. Target will have what we need, and the receptionist said there's a bar and grill near it that serves a good steak."

At the department store, they split up, and Kat bought a new set of pajamas for that night—no more teddies for the rest of the trip. Shorts, tops, and a package of bikini-cut cotton panties. Before leaving the clothing section, she scanned the clearance racks and pulled a long black skirt and black sweater from their hangers.

Together they cost less than five dollars, and at that price, she wouldn't feel bad asking Aiden to pay for the outfit she'd need to wear home. She chose an all-purpose bag from the purse department, and a pair of plain reading glasses. She didn't know what the prescription numbers meant, but Kat chose a pair that distorted her vision the least when she put them on.

She remembered a charger for her phone from the electronics department and added an armful of toiletries to the red basket dangling from the crook of her arm. She looked forward to washing her hair and soaking in a bath.

"Got everything?" Aiden asked when she met him at the check-out lanes.

"Yeah. I'm sorry you have to pay for my stuff."

"It's no problem, Kat. Forget about it."

After they were seated at a table tucked into a corner at the western themed bar and grill, Aiden asked her if she wanted anything to drink.

Kat reached for her purse to grab her driver's license but dropped her hands into her lap. "I'd love one, but I don't have ID."

Across the table, Aiden winked. "It's fine. I'll order what you want. In a place like this, I don't think they're going to pay attention anyway."

Kat conceded that was true—the place was dark, a lot darker than any restaurant she'd ever been in, and all the customers were talking amongst themselves. Some of them gave Aiden and Kat curious glances, but no one seemed unfriendly, and when their waitress served a rum and coke and a wine glass filled to the brim with red wine to their table without any trouble at all, she relaxed.

Country music blasted from the jukebox, though a dais in the opposite corner of the room indicated that the bar and grill also hosted live bands.

"This place isn't so bad," Kat said, licking drops of wine from her lips and inhaling the scent of chicken fingers from the large platter of appetizers they ordered in addition to their meals.

"It's all right. I'm too hungry to care, honestly," he said, grabbing a handful of French fries and dropping them onto a plane white appetizer plate.

The tabletop looked like a buffet, plates and plates of food covering every inch.

With her blood buzzing from the wine, she grinned at him. The alcohol gave her a sense of well-being and happiness. She was with Aiden, for a little while longer, and she could soak in a bath later and dress in clean clothes tomorrow.

"Will you order me more wine?" she asked, nudging his foot with hers under the table.

"Are you sure?" Aiden asked, his mouth full of steak.

His lack of manners pleased and amused her. He felt comfortable enough around her to talk with food in his mouth, and she laughed.

"Please?"

"Yeah, yeah," he mumbled, then swallowed, flagging their waitress with a slight wave of his hand.

Of course, she came running, and Kat tried not to glare. The waitress's attentiveness resulted in prompt service, and that's all that mattered.

"I need to go to the bathroom," she said, leaning over to speak close to his ear to be heard over a wailing Garth Brooks.

He only nodded, preoccupied with what remained of the appetizer platter.

Kat's stomach flipped, but in a good way, the neon lights fastened to the wall sliding together in a rainbow of dashing colors.

When she came out of the bathroom, a group of patrons were gathered on the dance floor in front of the dais, and they looked to be gearing up for a line dance.

"You want to dance, hon?" The waitress, the one Kat had been giving the stink-eye, smiled, and she enthusiastically bobbed her head, forgetting her animosity toward the woman dressed in a low-cut Gil's Bar and Grill lipstick-red t-shirt and a tight-fitting pair of jeans.

"Then get in there. They'll make room for ya," she said, pushing Kat on the shoulder toward the dance floor.

She couldn't make her way across the room fast enough, tripping over empty chairs and veering around a stick-thin woman with bottle-dyed blonde hair who stood near a table talking to someone.

Line dancing was one of her favorite kinds of dancing. There was a certain amount of pride she gleaned from being able to coordinate her movements with everyone else's, and she loved being part of a group who enjoyed dancing as much as she did. She didn't have many opportunities to share in common interests; caring for Neil and their small house took up most of her free time.

When the music started, she clapped with excitement before a woman standing next to her linked their arms.

The other dancers wore cowboy boots and made sharp stomping noises on the wooden floor, but the lack of boots didn't deter her. Soon her feet were moving so fast it didn't matter—had anyone been looking, they wouldn't have been able to see her feet anyway.

Kat's hair flew around her head; sweat covered her face and cleavage. Her heart pounded in tempo to the music. She'd forgotten what it felt like to be so free, the weight of her promise to her mother forcing her down, always.

But with Aiden near her, the music, and the wine, she pushed it from her mind, if only for the four minutes and thirty seconds the song lasted before the notes faded, and the dancers stopped, patting her on the back for a job well done.

Panting, she wobbled her way to their table, but instead of plopping into her seat, she wedged herself between the table and Aiden's body and sat in his lap.

He tensed for a moment but when he put his arms around her, she melted and rested her head on his shoulder.

"Thank you," she whispered into his neck.

"For what?" Aiden asked, rubbing her back.

"For some of the happiest moments of my life."

His jaw and beard brushed her cheek when he replied, but a sad song started just then, and his words were lost as Trish Yearwood sang about sitting on a bus to St. Cloud, Minnesota.

Aiden sat in the driver's seat, anxious to get on the road. He'd drive Kat home and go straight to the airport. He could book an evening flight and land in Miami by midnight, easily.

But his resolve faltered when she hopped into the passenger seat looking fresh and perky in a pair of denim shorts and a pink cotton t-shirt. He told her to buy what she wanted, but she hadn't spent more than fifty dollars.

She looked just as good in ten dollar shorts and a five dollar shirt as she had in the clothing from Luna Noir.

Maybe better.

"Sleep well?" he asked dryly. He knew she had—sometime in the middle of the night she ended up in his bed, and he'd woken with her head on his chest, his hands tangled in her hair, and a hard-on so painful it was all he could do not to turn her onto her back, rip her cute little pajama shorts off and thrust into her so deeply he couldn't find his way out.

"I told you, I went to the bathroom and when I came back, I fell into the wrong bed. Sorry."

Aiden wasn't sorry, and she didn't sound sorry, either. And no, she hadn't ended up in the wrong bed. Not at all.

He loved the way her skin pinked, and he ran the pad of his thumb along the soft skin of her cheekbone. "Today's the day," he said, starting the truck.

She lifted her chin. "Yep."

Pretending not to see her hands trembling in her lap, he navigated out of the pot-hole ridden parking lot.

"Anything on your mind?" he asked.

"You could catch a flight to Miami from Fargo and let me drive to Minneapolis. I'll drop the truck at a rental office, I promise."

"No."

"But I've taken so much of your time—and we both know the strike is over. I kept it from you because I wanted to spend time with you, but all it did was cause trouble. You could have been in Miami days ago."

"I've known, too," he said, setting the cruise control at a steady seventy-five miles per hour. "If I'd told you, you could have flown home before you lost your ID and your Blackout winnings. I would only fly now if you could, but you can't, so I'll drive you home."

"You're not mad I knew?"

"I didn't tell you for the same reason you didn't tell me, and I don't regret it." Aiden took her hand and brought it to his lips.

He drove with his hand in her lap for the next three hours.

"I know we're in a hurry, but can we stop for something to eat?" Aiden asked as they drove by a blue highway sign announcing several choices that made his stomach grumble. They cleared the North Dakota/Minnesota border not long before, and while the landscape looked the same, signs began to pop up declaring them only miles from little towns situated on one of Minnesota's various ten thousand lakes. They were about to drive by Serenity Bay, a small town of about two thousand people that boasted its own lake, beach, pontoon rentals and more. "Stretching wouldn't be a bad thing," he prodded.

"Sure. I've never been here. Looks like they have a cute main street, and some public accesses to the lake, if you want to take a walk."

Aiden blew out a breath. "Sounds good." He took the exit off the interstate and followed signs along the narrow two-lane road.

Serenity Bay hugged a lake that sparkled emerald blue in the high sun. In the distance, adults and children played in the sand of a beach that stretched for at least a quarter mile. Jet-Skis and boats dotted the lake, the surface rippling with the light breeze. Seagulls flew in the sky, looking for crumbs or castoffs from the fisherman spending a leisurely day in the perfect weather fishing for walleye.

Aiden parked after a car just backing out of a space near a city park, and he swiped his credit card at the meter to pay for two hours. That would give them enough time to stretch, walk around, and grab a bite to eat.

With the scent of barbecue and frying hamburger filling the air, Aiden shoved his keys into the pocket of the jeans he bought at Target. His mouth quirked at the thought of how much time he'd spent shopping for clothes. "Looks like there's a fair going on. Do you want to grab something from one of the booths?"

He hadn't had fair food in God knew how long. His palate usually ran on the more sophisticated side, preferring to eat at places like Top Hat over Gil's Bar and Grill, but hunger was hunger, and maybe a slushy and corn dog wouldn't be so bad. His stomach didn't seem to think so, not by the gurgling sound it made when he thought of funnel cake and cheese curds.

Kat stepped onto the sidewalk and gathered her hair into a high ponytail. "You don't look like the type who would enjoy food like that."

Aiden winced. She was getting to know him well . . . too well. "I like . . . grease, just like the next guy."

Kat laughed, though it sounded forced. "Sure, you do. Whatever you want. Lead the way," she said, gesturing to the park where little kids wearing swimsuits ran, chasing dogs, pulling balloons.

They passed booths selling Special K bars and Better than Sex Cake, food trucks, and tables selling locally made products like honey and wine from a local winery. There was something for everyone. Between the corn dogs he was thinking of, and fried macaroni and cheese on a stick, he'd have a hard time deciding.

But there wasn't any rush, besides the fact that he was hungry, and he held Kat's hand, content with the way her fingers curled around his.

The wind blew off the lake, and Aiden closed his eyes for a moment, wondering how it would feel to live in a little place like this. He could open his own office. Kat could open the clothing store she wanted, or she could work in the library, if she chose. They could bring their kids to the beach in the summer and take them sledding in the winter. Having grown up in Florida and then later, after Dylan moved to California, spending large chunks of time in LA, snow was a foreign concept to him. But now that the picture filled his mind, he had a terrible time brushing aside the thought of his daughter dressed in so many layers of clothes she could barely move, yet giggling all the while.

"Do you like living in Minnesota?" he asked as they wandered among the stalls of food, jewelry, knitting and crochet projects.

Kat looked up at him. "Sure. I love the seasons—they're everything they look like in the movies. The crisp leaves in the fall, the scent of wood smoke, the slight chill in the air of the oncoming winter. Winter brings sleigh rides, looking at lights in the snow. Snowmen. Hot chocolate. Have you ever had a white Christmas?"

Aiden shook his head and guided her around two children feeding a puppy pieces of hot dog.

"Then the snow melts, and the sun comes out. The trees green, the grass grows. And summer . . . summer is nice. Warm . . . slow, you know? People slow down, take vacations." She stared across the lake, a band of evergreen trees standing out in the distance. "But it isn't the ocean."

"Bugs," he reminded her.

The smile she shared with him was full of sadness, lost dreams, missed chances. If he looked in the mirror, he was sure that same expression would stare back at him.

"I'd take the bugs if I could have the ocean."

"Is that why you were sad? On the shuttle? Because you were going to miss the ocean in Santa Barbara?"

She shrugged.

"You can come visit me. My penthouse condo is oceanside— well, as oceanside as you can get. The part of the beach I live on is public access—six lanes of traffic separate my building from the sand, but there's a crosswalk right outside my door."

"Can you see it from your windows?"

He nodded, studying the dark depths of her brown eyes. "Yeah. I can hear it, too, at night, if I leave my balcony doors open."

"That sounds lovely," she murmured, then wrinkled her nose. "But a visit will be unlikely, don't you think?"

"Yeah, I guess so," he said, kicking himself for being a thoughtless bastard. Kat visiting him would be as likely as the cops finding their SUV and all of their things inside, intact.

They stopped at a few tables, and he bought her a bracelet made of white and pink stones. As he fastened it around her wrist, he resisted the urge to kiss her palm. Instead, he led her through the crowd. "Let's eat and get going. I don't think the meter has much time left on it."

He tugged her hand, and after a few feet, he stopped in front of a food truck offering an assortment of menu items. "Fish tacos?" he asked, his eyebrows raised. He loved fish tacos—the kind he ordered from a little food truck in Miami were the best he'd ever eaten.

"Gross. No thanks. But I'll have the truffle fries. A double order. And a raspberry Icee."

"Where are you going to put all that?" he asked after giving a teenage girl their order.

"I have to eat while I can—Neil is always telling me . . ." she trailed off and looked down at her feet. "Well, never mind."

Aiden could just about finish her sentence, but rather than press her, he gritted his teeth.

The girl manning the register handed him Kat's huge basket

filled with fries, still sizzling with deep fryer grease, and her blue Icee. He handed them to her and took the cardboard basket lined with parchment paper and filled with four tacos. They smelled amazing, and Aiden took a deep, spicy breath.

He looked around the park, down the expanse of beach and spied an empty bench. Nudging her in that direction he said, "There's a bench over there, do you want to sit?"

She mumbled something unintelligible around a mouthful of fries, but it sounded agreeable, and he grinned.

They walked across the grass, dogs and children running around them, squealing, and he felt like he stepped into a Norman Rockwell painting. Life couldn't be so simple.

"Don't you mind your money from Blackout was stolen?" he asked. She hadn't said one word about the missing money, and it impressed him. Not many people would let fifteen thousand dollars go without shedding a tear. Of course, she could have cried about it in private, but for some reason, he didn't think she had.

She licked her fingers, and he squirmed when the tip of her tongue darted out of her mouth.

"No, not really. I have no right to mind. It *was* my fault we stopped. I guess it was my payback for not listening to you. I feel sorry for TJ, though, what happened to him."

Aiden deliberately didn't think about that afternoon, but Kat's comment brought him back to the convenience store, the ice returning to his veins remembering when TJ took her. "That was a helluva thing."

"Yeah." She took a pull of Icee through her straw and handed it to him.

He hadn't ordered anything to drink, and he accepted it gratefully, wetting his mouth with the flavored ice.

"What are you going to do after you drop me off?" she asked, biting off a tip of French fry.

He rubbed his neck with the back of his hand—his fingers were greasy, and he didn't have a napkin. "I guess talk to Samantha. She's been patient, and it's only fair I hear what she has to say."

"You want to get back together with her, don't you?"

His impulse answer was yes, of course he did. When she left him, his world had fallen to pieces.

"I guess it depends on why she left me," he answered honestly.

"Right." She offered him her Icee again, and he took another pull at the straw.

"What about you?" he asked, handing the red and white cup back to her.

"I guess I'll talk to Neil, find out why he freaked out. Go back to work. I won't be able to help Nan now, with her office, but I'll do what I can. Go back to normal, I guess."

She didn't look happy about it, and he couldn't blame her. Falling back into the same routine, going out with Samantha on the weekends after working a seventy-hour week at work, *if* he went back to work, didn't sound the least bit appealing.

He finished his tacos and threw the basket into a trash barrel a few feet away from their bench. "I need a napkin, I'll be right back."

Aiden grabbed a handful from a picnic table nearby, and when he turned toward the bench, his breath caught.

Kat's shoulders slumped, her hair drooping in the elastic of her ponytail. She looked like a sad, lost little girl.

He handed her a wad of brown paper napkins and took the empty paper basket from her. "Let's get going. I don't know what kind of traffic we'll run into outside the city, and we may need to allow a couple hours to get through rush hour."

Kat threw her napkins and empty Icee cup into the trash, and Aiden held her hand. He liked it; he drew comfort from her presence.

"Do you want me to drive for a bit?" she asked as he pulled the truck keys from his pocket.

"Sure. Have you been up this way? Do you know the roads?"

Kat shook her head. "No, there hasn't been a reason for me to be this far west. But I know the area around the Cities pretty well, and if we run into some traffic, I can get us around it."

"Sounds good," he said.

He settled into the passenger seat and reclined the chair. By his estimation, they had four, maybe five hours on the road.

Ten minutes out of Serenity Bay, his stomach started gurgling and churning. For a moment he thought it was motion sickness, and he slid down his window, hoping fresh air would calm him.

His skin started to prickle and sweat gathered under his arms.

"Are you okay?" Kat asked. "You don't look very good. You're all white and pasty. Maybe you should've had some water with your tacos instead of my Icee."

"My stomach is a bit off, but maybe I just need a nap," he said, reclining his seat as far as it would go, hoping he could sleep off the nausea.

"Okay, get some rest," she said, turning her eyes back to the road. "We'll hit the entrance for the interstate in a couple minutes."

Aiden closed his eyes, but that made him feel worse. He snapped them open as his stomach lurched and through the trees watched slivers of the lake go by. The aftertaste of the fish tacos filled his mouth, and he tried to swallow it back.

"Kat, I need to stop."

"What?" she asked, alarmed.

"Stop the truck."

Quickly, she pulled the truck onto the narrow shoulder, and he was heaving into the ditch before she could shift into Park.

"God, Aiden, are you okay?"

He shook his head, his stomach rolling. "I need a bathroom. Fast."

"We're going to have to go back to Serenity Bay," she said. "The next town is a half an hour away."

"I need a bathroom," he repeated, not caring how pissed he sounded or where they had to go to find one. "I have to—"

Another round of heaving cut him off, and he knelt on the

grass, little rocks biting into his palms. Beyond caring he was spraying vomit onto his clothes, he prayed against hope he kept his skivvies clean.

"Oh, God," Kat said, patting his back. "I think those fish tacos gave you food poisoning."

Chapter Nine

Kat searched the truck for anything that could help Aiden, but all she found was a bottle half full of water.

He sat with his back against the wheel of the truck, sucking in air through his nose, his shoulders shaking.

"Rinse your mouth out, maybe," she said, handing him the warm bottle. "Can you make it back to town? Do you want me to call nine-one-one?"

"No, I just need a bathroom. If you go as fast as you can, I think I'll be okay. I feel like I've thrown up everything I've eaten in the past three days."

Worrying her bottom lip between her teeth, she opened the passenger door and waited as he pulled himself to his feet, leaning against the vehicle for support.

"I'll try to be quick, but where do you want me to go?"

He threw the bottle of water into the backseat. "You'll have to find a hotel or something. I can't travel this way."

Kat knew that. She had a terrible case of food poisoning once after eating at a little dive, foolishly ordering bleu cheese dressing on her salad. If he was as sick as she'd been, they wouldn't be going anywhere for three or four days.

The minute he shut his door, she stomped on the gas, the tires skidding on the loose gravel as she made the tight U-turn. She wouldn't have much time; she believed him when he said he needed the bathroom for something else.

A sign for the Serenity Bay Motel said it was three miles up ahead, and Kat didn't ask Aiden if it was okay. The little town sat near a lake with a pretty beach, and it was the middle of June— prime tourist season. They would be lucky if any motel had a vacancy.

She pulled into the lot and parked directly outside the office. "Let me see if they have any rooms. Places like this get booked up with fisherman and families on vacation."

"Just hurry," Aiden said through clenched teeth.

Kat grabbed his wallet from a cubby in the dash, and she ran into the office.

A middle-aged woman wearing a Serenity Bay t-shirt and jeans sat behind the desk reading a thick book.

"Excuse me, do you have any rooms available for the next . . . four nights?" Even if he got over what he'd eaten, he'd be weak, and maybe he'd need an extra day to rest.

"Yeah, but you're lucky we do. A family of four canceled their vacation not an hour ago—their youngest came down with chicken pox. What's your hurry?" she asked as Kat threw Aiden's credit card across the desk.

"My . . . " What was he? It would be easier if the woman thought they were married. ". . . Husband ate at a food truck in the park, and now he's not feeling well."

Aiden climbed out of the truck and leaned against the front bumper, bent at the waist, his fingertips white, gripping his thighs.

"Oooh," the woman whistled, peering through the grimy window. "He ate at Trudy's Taco Truck, didn't he? You know," she said, placing a fisted hand on her padded hip, "she's been told time and time again to clean up her truck. The health department has shut her down twice." She leaned against the counter. "If you have a mind, you could sue her."

"Well, right now Aiden really needs, ah, a bathroom, but I'll let him know when he's feeling better."

"Oh! Right." The woman wrinkled her nose. "Coming out both ends, huh? That's what Trudy's tacos do to ya. Here. You'll be in number seven. Seems like you could use some luck." She handed a key to Kat that was attached to a silver keyring in the shape of a seven. "You ain't gonna wanna use your bathroom, darlin', not while he's in there, so you come use the one here in the office. And we have a washer and dryer, you know, because his clothes aren't gonna be fit for wearin' until you wash 'em."

"Thank you, ma'am," Kat said gratefully. She hadn't had much of a thought about what she would do for her own needs, but knowing she could use the bathroom here was helpful.

"You better get going, now, your husband's looking downright pissed."

"Yeah, right. Thanks," she said, shoving Aiden's credit card into his wallet.

"You know, if I wouldn'ta known better, I would have said you remind me of that girl from that one movie about the singing girls? The a cappella group."

"*Pitch Perfect*, yeah. I've gotten that. Thanks again!"

When Kat ran out of the office, nearly banging her forehead against the glass in her haste to open the door, Aiden barked, "What took you so fucking long?"

Trying not to take offense, he was sick after all, she tried to quell the hurt. "Apparently, you're Trudy's newest victim. Her tacos are, ah, yummy."

"Do they have a room or not?"

She gestured across the small parking lot to their door. "Number seven. We got a room for four nights, but we were luck—"

He tore the key from her grasp and bolted across the empty lot.

By the time Kat moved the truck and parked in front of their motel door, Aiden was already inside the bathroom, retching noises filling the little room.

Kat winced.

The motel was clean for the type it was, not that much different from the one they'd stay at in Harmony. At least she wouldn't have to worry about scorpions. Kat was on familiar ground. Besides a spider or a stray wasp, there wouldn't be any insects to worry about.

"Aiden, is there anything I can do for you?" she asked through the bathroom door when there was a pause between his heaving.

"Just leave me alone."

"Okay. Tell me if I can bring you anything . . ." But her words were drowned out by Aiden gagging.

She brought in their things from the truck. Aiden's phone, his wallet. Her phone. The clothes they purchased at Target, which were, suddenly, not enough to see them through the next few days. She could do their laundry at the office, if need be, and it wasn't like she wasn't going to have time on her hands. But she needed to stay close to Aiden; he might need her help at some point. Food poisoning could turn from bad to worse in a second.

Hearing him vomit made her own stomach churn, and she turned the TV to HGTV to drown him out.

Kat plugged in Aiden's phone to charge, then she sat on the bed, at a loss.

She brought up Nan's phone number. Nan hadn't called her back, and she was ashamed to admit she hadn't thought about her friend since they'd spoken in Denver.

"Hey, girl," Nan said in greeting. "You home yet?"

"No, but we're in Minnesota. Aiden ate some bad fish, and now he's sick. We're stuck in a little town about two hours out of Moorhead, Minnesota. I'm afraid it's going to be a while before we can leave."

"Kat, why didn't you grab a plane in Fargo? You know the flight from Fargo to Minneapolis is less than an hour. You gotta let this guy go, hon."

"I would have, but . . ." Kat updated Nan on what happened with TJ, how he put a gun to her head, and later, when she insisted on helping the older couple who had stolen their truck, taking her purse and ID with them.

"My God, are you all right?" Nan asked.

"Yeah. Yeah, I am," she said, surprised she was telling the truth. "Aiden, he's been really sweet. The night TJ put a gun to my head . . . I wasn't doing very well, and we—"

"You slept together! Oh, Kat, I am so happy for you! I never liked Neil and—"

"We didn't sleep together, well, he got me off, but, what the hell do you mean you never liked Neil? You've supported me all these years!"

"Never mind that, what do *you* mean, he only got you off? Katrina Ford, you had the guy eating from your hand that night, and all you did was let him finger you? Are you for real?"

"Try having a gun to your head, Nan," Kat hissed, her eyes darting toward the bathroom door. She didn't want Aiden to think something was wrong. He had enough to deal with. "I wasn't thinking about sex."

"You were thinking about it enough to somehow make it into his bed," Nan pointed out.

"He's a gentleman. God, you're such a ho," she muttered.

"You were gonna be one, too. How many men would you have screwed if you'd stayed in California?" Nan mused, sounding not the least bit offended Kat had called her a slut.

"That was a bad idea."

"No, it wasn't, but at least you met Aiden instead. Are you gonna get in on that before he drops you off at home, or not?"

"He's got his head in the toilet. He's not thinking about sex right now."

"Men are always thinking about sex. He's probably pissed he feels too sick to bang you."

"Whatever you say. Now tell me what you meant by that comment about Neil. I thought you were on my side."

"Kat, I love you—we've been friends forever. But I never once thought it was a good idea for you to marry that loser. Your mother wanted you taken care of after she passed away, I can understand that. I really and truly can. But if your mother knew how unhappy you are with him, she never would have made you promise. Never. She'd never want that for you."

"Neil doesn't make me *un*happy," she said, but her voice sounded unconvincing even to her own ears.

"Like hell he doesn't. Listen, I've never said anything because marrying Neil was what you wanted. Your reasons were your own, but he doesn't care about you, he treats you like a maid, and lets you pay his bills. Your mom is gone," Nan's voice lowered. "She won't know if you don't go through with it."

"Then who would take care of me?" Kat whispered over Aiden's moans.

"It's not who would take care of you, baby, the question is, who do you want to take care of? Anyway, I'm flying out of LAX the day after tomorrow. At this rate, I'll beat you back. Give me a call when you get into town, okay? We'll meet for coffee. And Kat, I'm glad you're okay."

"Thanks."

Kat disconnected the call and tossed her phone onto the bed.

The bathroom was suddenly quiet, and that made her worry. "Aiden," she said, lightly tapping on the door, "are you okay in there?"

"As okay as I can be puking my guts up," he said. "I'm sorry you can't use the bathroom."

"It's fine. Don't worry about anything but feeling better. Let me know if I can get you anything."

In answer, Aiden made noises indicating he was done throwing up and had moved on to another way his body could get rid of the putrid fish.

Kat backed away from the door.

He hadn't sounded better, but he hadn't sounded worse, thank God.

The motel room contained the usual—two queen beds, a nightstand between them, an old TV Kat already flipped on, and a low dresser made of particle board that looked like it came from Walmart. The carpet was dingy, a strange hue between green and brown. Light brown paneling covered the walls; a large window looked over the parking lot.

At a loss, but wanting to be helpful, Kat grabbed Aiden's wallet, and with a quick goodbye Aiden didn't acknowledge, let herself outside into the bright summer afternoon.

She chose a direction at random and walked until she found a small corner grocery store. As she wandered the aisles, Kat wracked her brain for the foods her mother used to feed her when she had the stomach flu.

Ginger ale, she knew that one.

The BRAT diet, that's what it was.

Bananas, applesauce, what did the R stand for? Rice? And the T. The T stood for toast, but there wasn't a toaster in their room; she'd have to make do with Saltine crackers.

She grabbed little cartons of Jell-O as well, going with the Original rather than taking a chance the aspartame in the Sugar-Free variety wouldn't bother Aiden's already sensitive stomach. She hoped there was a refrigerator in the room.

Browsing, she bought a few things for herself, including a book and a couple beauty magazines. She wasn't much for TV and the constant noise might grate on Aiden's nerves.

Her arms were aching by the time she carried everything to the motel, and she blew out a sigh of relief when she spied a little black fridge with a coffeemaker sitting on top of it.

After putting everything away, she read her book on one of the beds, propped against a large stack of pillows.

When she realized Aiden hadn't made any noise for quite some time, she checked her phone and frowned.

Two hours had gone by.

Kat set her book aside and leaned against the bathroom door. "Aiden? Are you okay?"

He didn't reply, but the toilet flushed. She blew out a sigh of relief; at least he was alive in there.

Not knowing what she would find, Kat wet a washcloth in the sink and slowly, so she wouldn't hit him in case he was sprawled on the floor, she opened the bathroom door, grateful he hadn't locked it.

"Hey," she whispered, kneeling.

He leaned against the side of the tub, deep circles under his eyes, lines of fatigue and pain framing his mouth.

"Get out of here," he croaked, but Kat wasn't afraid. He looked too weak to force her to go.

She held the cool cloth to the side of his face, smoothed it over his forehead, and cleaned his mustache and beard.

Kat rinsed the washcloth, saturating the material in cool water, and again, sat down beside him. "Are you feeling any better?"

She lifted her hand to his face, meeting his gaze, the haunted look in his bloodshot eyes stealing her breath.

"What are you doing?" he rasped.

"I was worried about you. You didn't sound good in here."

"I've never been so sick in my entire life," he said, sagging against the edge of the beige bathtub.

Kat pressed the washcloth to his forehead. "Do you think you're done?"

Aiden groaned. "No. My stomach is in knots, and I'm taking a chance not sitting on the toilet, but my body aches from puking so much, I couldn't sit there another minute."

Kat rubbed his shoulder. "Take all the time you need. I'll be right here if you want me for anything."

Aiden shook his head and held her hand, his skin clammy. "No. You should go. You're only a couple hours away from home. What time is it? You could make it before it gets dark."

"Aiden—" she started, but he cut her off.

"Take the truck, and I'll figure out a way to Fargo and fly out from there. You should go, Kat."

"Aiden, look at me."

After he met her eyes she said, "I'm not leaving you here by yourself, not while you're sick. I won't. Don't ask me again." She gathered him into her arms, and he rested his head on her shoulder. "I'll stay with you. Let me stay with you."

He tightened his arms around her, and she rested her cheek on the top of his head.

"For as long as you want," he murmured.

How about forever?

She held him while he dozed, and when he woke to heave into the toilet, Kat patted his back, helpless, her skin prickling with discomfort.

"Why don't you give me your clothes?" she asked after he was done. "The woman who checked us in said we could use the washer and dryer in the office. You might feel better in something clean."

"Can you bring my body wash in here? I get dizzy if I stand, but washing up in the tub sounds doable."

Kat pressed her lips to his cheek. "Okay, but be careful and call me if you need help."

"I'm not sick enough for that. I can take a bath by myself."

She appreciated his bravado, but it didn't reassure her and wouldn't keep her from worrying. His skin was the color of ash, and even though she wiped his face, his forehead beaded with sweat.

"Don't be like that. If you need me, you need me." Kat realized how that sounded and looked away. He'd never need her, not the way a woman prays a man will need her. For love, for companionship. To have an equal partner by his side.

He parted his lips to respond, but he jerked toward the toilet instead.

"I'll bring in your things," she said, but she doubted he heard her over the retching.

Against her better judgment, but at his insistence, she left him in the bathroom, the water running into the bathtub, to use the washer and dryer in the main office.

While their clothes washed, Kat passed the time talking to Carla, the woman who checked them in. After Carla found out Kat was a librarian, the woman spent two hours pumping Kat for information on all the latest bestsellers.

"I better go check on him," Kat said, folding their warm clothes on the front desk. "But thanks for keeping me company, and for letting me use the washer and dryer."

"Thank you, darlin'. You gave me some good ideas for my book club. Appreciate it."

The bathroom was quiet when she came back to their room. "Are you okay?" she asked, just to be sure he was able to clean up without falling and slamming his head. She would never forgive herself if he'd gotten hurt while she was gone.

"Yeah, but I'll be spending the night in here."

"I figured as much," she murmured. "It's all right. I washed our clothes, so I'm in for the evening. If you need anything, call me."

Aiden grunted.

Kat was in the middle of eating the sandwich she bought herself for dinner and munching her way through a bag of Cool Ranch Doritos when Aiden's phone started buzzing, dancing with the vibration on the dresser near the TV.

Dylan's name flashed on the screen.

Aiden's brother.

She looked toward the bathroom, and just when she thought maybe Aiden would be okay to talk, a low guttural moan seeped under the door.

Maybe not.

Kat answered it before it went to voicemail. She didn't want his brother to worry about him.

"Hello?"

"Who is this?" Dylan's voice, full of curiosity, filled her ear. "I was calling for my brother, Aiden."

"This is Kat."

"He's still with you?"

"He's not feeling well. He could have dropped me off by now, but we stopped for a bite to eat and now he has food poisoning."

"Jesus Christ," Dylan muttered, and Kat winced. "You're his lucky charm, aren't you?" Sarcasm oozed through the line.

"It's not my fault he ordered fish tacos from a food truck," she retorted, resenting being pinned the blame.

Dylan didn't know her, but it sure sounded like he didn't like her.

"Fucking fish tacos," Dylan said. "He's always liked them."

"Well, he's paying for it now," she said, breaking a Dorito into crumbs. She regretted answering Aiden's phone.

"How long has he been sick?"

"Since this afternoon. We have a motel room for three more nights after tonight; he has plenty of time to get better."

"Are you going to look out for him, at least?"

Kat took umbrage to the idea she would abandon him. "He wanted me to go—we're not far from Rosemont Valley, where I live, but I'd never leave him this way. This sick, he shouldn't be alone."

Dylan blew out a breath. "That's something, at least. What's going on between you two, anyway?"

"Nothing." She lifted her chin to give herself courage. "I know he's not available, and I know Samantha's waiting for him. He hasn't even hinted at a future with me, and he's never made me any promises."

"Yeah, he has, Kat. He doesn't want to bring you home. Can't you see that?"

Kat paused. The detour to Mount Rushmore had seemed unnecessary, but she'd went along because she wanted every second she could with him. He admitted he hadn't told her about the strike being over because he wanted to spend time with her, but stretching out their road trip was a far cry from having a future together. "That might be true, but he never said he wouldn't, either. He wants to work things out with Samantha, and I'm engaged. We both know we won't see each other after this."

Kat pressed her lips together.

"He's told me that too, but you both sound pretty damned miserable when you talk about going separate ways."

"That's not for me to say," she said, refusing to let Dylan's words spark a hope in her heart.

"I know my brother. He's always been looking for something. He thought he found it in Samantha."

"He did," Kat said. "She ran away from her wedding to be with him. Nothing is standing in his way."

"Not even you?"

"Not even me."

"Take care of my brother, Kat."

"I will. Until he doesn't need me anymore."

Kat wrapped what was left of her sandwich in the waxed paper and threw it into the garbage.

She lost her appetite.

Aiden stumbled out of the bathroom as the sun peeked over the horizon. A piercing pain picked at his head, and his joints and muscles ached. His throat burned like it was on fire.

He splashed lukewarm water onto his face and rinsed his mouth out in the sink. After dabbing a bit of toothpaste on the tip of his finger, he sucked it off. He breathed a sigh as the minty flavor replaced the sour taste on his tongue.

"How are you feeling?"

Aiden shuffled toward Kat's voice.

She'd closed the curtains, and he could only make out her silhouette in the shadows.

"My asshole feels like I've been shitting lava, but otherwise, I think the worst is over," he said, too tired to care how crass he sounded.

Sitting in the middle of one of the queen beds, one strap of her tank top falling off her shoulder, her long hair in a tangle around her head, Kat clamped a hand over her mouth in amusement or disgust, he didn't know which, and he was too tired to care.

He dropped into her bed, and stretching, pulled the surprisingly soft sheet to his chin.

"What are you doing?"

"I'm exhausted." To prove it, he stifled a yawn. "You might have missed it, but I spent the entire night puking."

"I didn't miss it. You kept me up all night. But there's a bed over there."

"You're not in that one," he said, arranging the bedspread over his torso. "Why are you giving me a hard time?"

Kat stretched beside him and rested her head on a hand, leaning over him. "I'm not. I'm glad you're looking better."

He closed his eyes when she pressed a kiss to his cheek. "Let's go to sleep."

She curled her small body around his and nestled her head onto his shoulder.

He wrapped an arm around her, and he was asleep in seconds.

When he opened his eyes, his arms were empty, but Kat still lay in bed, reading a book. "What time is it?" he asked. Gauging from the sun trying to dodge the curtains, he guessed it was late afternoon.

Kat confirmed it. "It's two-thirty. You slept without moving for over eight hours. Do you feel better?"

Besides feeling like he was getting over the flu—body aches and chills—he did feel better. The queasiness had been replaced with a hollowness resembling hunger. "Not terrible. Maybe a little hungry. Maybe."

"I went to the store yesterday. I bought you some ginger ale. Do you want some crackers?"

Aiden's throat worked with emotion, taken off guard by her thoughtfulness. No one had ever gone out of their way for him like that, not a woman who wasn't his mother, at least. His employees were paid to go above and beyond. Those who didn't were replaced by those who would. If he needed anything, Samantha was quick to make a call, but she never took the time to do anything for him herself. If he was hungry, she called out for delivery. If he needed something repaired, someone picked it up and returned it, good as new. Samantha didn't do anything a personal assistant couldn't do. Aiden had never thought much about it, always willing to pay for convenience. But Kat had gone to the store, had thought about him, had anticipated his needs, and that simple kindness shook him. When he could speak he said, "You didn't have to—"

"I wanted to. Besides," she smiled over her shoulder as she scooted off the bed, "I didn't want to sit and listen to you throw up. So there."

She handed him two inches of chilled ginger ale in a plastic cup and a sleeve of Saltine crackers.

He sipped at the bubbly liquid, swearing it was the best tasting thing he'd had in years.

As Kat crawled back into bed, he set his cup aside on the small table between the two beds and opened his arms.

When she hesitated, he thought maybe he'd gone too far, and his chest tightened, waiting for rejection. But she smiled, positioned herself between his legs, and he wrapped his arms around her, pleased she let him hold her. He sank into the pillow, his body relaxing into the mattress. Her damp hair smelled of vanilla shampoo. She took a shower while he was sleeping, and he gave into the temptation to run his fingers over her skin now smooth and dewy with body lotion.

"Thank you for not leaving," he said. It would have been dangerous for him to be alone. He'd known that, even as he tried to shoo her away.

She rested her cheek on his chest, wrapping his arms around him. "I said I wouldn't."

"I appreciate it." He struggled with something else to say.

Filling the silence, she said, "Dylan called yesterday."

"Did you talk to him?" Aiden could just imagine what a conversation between them would sound like, and he hoped Dylan hadn't given her a hard time. His brother hadn't exactly kept his opinions to himself during this whole mess.

"Yeah. I hope you don't mind. I didn't want him to worry when you didn't answer."

"It's okay, but he's not happy with the situation I'm in with you. He doesn't want to see me hurt after this thing with Samantha."

"He said a few things, but it didn't upset me. He didn't tell me anything I didn't already know." She paused. "Aiden?"

"Yeah?"

"Will you tell me about your job? About that case?"

He took another sip of ginger ale, though he suspected Kat being in his arms calmed him more than the fizzy drink.

He wound one long brunette curl around his finger, the silky strands catching on a hangnail. "Why do you want to know?"

"I'm just curious. We've been on the road for days now, and you haven't mentioned it once."

As he organized his thoughts, wasted a moment nibbling on a cracker. "Do you remember the OJ Simpson case?"

Kat wiggled, the top of her head brushing his chin. "Not really."

"During his trial, the prosecution presented into evidence a glove found at the scene. They said it was his, and it would prove he was there."

"Right. I remember. It didn't fit him, and it caused a huge scandal."

"More than a scandal. It blew the case apart. It got him off; that one little thing."

"What does that have to do with your case?" Kat asked, shifting, rubbing her belly against his cock. He prayed he was too weak to get hard.

"My case involved a similar scenario. A teenage girl was taken from a mall parking lot and dragged into a wooded area nearby. A man killed her there, and we got a partial facial ID of a potential suspect from a parking lot security camera. He had a solid alibi, but when we searched his house, we found an old pair of work boots. There were trace amounts of blood on them, and they were a match to the victim."

"Was his alibi a lie?"

"Maybe. We had the boots, and they were found on his property. We dismissed his alibi, didn't check into it any further. My team and I thought the boots were everything we needed. The only problem was, when we had him try them on during the trial, they didn't fit."

Kat sucked in a breath.

"He could force them on, but it was clear they weren't his boots. Further testing confirmed it. The molding of the sole didn't match the suspect's foot impression."

"That doesn't mean he didn't wear them to kill that girl."

Aiden tightened his arms around her. "That's what we thought. The jury didn't buy it, though. He had an alibi, or enough people willing to lie for him, at least, and the boots didn't fit. They let him off." He fisted the floral comforter in an angry grasp. "I was a pariah. I prosecuted the wrong man, which meant the real murderer is still out there."

"Do you really think that?" Kat whispered.

"No. I knew the son of a bitch did it—I could see it in his eyes. I've been prosecuting the shit out of guilty people for years. I know pride when I see it. He had the boots in his possession. The blood on them matched our victim. But it wasn't enough."

"You can't do anything else?"

"Cases come, cases go. And you can't try the same man for the same crime. Even if there weren't a million other cases to close, finding concrete evidence wouldn't do anything to help us now."

"But if you kept looking—"

"There's no point, Kat. There's not enough resources to open a closed case."

"Why is it closed?"

"We thought we had the guy. We didn't. Or we did, but not enough proof, which amounts to the same thing. Her parents were devastated. After the verdict, her mother spit in my face. I've tried to come to terms with it, but I don't know if I ever will. I can't get the hate in that woman's eyes out of my mind."

"You're not the first attorney to lose a case," she said, running her fingertips over his chest, through the sparse hair that peeked from the neckline of his white ribbed tank.

Aiden took the comment for what it was: consolation. But there weren't any consolation prizes, no ribbons for participation, not for something like that. "You weren't there, Kat. And it was my own fault. My team didn't do the work. We thought the boots were enough. We needed more. That's what America is known for, sweetheart. I believe in the system. I failed. It didn't fail me."

"Is that why Samantha left?"

"Of course—" Aiden stopped. No. That wasn't why she left him. He'd lost cases while they were dating. It didn't matter this was such a high-profile case, or that her name had been linked with his in the papers. She didn't care about things like that. Why she left didn't have anything to do with the case. No, it had to do with Max. The timing was just a coincidence.

"No. She said it had something to do with Max and I believe her, but I won't deny it was shitty timing. I could have used the support."

Kat propped herself up on her arms and looked into his eyes. "She's waiting for you. She can help you ease back into work."

He stared at her irises, the pupils large in the dim room, searching for light, and she looked . . . aroused, sexy. Her eyelashes were bare of mascara, the lids clean of eyeshadow. She didn't wear any makeup at all, her lips sparkling with a natural pink color and a little saliva. Gorgeous. She was simply gorgeous in a delicate small-town girl kind of way. She appealed to him on that level. Wholesome. Kat possessed the demeanor and manners to match. A quietness about her that calmed his heart, eased his anxiety. She listened when he spoke.

Like he mattered.

Like she mattered to him.

"I don't know if I want that. Not anymore. Kat," he whispered, cradling her face in his hands. Gently, he drew her to him, and pressed his lips to hers. "What are we going to do?"

Kat swallowed. This was her chance. Just one night. "How do you feel?" she asked, studying his face. Telling her about the case, and his memories about the victim's mother, and Samantha leaving him at a time in his life when he'd needed someone the most, made the shadows in his eyes more pronounced.

"Better," he said, bringing her hand to his lips and kissing her fingers.

Katrina made her choice. "Will you make love to me, Aiden?"

He stilled. "Are you sure that's what you want?"

There wasn't anything in life she wanted more. She nodded.

"I don't have any protection," he said, smoothing her hair. "Did you buy condoms?"

She bit her lip. She hadn't been thinking about that while she was in the grocery store, but . . . "I'm due to have my period soon. Really soon. I'm not in a place in my cycle to get pregnant."

"Aren't you on birth control, honey?" he asked.

Kat knew what he was thinking. She lived with a man and had been engaged for years. Surely she was using something. "Neil and I don't sleep together. We don't have sex."

Aiden huffed out a laugh. "Never?"

Self-conscious now, she stiffened and tried to pull away. "I told you. We're engaged because it's what my mother wanted for me, and his mother, too. He went along with it, but he doesn't . . . he's not interested in me that way."

No, not sex, she thought bitterly. But her paycheck, that was something else. She'd known all along, but she hid from the knowledge under the pretext she was doing what her mother wanted her to do. Nan, finally saying the words aloud, made them true.

"Wait, I'm sorry," he said, pulling her back onto his chest. "I'm sorry. I'm just having a hard time wrapping my mind around the idea he doesn't want . . . From the moment we met . . ."

He captured her mouth with his, drawing her closer, slipping his hands under her tank. His cock was hard beneath her, and she pressed into him, wanting him inside her.

When he tried to pull her tank top over her head, she said, "Wait."

She wouldn't sleep with Aiden while ties to another man remained on her hand. She slipped the silver engagement ring off her finger and set it on the night table. She should have felt guilty, sad, but all she felt was relief, like she suddenly dropped a hundred pounds and she could fly, free, like a bird, into the sky. "Are you sure you feel good enough?" she asked. Her question made him pull his gaze away from her ring, abandoned, on top of a notepad featuring the logo of their motel.

"I've never felt as good as I do now," he said, twisting onto his side so she rested on the mattress, her head propped on a large feather pillow.

"Good," she whispered before he pressed his mouth to hers.

Kat pushed her hands under his white ribbed tank top. His muscles constricted under her touch, hard, yet delicate and fragile, skin and bone and all heart, and she skimmed her fingertips over his ribs as he did the same to her to caress her breast.

Wetness flooded her panties, and a flare of heat sprang from her core. Not from between her legs, though she felt on fire there, too. No, the searing warmth came from her heart, from her soul, and how she felt for this man who cradled her like she was the most expensive thing on earth, the most precious thing he'd ever held in his arms.

She knew she was falling in love with him, had known as early as Blackout, but their legs tangled under the sheets, their hearts beating in tune, their breathing in rhythm, she knew what she felt for him was irrevocable, that she'd never feel this way for another man, ever again.

Kat ran her fingers through his beard, down his neck. She replaced her touch with her lips, and he sucked in a breath.

"We're wearing too many clothes," he murmured, running his fingers along the waistband of her pajama shorts.

She didn't want to be away from him for any amount of time, but she took the few seconds she needed to pull her tank top over her head and wiggle out of her shorts and panties while he threw his tank onto the floor and pushed his boxers from his legs.

Laying on her back, her throat clogged watching him watch her. No one had looked at her that way, like he was witnessing the eighth wonder of the world.

"You're so beautiful, Kat," he said, running a finger down her cheek.

"Thank you." She blushed.

"Ah, a woman who can take a compliment. I like that. You deserve it, you deserve all of them. So much more than—well, no more talking, huh?"

"Yeah, no more talking," she whispered, easing him to her with her hands on his strong shoulders.

"Open up for me, sweetheart," he said, sliding his hand down her hip, to the apex of her thighs.

She did as he asked, widening her legs, and he slipped a finger into her.

"I don't want to hurt you."

As her muscles contracted, grasping onto his finger, she shook her head, her hair tangling on the pillow. "You could never hurt me, Aiden." But even as she said the words, she knew she was lying. He would hurt her, oh, would he hurt her.

Not this way, though, not now.

He pushed two fingers inside her, twisting them. "You're so tight. Are you sure you want—"

"Please," she begged. "Please, Aiden. I want this more than anything."

He settled between her legs, and she prepared for the pain. She wasn't a virgin, but it had been years since she'd been with a man, and he would know it, too.

Pushing into her, he groaned. "My God. Slow, slow," he whispered, his neck muscles straining in an attempt to stay in control.

She was wet, soaked with desire, and she lifted her hips, opening for him. She reveled in the fullness, the small amount of cramping, the completeness when he settled all the way inside her.

"Are you okay?" he asked.

"More than okay," she said, touched he asked.

He sucked on one of her nipples, and she arched her back, running her fingers through his hair.

"I'm going to move, okay, baby?"

"Okay." Kat gripped his biceps as he started to withdraw then push inside her again. After a few moments, she caught the rhythm, and he kissed her, their tongues tangling as his body pushed her into the mattress.

She wrapped her legs around his, and he pulled her closer with his arms under her back.

"I'm going to come in a second, sweetheart, I can't wait any longer," he said, and pressed his lips to her forehead.

"I want to feel you come inside me," she said, looking into his eyes.

She did. Thrusting, hard enough the tip of his penis jabbed at her center, he pulsed inside her, shuddering, and what he left behind was hot and slick.

He braced himself on a knee, lightening the weight of his

body on top of hers, and immediately, she missed the heaviness, the comfort. "You didn't come," he said, nibbling her jaw.

His beard tickled her sensitive skin, and she pressed her face against him, enjoying the sensation. "No." There was no point in lying. He was more experienced than she was, and he knew she hadn't. It hadn't occurred to her to fake it; he would have known that, too. That he was kind and considerate, even in bed, was now her downfall.

Slowly, he pulled out of her. "Did I hurt you?" he asked, a worried frown puckering the skin between his eyebrows.

She smiled, meeting his smoldering blue eyes. "No. You felt good, you really did," she said, when doubt flashed across his face.

"I've made you come, so I know you can," he said, turning to his side, and resting his head in his hand. "Let me do it for you now."

She ached to be touched, and her legs opened of their own volition. "I won't say no."

His fingers found her engorged nub, and she moaned.

Aiden took her mouth, slipped his tongue between her teeth as his fingers feathered over her skin, her nerves on fire with arousal.

When he kissed his way to her breast and bit the delicate tissue of her nipple, the pressure grew, and she needed only one last touch to shatter into a million pieces. Her hips came off the mattress, pressing into his hand as he teased the orgasm from her.

Turning her face into his shoulder, she whimpered in pleasure.

"There, that's what I wanted," he said, cuddling her to him.

She paused to catch her breath, and steel herself against what she knew would be the most painful moments of the rest of her life. "Thank you, Aiden. For all of it."

"Kat," he murmured into her hair.

"No more talking," she whispered, tucking her head under his chin.

"No more talking," he agreed.

She memorized his every feature as he dozed; the haunted, hurt, look he carried with him, almost gone. That's what she wanted for him. To be happy.

He would do what he needed to do to get his career back on track, he'd make amends with Samantha, and he would be happy.

Now the only thing was, she had to figure out her own life, so she could do the same.

Chapter Ten

T hey used every minute, every second, of their time in Serenity Bay to make love, talk, learn each other's secrets, and simply enjoy being with each other. Aiden relished the time with her, the laughter, the jokes, the stories, and when the fifth morning dawned bright and sunny, his stomach rolled with nerves. Their little bubble they hid themselves in popped, and they landed with no cushion beneath them.

She didn't speak as she gathered her clothes, and Aiden wracked his brain, coming up with a million things to say and discarding them just as quickly.

There wasn't anything to say.

"Ready?" he asked after he went over the room one last time.

"Yes. While you were in the shower I called my work and took a few more days. There's no way I'll feel like working tomorrow."

Aiden hadn't been in touch with the DA's office. They'd want proof from a psychiatrist he was attending his sessions, and he had nothing to give them. His time with Kat had done more than enough in that regard, but he didn't think his boss would allow him to go back without documentation he was in the right frame of mind to take on new cases. "Did they give you any trouble?"

"Oh, no. I explained what was going on, and the head

librarian insisted I take another week off. We should get going so you can make your flight." Her voice sounded light, but her lips trembled.

"Right." He made his own phone calls while she was cleaning up in the bathroom, calling the airlines to reserve a seat to Miami by way of Minneapolis. After these several days of being with Kat, he also had the courage to call Samantha. She'd been relieved to hear from him and said she was waiting to speak with him.

His body rigid, waiting for the next catastrophe, he drove them across Minnesota, but nothing happened. There weren't any broken down cars with their passengers flagging down help. They didn't stop for coffee, or a restroom. Aiden's stomach still wasn't its best, and he'd been eating light since he stopped throwing up. Even coffee and Monster drinks sounded too harsh, and he sipped small amounts of ginger ale instead.

They made record time, and he thought with not a little amount of sarcasm that if their trip had gone that easily the entire time, he could have gotten Kat home days and days ago.

But then he'd never have had the pleasure of lying in her arms, telling her childhood stories, making her laugh. He'd never have had the pleasure of watching her shatter to pieces in his arms when she came, or the naughty glint in her eyes when she kissed her way down his stomach to give him a blowjob.

He felt like he'd lived a million years with her, wrapped up into one second, and no matter how much time he spent with her, it would never be enough.

About half an hour outside Minneapolis, she crawled into the backseat and started undressing. When they left the hotel, she was wearing the clothes he bought her at Target, but now she slid the jean shorts off her legs and shimmied out of her t-shirt.

"What are you doing?" he asked, watching her in the rearview mirror.

She didn't answer, pressing her lips together in an attempt not to cry.

His gaze tore between the road and the mirror, unable to keep his eyes away from flashes of her bared skin, where only hours before he'd skimmed his lips, until he realized what she was doing, and furious, a growl gathering deep in his chest, he glued his eyes to the interstate.

She picked up the clothes from somewhere; he didn't know where. When she crawled into the front seat she wore a long black skirt, and despite the heat of the sunny day, a turtleneck sweater. She bound her glorious hair into a tight bun at the back of her head, and she bought glasses, too, that perched on her nose. Her engagement ring circled her finger.

Kat erased every trace of the woman he'd fallen in love with.

He gritted his teeth.

With her direction, he drove into a quiet neighborhood situated in the middle of a peaceful suburb of Minneapolis. He parked across the street from a little house that seemed comfortable and well-kept, if a little worn. A flower garden grew beneath a large picture window and a massive pine tree took up most of the postage stamp front yard.

A family-oriented residential area, he could picture Kat raising her children there, and he stared bitterly at the house, where presumably Neil sat, not knowing how good he had it.

Or taking it for granted if he did.

He swallowed a mouthful of dirty names he wanted to call her fiancé, and expletives in general to express the resentment storming inside him.

"It's a pretty house," he said, choosing his words carefully. This was the moment he was dreading, and if he didn't keep his feelings in check, he'd punch something.

"Thanks. It was my mother's. She left it to me when she died. Listen, Aiden—"

He stared out the window, too angry to meet her eyes. A woman pushed a bright pink stroller down the sidewalk. He swallowed against the bile rising in his throat. One day, maybe one day soon, that would be Kat. "You don't have to say anything. I wish you luck, sweetheart. All the very best in the world."

She slid out of the seat onto the sidewalk, and he stepped into the street. He pulled her bag out of the back, and after she rounded the hood, he handed it to her.

He stood for a moment, staring at the pavement.

Kat touched his arm, and he finally met her eyes. If he fucked up this goodbye, he'd regret it for the rest of his life.

"Good luck, Aiden. I hope you and Samantha work it out." She lifted her chin, her face frozen in stony determination, her brown eyes hidden behind the sun's glare off the glasses she didn't need.

He swallowed around a fiery lump in his throat that threatened to cut off his air supply. "Thanks. Take care."

Not able to help himself, Aiden watched her walk across the street. She stopped when she reached the side door of the house. Kat looked over her shoulder at him for just a second and lifted her hand.

He nodded, rooted to the spot in the street. He wanted to call out to her, tell her to wait, to stop. To let him . . . he didn't know. Love her? Marry her? At the very least, talk her out of her stupid plans. But he couldn't do any of that, and with his heart pounding, Katrina disappeared inside.

Sitting behind the wheel, he set the directions to the airport on his phone's GPS.

He did it. He'd seen her back to her house, to her fiancé, just as he promised, and he didn't think anything would hurt more than when he drove away.

He made his flight with plenty of time to spare, and he called Dylan while he sat at his terminal waiting to board. As the line rang, he couldn't help but torture himself wondering what Kat was doing at that moment. What she was telling Neil about the picture, hoping to save what was left of her engagement.

"Hey, tell me you're finally on your way home, and not in

some fucked up situation, like in the woods, up a tree, cornered by a bear."

Aiden wished. He wished he were. He wished he were anywhere with Kat by his side. "Nope, you'll be happy to know I'm at the airport waiting to board."

"Feeling better?"

Aiden rubbed at his chest over his heart. "No."

"You're still sick—oh." Dylan fell silent for a moment. "You miss her already, don't you?"

"There's no point in missing her," he said, picturing the woman he dropped off. She wasn't the same woman he'd gotten to know during their road trip. "I'm never going to see her again."

"Not going to keep tabs on her? Maybe she won't—"

"It won't matter," he said, cutting his brother off. "How are you? How's Natalie?"

"You win some, you lose some."

Hurt and resignation highlighted his brother's voice, and Aiden pinched his nose between his eyes in sympathy and fatigue.

"I guess the Price men are unlucky in love," he said, his gaze drifting around the terminal full of people.

"Then you admit you're in love with her," Dylan said.

"I was talking about Samantha."

"You two will work it out," Dylan said, "if that's what you want. She's waiting for you, and Nick, too. He scrammed out of here after I told him you finally made it to Minnesota. Listen, Aiden, I'm thinking about moving back to Miami."

"Oh, yeah?"

"Yeah. I miss Mom and Dad, and without Natalie, there's nothing for me in LA."

"Are you sure you want to give up?"

"We've been together for a couple years now," Dylan said. "Either you know or you don't."

Aiden didn't think relationships were that black and white, but it sounded as if his brother had made up his mind. "Yeah. I need to board my flight—we'll talk when I get home. Don't do anything you'll regret. Can you do me a favor?"

"Yeah, sure. I've got nothing else to do."

"Can you go to LAX and hunt down Kat's suitcase? I asked her to leave it behind to make it to the rental place faster. She might have forgotten about it, but could you have it sent to her? I'll text you her cell number and her address."

"I think the airport will take care of that, Aiden."

"Please? Just this one thing. I just want—" Aiden's voice broke.

"To do this one last thing," Dylan murmured. "Are you sure there's no way that you two could—"

"It's over, Dylan, let it go."

"Yeah, yeah. I'll run over there tomorrow."

"Thanks. I need to go, my section is boarding. I'll call you later."

"Have a safe flight."

He settled into his first-class seat, ignored the stewardess when she asked him if he wanted a pre-flight drink or a pillow.

There was nothing she had that he wanted.

As they flew over the city, the buildings bathed in sunset, he didn't think he'd ever be able to fly again without thinking about how he'd met Katrina, his life forever changed by just that one chance encounter with a woman who was wasting her entire life to keep a single promise.

Kat stared out the window into her almost-mother-in-law's backyard. A large brown rabbit sniffed through the grass, his ears pricking at the sound of a lawnmower's engine revving in the neighboring yard.

Her heart raced and her palms were damp.

Neil had listened to her explanation and desperate pleas, and after an hour of poking and prodding, he finally admitted he saw the picture and her compromising position as a way out of their engagement. He was having doubts marrying her was what he wanted, but as the days went by, he realized he couldn't make it on his own. Happy to have her back, he'd given her a chaste kiss on the cheek and asked if she could do his laundry as all his under-wear were dirty, and could she make him a sandwich after she went to the store for groceries? He hadn't taken it upon himself to go while she'd been gone.

It was like she'd never been away, except she had a mountain of Neil's laundry that needed doing, dishes stacked in the sink that needed washing, and a pile of junk mail that needed sorting.

As she lay in bed that first night home, exhausted from trav-eling and housework, she realized she couldn't do that anymore, didn't *want* to do that anymore, and the next morning, she woke with a plan.

Neil barely looked at her over the eggs she made him for breakfast, and two hours later she stood in Neil's mother's house waiting for her to fix coffee and cake for their chat.

Wearing a white and pink blue housecoat under a white apron, Marion shuffled into the living room carrying a tray laden with mugs full of coffee, a little canister of sugar, a ceramic container full of cream, and two dessert plates holding thick wedges of chocolate cake. "It sure is good to have you back," she said, beaming at Kat.

She carefully placed the tray on the coffee table and waved Kat over to have a seat on the pink and green floral couch. "You're looking more and more like your mother every day."

Kat wished Marion wouldn't have mentioned her mother; she didn't want to bring her into this. This was her life, her choice. Her mother wasn't around anymore. She'd never know if she kept her promise or not, but she liked to think her mother would only be concerned with her daughter's happiness—no matter how that came to be.

"Thank you. I miss her a lot," she said, sitting next to the woman who had birthed her fiancé. No, not her fiancé, not anymore. Though she still wore her ring, Neil didn't feel like her fiancé and hadn't for a long time. If ever. The years blended together, and she couldn't untangle the days and months of unhappiness and complacency.

"She'd be so proud of you," Marion said, patting Kat's knee. "You have a wonderful job, and you've been keeping her house looking brand new. All you need now is to get over your cold feet and marry Neil. You living together, but not married, it's not right."

"Marion, that's what I came to talk to you about."

Marion's frown smoothed into a delighted smile. "You finally set a date then."

Kat shook her head and turned the ring on her finger. "No. Marion—"

Marion's smile faltered, and her faded blue eyes slid away. "I don't want to hear it, Katrina. Your mama and I, we raised you two hoping, and nothing made your mother happier, more content, than when you told her that you were going to marry my son."

Smoothing the skirt of her sky blue sundress, Kat thought of Aiden's face to give her courage. He was a brave, strong man, always doing what was right. She would do the same.

"Marion, I'm sorry. My mother was under the illusion he would take care of me."

"Now, I know he hasn't been himself these past few months—"

Kat gaped and tried to still her anger. This was a woman who had been there for her in every way since her mother died, and she didn't deserve Kat's temper. "He hasn't done anything for years," she corrected the older woman gently, placing a hand on her shoulder. "His doctor cleared him to go back to work a long time ago, and he hasn't been eligible for disability payments for several months. You know how hard it's been on us to pay our bills with only my salary."

"He just needs a little time."

"I know you don't want to hear it, but Neil won't find work as long as I keep paying the bills and doing everything for him. He sits at his computer all day long—how do you think he saw that picture so fast?"

"That picture was an embarrassment," Marion snapped. "You sidling up to that man like a tramp."

Kat bit back a vicious retort. Marion was angry on Neil's behalf; she wouldn't expect a mother to act any other way. "It wasn't my fault. Just like it wasn't my fault the pilots went on strike. I tried to get here as fast as I could to work it out, but I realize now it was for nothing. You have to face the truth. I was only trying to hang in there because of the promise I made to my mother, but I don't want to marry Neil. I know you like the idea of me taking care of him, and believe me, he likes it too, but a marriage is supposed to go both ways. It would be nice to be in a relationship and not feel alone. I'm nothing but his glorified maid, and he could hire one if he got a job."

With shaking hands, she picked up her coffee and sipped the tepid liquid. The only thing that made Kat finish the conversation was imagining the look of pride in Aiden's eyes if she ever told him what she had the courage to do.

Six years.

Six years of her life lost in a promise.

Marion deflated, her shoulders hunching, chin wobbling with suppressed sobs. "I'm sorry. You're right, and I've been taking the easy way out, shoving my burden onto you. That boy's going to end up in my basement."

Kat slipped the engagement ring off her finger and pressed it into Marion's hand, wrapping the woman's fingers around the symbol that should have meant everything, but only represented a cage she was all too eager to escape. "I'll be selling the house. It's full of my mother's memories, but I don't want to live there anymore. If Neil doesn't want to buy it from me, well, what he'll do isn't my concern. He's a grown man, and he's too old to be living the way he has. We're *both* guilty of letting him have his way."

"You don't want to live there? Where are you going to go?" Marion rubbed her fingertip over the ring's small stone.

"I don't know, but I need a fresh start."

Marion squinted at her. "You're not the same woman you used to be. You've changed, grown up."

Kat stood. "Maybe I was never the woman you thought I was. Maybe I'm more than I thought I was, too. I'll stay in touch."

With a straight spine and stiffened shoulders, Kat walked out to her car.

Her life was now her own.

It was time to start living it.

Chapter Eleven

L ater that day, while Kat packed her suitcase, the doorbell rang.

Neil never answered the door—she wasn't counting on him to start now—and she rushed from her bedroom. Kat gasped when she found a UPS man standing on the front stoop holding her hot pink suitcase that matched the carry-on she lost in Aiden's stolen SUV.

"Katrina Ford?"

"That's me."

"Sign here, please."

"Where did this come from?" Truthfully, sending for her suitcase from LAX had been the last thing on her mind. In fact, she gave little thought to her carry-on and the money she lost, and she hadn't shared any stories about her trip with Neil or his mother.

Not that they'd asked.

"A . . ." the UPS man consulted a packing slip, ". . . Dylan Price sent it? This isn't the first suitcase we've had shipped. That pilots' strike messed up a lot of plans. I'm sorry you were affected."

"It changed my life," Kat whispered, gripping the handle of the case.

The UPS man raised his eyebrows. "For the better, I hope."

"Yes. I hope so, too. Thank you."

Sitting on her bed, Kat bit her lip. Aiden must have asked Dylan to send her the suitcase. She wanted to call him and thank him. Since returning to Rosemont Valley, she tried to keep thoughts of him at bay, unwilling to picture him reconnecting with Samantha, the way she encouraged him to do. But now their adventures flashed through her mind like a filmstrip, and only the doorbell ringing stopped her tears.

"What's going on?" she muttered to herself, wiping her cheeks.

A man wearing grey dress pants, a white dress shirt, and a grey suit coat despite the heat, stood on her porch, his silver watch glinting in the afternoon sun.

"Can I help you?" Kat asked through the screen door.

"Are you Katrina Ford?" he asked, sliding his sunglasses from his face and squinting as he studied her.

"Yes, that's me."

"I have a few things that belong to you. I'm Detective Osmond from the Rosemont Valley Police Department," he introduced himself as he flashed his badge at her. "May I come in?"

"Yes, of course. I'm so sorry."

She led him into the kitchen. As she made coffee, she listened to Detective Osmond explain how the Pennington County Sheriff's office found Aiden's SUV. "Seems the wife had a penchant for ghosts and they stopped to spend the night at the Hotel Alex Johnson. Have you heard of it?"

Kat offered him a mug of plain black coffee and shook her head. "No. Is it haunted?"

"It's a tourist attraction in Rapid City." The detective blew on the coffee before taking a small sip. "The hotel is known for ghosts and such, and after spending less than five hours in their room, they hightailed it out of there. A bored patrol stopped them for speeding, and he ran the plates. The BOLO on the SUV popped damned fast. They must have spent through some of your casino earnings, unfortunately. The receipt in the briefcase said you won twenty-five thousand dollars? But there was only fifteen thousand when the boys back in Rapid City counted it out."

"I gave some of it away," Kat said, then went on to tell him about Danny and May's horse ranch in Utah.

The detective nodded in satisfaction. "I always did say good things happened to good people, and you getting your money back proves it to me. I just need you to sign this," he said, pulling a piece of paper out of the inner pocket of his jacket, "and we can close this case. Your money, purse, and carry-on are in my car."

"I appreciate you bringing them to me. I could have come by the police station."

"If you don't mind me saying so, ma'am, I personally wanted to see the woman who the boys in South Dakota swore up and down looked like Anna Kendrick." The detective tilted his head, considering her. "I don't see it."

Kat laughed. "It's caused me some problems."

Some delicious, sad, heartbreaking problems.

The detective stood from her kitchen table and pushed his sunglasses onto his face. "Well, I hope this will end some of them."

"It will go a long way. Thanks again."

After Detective Osmond retrieved the cardboard box that contained her things and said another round of goodbyes, she sagged against the door.

She hadn't been worried about money since Aiden paid for most of what she needed on their trip, and with her bank card stolen, what she saved for California had, for the most part, remained untouched. Having her casino winnings returned would come in handy, and she wrote a mental note to deposit the cash into her account before she left.

She wondered what Nan would say when she told her best friend her plans.

"You're really going to do it? I have to say, it's not like you."

"It's not? I was going to meet you in California and get my brains fucked out by as many men as I could find in Santa Barbara."

In that regard, Kat was glad things hadn't happened the way she planned. Nothing would ever compare to the way Aiden made love to her in Serenity Bay. Nothing would ever compare to the days they spent in the motel while his strength came back, talking, laughing, making love. She'd take four days of Aiden over a million men for a million days.

Nan sat back and studied her over the scarred table of the Starbucks in Rosemont Valley, and she blushed. She'd never been able to hide anything from her friend, and thinking about Aiden probably made all her feelings for him plain on her face.

"You really love the guy, don't you?"

"It doesn't make any difference. He hasn't reached out, and I doubt he will."

"Then what's the point of the road trip?"

Kat poked at a large chocolate chip cookie laying on a plain white plate. "I just feel like I need some time alone. I've been with Neil for so long, I've forgotten what it feels like to be by myself. A road trip will clear my head, help me think. Do I want to stay here? Do I want to keep my job at the library? I only went into Library Science because that's what Neil told me to do. After my mom died, I did whatever he said."

Nan took Kat's hand and squeezed. "I remember."

"But you have a point. She won't know I don't marry Neil, and I hope my happiness would mean more to her than me settling down with a man who won't lift a finger for himself when I'm around. Not that he did while I was gone, either. The house was completely empty of food, and I did laundry for an entire day because he never bothered to shove a couple loads into the washer."

"Then what?" Nan asked, brushing her blonde hair away from her face.

"Then I start living the way I want to live."

"Without Aiden?"

"If it comes to that, then yes. Without Aiden."

Before she told Nan goodbye, she pushed a check drawn from her bank into Nan's hand. "Here, I want to invest in your insurance agency."

Nan looked at the amount of the check and tears filled her eyes. "Are you sure? Are you sure you can spare this much?"

They stood in the Starbuck's parking lot, her hair flying around her head in the wind, and she pulled a long strand from between her lips before she answered. "Yes. It's only a little bit of my winnings from Blackout, and besides, I'm selling the house. Mom left it to me free and clear, so everything from the sale will go straight into my savings account. It's the least I can do, Nan. You're my very best friend, and I love you like a sister."

"Thanks." Nan wiped her eyes. "You know I feel the same way about you. Keep me posted, okay? I want to know you're safe. The last road trip you took didn't work out so well."

She drew Nan into a fierce hug. "I learned a few things on that trip. I hope I learn a few things on this one, too. Now stop acting like we'll never see each other again." She nudged Nan away. "I'll see you soon. Bye. Good luck."

Nan pressed a kiss to her cheek. "The same to you."

Kat trembled in the driver's seat, her hands shaking on the wheel as she drove out of the parking lot. She had her suitcase stowed in the trunk. The house was on the market with strict instructions to Neil he move out as quickly as possible. He hadn't cared she was taking off, only grumbled he'd have to cook his own meals from now on. Which wasn't entirely true, if he did end up living in his mother's basement the way Marion predicted.

That he felt so little for her made Kat sad, but at the same time, she was relieved he was letting her go without a fuss. If he really cared, it would have made it harder for her to leave.

But his attitude shoved her out the door, and now as she cleared Rosemont Valley and the cars started to thin on the interstate, she cranked the radio and headed west.

When Aiden opened the door to his penthouse condo, he knew he wasn't alone.

His heart sore and empty, he resisted the urge to turn tail and walk out, instead forcing himself to confront Samantha, who had laid out a late evening meal.

Candles flickered everywhere, and Aiden ignored them and the romantic atmosphere they created.

"Samantha," he said, dropping the duffle he purchased at Target onto the floor and kicking off the loafers he bought at Blackout.

She opened a large plastic takeout container of what looked like noodles and pried the white cover off a quart container, the name of their favorite Italian restaurant written in gold script on the side. "Aiden," she said, turning toward him, a guarded look in her eyes.

The tangy scent of spaghetti sauce turned his stomach, already soured by the flight. He still didn't feel back to normal, and he hadn't had a real meal since before eating at the fair in Serenity Bay. The spices and garlic drifting from his open kitchen made his mouth water, and not in a good way. He swallowed, trying to tamp down the urge to throw up.

"How did you know I'd be home tonight?" God, he wanted a drink, but the idea sounded even worse than what Samantha was serving.

"Nick told me."

As she unwrapped a package of breadsticks, Aiden studied

her. How could two women be so different? Where Samantha was tall, Kat was petite. Where Samantha wore designer clothes, Kat looked fine in Target clearance. Where Samantha did a million things at once, Kat took her time, and had an easy, peaceful calm about her.

Aiden dropped onto the couch and rubbed his fingers through his beard. He wanted to chug some Pepto-Bismol and go to bed. "I don't suppose we can talk tomorrow?"

"If that's what you want," she said, walking across his living room, her hips swaying. She untied the bow to her wrap dress, and let it flutter to the floor. She stood only in a black bra, garter belt, stockings, and her black stiletto heels.

"Not like that, Sam," he said, averting his eyes. He could still taste Kat on his lips, and it seemed dishonest, somehow, to see Samantha that way, stripped down, bare, offering him something he didn't want anymore.

"What's wrong with you?" she snapped, bending to pick up her dress. She shoved her arms into the sleeves, and with angry jerks, knotted the tie around her waist. "You've never turned me down before." She narrowed her eyes and dropped onto the couch next to him. "You were driving some girl across the country because of the pilots' strike. What happened between the two of you?"

Aiden rested his elbows on his knees and stared at the greyish-blue carpeting his decorator had chosen when he purchased the condo. "Why did you leave me?" he asked instead of answering her question. "Why aren't you married to Max and on your honeymoon?"

"I guess you deserve an explanation," Samantha whispered. She kicked off her stilettos, padded across the room, and lifted a glass of red wine to her lips. "It's only fair."

Aiden followed her gaze to the lights of tanker ships twinkling on the water. "It'd be nice."

"I was going to finally break it off with him," she started, not turning to look at him. She stood, back straight, the blonde wavy strands of her hair curtaining her shoulder blades. "But the day I was going to tell him I've been seeing you all this time, I found out I was pregnant."

Aiden pushed his thumbs into his eyes, trying to ease the pressure building in his head. "Is the baby mine?"

Samantha huffed a sad laugh. "Honestly? I don't know."

"That doesn't explain why you left me, Sam. I would have been a father to your . . . our . . . baby. You know I wanted to marry you, but you never said yes, remember? I loved you."

"Loved me? As in, you don't anymore?"

"As in, I don't know what I'm feeling right now. Why did you run out on Max? How did he take it?"

"He was hurt, of course. Confused. I lost the baby. The morning of the wedding I started bleeding, and I used it as an escape. I missed you, and I realized, sitting in the dressing room of the church, I'd made the wrong choice choosing Max over you."

Aiden silently crossed the room and took Samantha in his arms, her back against his chest, her temple resting against his neck. "I'm sorry. I didn't know you wanted children."

"I didn't know I did." She linked her fingers with his. "But it's different, you know? Once you see the two lines, you suddenly have a future."

Aiden stiffened. "A future you evidently saw with Max and not me."

"I was confused. You know we've been engaged for a couple of years, and pregnant, I felt I owed him to go through with it. He never knew about you, never knew I had doubts." She twisted in his arms and rested her head on his shoulder.

Aiden bristled, but he tried not to let it show. In one second, Samantha had relegated her entire relationship with him into having "doubts."

No wonder she was able to walk away from him so easily.

"I want to start over, Aiden. Max is gone, he's in my past. I want you to be my future."

Aiden inhaled the heavy scent of Samantha's perfume. So

different from Kat's sweet vanilla. "Did the case have anything to do with this?" He almost hated Kat for putting the idea into his head, and he tried to forget it. Tried not to believe Samantha would do something like that to him. But the timing was too coincidental, and once Kat said it, he hadn't been able to brush it aside.

Samantha paused. "No. No, I mean, I wasn't . . . I thought you could use the time alone to think about things. You didn't want to go out, just sat here and brooded. It did you some good, didn't it? The time alone to think?"

Time alone. That's what she called running out on him. "I needed you here."

"I'm sorry. I'm so sorry, Aiden. I'm here now. You can go back to work, and I'll help you. I can run some PR, spin the case in your favor. It's what I should have done in the first place. I'm sorry. Let me make it up to you, and we'll go back to the way we were."

She wrapped her arms around his neck, and he let her.

Kat's first stop on her road trip was the motel in Serenity Bay, and it was perhaps, the most difficult.

She could have gone in and spoken with Carla, thanked her again for her kindness, but staring at the motel and the silver number seven on the maroon-colored door made Kat's throat burn, and she wouldn't have been able to speak anyway. Tears filled her eyes, and she slid into her car. Unable to stand the pain any longer, she rested her forehead against the steering wheel and cried.

She missed Aiden so much.

As she drove through South Dakota, she tried not to guess what he was doing. Besides having Dylan ship her suitcase, he hadn't called or texted, and the lack of contact deepened the hole in her heart.

She drove to the gas station TJ tried to rob, and she made herself fill her car with gas and go inside the building to pay, rather than swipe her card at the pump. Mrs. F wasn't behind the counter, and the refrigerator case had been repaired.

This time, she bought a coffee, and with her eyes closed, she stood briefly where she and Aiden sat on the floor holding each other.

In Denver, she checked into the same Hilton they stayed in, thought about how hurt he'd been when he told her about Samantha turning down his proposal.

She hoped they were engaged now—if that's what it took to make him happy.

As she crossed the Colorado/Utah border, Kat pushed Aiden from her mind the best she could and looked forward to her last stop.

Even with the GPS on her phone guiding her way, she took two wrong turns, but on a warm, sunny morning she found Danny and May's horse ranch.

Jack was playing fetch with Portia in the large yard, and he greeted her with a huge smile lighting his face when she stepped out of her car.

"Kat!" he exclaimed, hugging her, securing his skinny arms around her waist. "You came back!"

"I missed you," she said wrapping her arms around the boy who was her height now. "Are your parents home?"

May stepped out of the house just then, her stomach flat, looking as if she'd never been pregnant, her blonde hair twisted into a messy bun near the top of her head. "Kat," she said warmly, holding out her hands, "hello."

Kat's face crumpled when she saw May's kind expression.

"Are you all right?" May asked, meeting Kat between her car and the porch.

"I need some time," Kat said around a lump in her throat.

May embraced her, and she let the tears she bottled up on her drive across the country flow down her cheeks.

"Of course, of course," May murmured, rubbing her back. "It's Aiden, isn't it?"

Kat nodded.

"Stay with us for as long as you need."

Kat enjoyed her time on the farm. She spent time with Jack, talked with May, and rocked Abilene, or Abby, as they called the baby, for hours on end.

One afternoon, two weeks after her arrival, while having a quiet conversation with May, Kat realized she'd needed the connection to people who had known her and Aiden as a couple. Spending time with May, Danny, Jack, and Abby gave Kat much needed peace. She rode horse with May over their acres of bright green grass. The breeze cooled her skin, but the bright buttery sun warmed her as did May's friendship.

The white mare Kat rode ambled along, allowing her to relax into the saddle; she'd never ridden a horse before, and the large animals made her nervous.

May tried to give her lessons on the different breeds of horses they'd boarded on the ranch at one time or another, but all the names, descriptions, and ailments of horses gone by went in one ear and out the other. Kat focused on enjoying the companionship of both the animals and the people, and she let the Utah plains soothe her soul.

"Will you tell me now, what's going on, Kat?" May asked, riding a chestnut horse next to her.

Kat didn't answer, trying to formulate her feelings into words.

"Where's Aiden?" May asked, breaking the silence. "Your ring is gone. Did you separate?"

Staring far into the distance at the mountain ranges miles away, she murmured, "We were never together, not the way you and Danny thought we were." She rubbed her horse's neck.

Kat explained meeting him at LAX and the pilots' strike.

May made sympathetic noises as Kat recounted what happened after she and Aiden helped find Jack.

"And you fell for him, didn't you? Literally and figuratively," May said, urging her horse along a path that had seen hundreds of horses throughout the years.

"Wouldn't you?" Kat asked, trying to smile.

"I prefer blonds," May said, and laughed when Kat rolled her eyes. "Yes, I see your point. He was very handsome, and a gentleman, too. He's been working with Danny, helping us turn our farm into a nonprofit to avoid so many financial problems. He's been a real help. But he's back in Miami with this other woman now? As far as I know, he doesn't give Danny any personal information. We had no idea anything was going on between the two of you."

Her eyes shot to May's in surprise. "That's nice of him. He seemed so put out being here, I didn't think he'd give our visit another thought. But I'm glad you're getting the help you need to keep the farm going." Kat worried the horse's reins between her fingers. "He hasn't called or texted. There's got to be a reason why he hasn't reached out."

May scoffed. "Yeah, that reason is your fiancé, Kat. What's stopping Aiden from thinking you're married? That you really went through with it? What if both of you are single?"

Kat paused to consider that idea. "Maybe. But you didn't see the pain he was in when I met him. He loved her."

"No, I didn't see how he looked, not then, but I saw the way he looked at you while you were here. He couldn't take his eyes off you."

She wanted to believe her. "Really?"

"Really. Go find him. What do you have to lose? If you want to start a new life, then you need closure. Maybe he does, too. You'd be doing him a favor."

"How would I get to Miami?"

May laughed. "You're going to have to drive. You've come this far, and besides, Jack has something to give you."

At May's insistence, Kat spent more time at the horse ranch than she was comfortable with. She didn't want to be a drain on their finances, even going so far as shopping with May and Abby and paying for a month's worth of groceries.

On the morning she planned to leave, a truck pulling a trailer parked in front of May and Danny's house.

She sat with Abilene on the porch rocking the baby and feeding her a bottle; holding the infant made her biological clock start ticking.

She and Aiden hadn't spoken of having children—with each other or anyone else. She assumed he would have kids with Samantha one day. Usually when people married, children were part of the package. Neil hadn't wanted anything to do with her, not that way, and it took two to get pregnant.

Looking into Abilene's bright blue eyes, Kat, for the first time in many years, considered the possibility of having her own children.

With someone.

Someday.

The young man driving the truck jumped out of the cab and adjusted a worn cowboy hat, running his hands through his greasy brown hair. "You the woman who takes horses?" he hollered at May, his voice rough with anger.

"We do," she said, squinting, her hand shading her eyes, her other hand holding onto the lead of a horse she was brushing out.

"Got a pregnant mare here," the man said, jerking his thumb at the trailer. "Can't afford her—not anymore."

"We can't pay you," May said, handing the horse's lead to Jack who popped his head out of the barn.

"Don't want your money," he said, undoing the latch, "just gotta get rid of her."

The atmosphere in the yard grew thick with tension, and Kat wished Danny were there and not at work in Silver Bullet.

The man wearing jeans and a light blue and black plaid button-down shirt let the ramp fall to the gravel driveway with a loud clatter.

The horse pounded her hooves on the floor of the trailer, and a muffled but frightened whinny met Kat's ears. Goosebumps crawled over her skin.

"Will you put Belle in her stall?" May asked Jack.

Kat gripped Abilene closer as May move toward the truck; she didn't like the funny feeling in her stomach.

The man disappeared inside the trailer, and she met May's dismayed eyes across the yard.

Slowly, a dark brown horse came into view, her muscles quivering, her belly low.

Even from the distance Kat sat away from the truck, she heard May gasp and exclaim in anger.

"She's due any day," May said, horrified. "Has she had medical care?"

"Couldn't afford it," the livid man snapped, hoisting the ramp in place and slamming the doors closed.

"Can you tell me her name, at least?" May asked, grabbing the horse's lead as she skittered nervously, her hooves dancing.

"Snickers."

It was the last thing he said before he climbed into his truck and slammed his door shut.

Kat relaxed after the truck disappeared in a cloud of dust and strain. She couldn't understand why he was so angry when May had taken the horse without argument or recrimination. The jerk hadn't even bothered to say thank you.

"Belle's in her stall," Jack announced, bouncing out of the barn.

The sound of Jack's voice spooked Snickers, and she tried to break from May's grasp, kicking her hind legs. She clipped Jack's shoulder in the process.

Terrified, Kat stood and screamed, "Jack!" startling Abby and making her cry.

With shaking hands, Kat nestled the baby to her shoulder and patted her back, trying to console her to stop her crying. She wanted to see if Jack was okay, but she was afraid to go into the yard with the baby while the horse was anxious and scared.

May rushed to Jack, letting go of Snickers' rope.

Kat breathed a sigh of relief when Jack stood, looking bewildered and off-kilter, rubbing his shoulder. He wasn't crying, and that was a good sign. The kick looked vicious, and Jack was lucky he wasn't seriously hurt.

Abby quieted, and Kat pressed a kiss to the baby's head. "I'm sorry, sweetie," she murmured.

May patted Jack down, and he swatted her away in embarrassment. After May grabbed him and kissed his cheek, Jack ran to the porch and plopped onto the top step.

Snickers calmed, and she sniffed along the side of the barn at stray blades of grass.

Kat's heart pounded as May approached the horse and grabbed the reins hanging from the horse's halter. She held her breath until May came out of the barn, wiping her forehead with the back of her hand.

"Do you have a few more days?" May asked, approaching the porch. She sat next to Jack on the step and patted his leg.

"Sure, why?" As eager as Kat was to get on the road, she was scared, too. She'd never driven to Florida before, never had a reason to visit Miami, and she didn't know where Aiden lived. She didn't want to face what she'd find when she found him, but she needed closure, as May pointed out. If that meant knowing Aiden had moved on with Samantha, then so be it.

"Snickers is due any time. Have you ever watched a horse give birth?"

Kat shook her head.

"Then stay. You don't want to miss something like this."

Abby's milky breath floated over Kat's skin. She would give May, Danny, Jack, and Abby a few more days of her time, then she needed to go.

If she wanted what May had, then she needed to face her fears and fight for what she wanted.

Chapter Twelve

T wo days later, May shook Kat awake.

During her visit, she'd been sleeping in the room she shared with Aiden. As the days turned into weeks, the sounds of the old house no longer woke her, and besides the nights she got up to feed Abby to give May a chance to rest, Kat slept soundly.

"Kat," May said, nudging Kat's shoulder.

"Hmmm?" Kat murmured, burrowing into her pillow.

"Snickers is ready. Do you want to go down to the barn?"

Kat jolted awake. She didn't want to miss the birth of Snickers' foal. "I'll be right there. Let me change."

"Okay, hurry. Danny called the vet just in case. The baby's sleeping, and Jack's in the barn waiting for us."

Kat dressed as quickly as she could, scrambling for clothing in the dark, and met May in the barn.

May had turned on two lanterns, but they did little to fight the darkness inside the cavernous space.

Kat rubbed her nose. During her time on the farm, she'd grown used to the smell of manure, hay, and horse, but tonight the scents were particularly strong, blood and the pungent smell of amniotic fluid adding to the mix.

She crouched on the floor with Jack, and he leaned into her, resting his head on her shoulder.

Watching Snickers give birth was perhaps the most beautiful thing she'd ever experienced. Tears filled her eyes as the horse pushed the foal from her body.

Kat sat in the barn with Jack and May, the vet waiting silently behind them on the off chance he was needed, until the first rays of sunlight broke over the horizon. Kat's butt was numb from sitting on the hard wooden floor, and she stretched, breaking the spell.

Claiming hunger, Jack scurried into the house, but Kat didn't want to leave. She leaned against the wooden stall, watching the foal and Snickers through the slats.

"Thank you," she whispered to May.

May gathered her into her arms, and she melted into the woman's embrace. "You're welcome. It's been a joy having you here, but this isn't your place."

"I wish it were." It would be so easy to stay with May and Danny, help take care of Jack and Abby.

"No, you don't. You want a husband, and a family of your own. I'm not saying you couldn't find a man in Wolverton, I'm sure there'd be plenty of takers, but Aiden isn't here, and he's who you want."

"It's been months since he dropped me off. What if he's forgotten about me?"

"You never forget someone you love," she whispered, rubbing her back.

As she watched the foal struggle to her feet, she hoped that was true. A brave little thing, coming into the world with such innocence. If May and Danny kept her, she'd never lose it. "What will you name her?"

May rubbed her eyes. "You already have."

Her heart breaking a little more, Kat murmured, "KitKat."

"Yes." May kissed Kat's cheek. "I love having you here, but it's time for you to go home. Wherever that may be."

Kat opened her mouth to agree, but Jack interrupted, scampering into the barn holding out a piece of toast. "You're leaving today."

Accepting the small breakfast, Kat nodded. "Yeah."

"Come on, then," Jack said, tugging on her hand.

"Where are we going?"

Jack led her to the corner of the barn where Portia and her puppies spent the night. May and Danny gave the dogs the freedom to go where they liked, and the dogs padded in and out of the house. But Portia was strict with her pups, and this early in the morning, they were rolling around in fresh hay in an empty horse stall.

Portia had six puppies in her litter, and Jack was told he couldn't keep them. Quietly, May and Danny asked around if they knew of anyone who wanted a puppy. They could safely be taken from their mother now, and May and Danny didn't want Jack to become attached.

"Ted and Amanda are taking two," Jack said.

"I bet they'll like that after having to give up Portia," Kat said, bending to pet one of the puppies.

"They were pretty happy," Jack said, though he sounded less than excited at the idea of having to give Portia's puppies away. "I want you to have two, too."

"Oh, but Jack—" Kat started.

"Please, Kat?" Jack settled next to her, his blue eyes pleading. "I trust you to take care of them. Then I can give Amanda and Ted their two . . ." he lowered his voice, ". . . and then maybe I can convince Mom and Dad to let me keep the other two. One for me and one for Abby."

"You don't want to give them to strangers, huh?" Kat asked, flicking a lock of hair out of his eyes.

Jack shook his head.

"I'll take them on one condition," Kat said.

"I'll do anything you want," Jack agreed, nodding.

"Ask your Mom to take Portia to the vet to get her fixed. If she gets pregnant again, you'll have more puppies to deal with, and I know your Mom and Dad can't afford to keep any more. Okay?"

"I promise."

"Then I'll take two of the little guys. Thank you for thinking of me."

"I'll miss you when you leave," Jack said, digging his thumbnail into a board, peeling off a sliver of wood. "I wish you could stay and babysit me and Abby when Mom and Dad are busy."

"I wish I could too, sweetie, but I've been using my visit to hide from scary responsibilities. A large part of being a grown-up is doing stuff you don't want to do, and I think you learned a little about that when your mom and dad tried to give Portia away."

Jack smiled as one of the puppies licked his hand. "Yeah, but Mom says everything works out for the best." He brightened. "Come on, let's go eat. Dad made pancakes to celebrate KitKat being born!"

After a huge breakfast and a hot shower, Kat thought she'd never said truer words than when she was driving away from May's and Danny's house, her suitcase in the trunk and two puppies sleeping in a large crate in the backseat.

With a dry mouth, she pointed her car east, calculated how many days it would take to drive from Utah to Florida, and she prayed she had the strength to face what she would find.

Kat had been in Miami for two weeks when Nan called her. The ringing stopped her in the middle of the busy sidewalk, and the pups took the opportunity to sniff at a parking meter. With the handles of their leashes looped around her wrist, she pulled her phone out of her purse. She wore the strap across her body to keep her hands free.

"Hey," Nan said, after she connected the call.

"Hi, how are you?" Kat asked, her friend's voice bringing on a wave of homesickness.

"Great! All your things are moved into storage. Neil's been living with his mother for a few weeks now."

"I appreciate you doing that for me." When the realtor called and told her the house sold, she was stabbed with disappointment. She'd had no idea the little house that still needed a new roof would be on the market for only a few short weeks. Kat needed to empty the house, but she didn't want to have to drive back to Minnesota. Like a guardian angel, Nan stepped in, hired movers, and rented a storage unit for all her things.

"It was no problem, but I'm afraid you'll want to go through that storage space sooner rather than later. You're paying to store a lot of junk."

"I know. I didn't have the heart to throw anything out after Mom died, but I don't know when I'll be back to do it."

"Have you found a space to rent yet?" Nan asked.

"I might have found something, but everything is so expensive here."

"You're in Miami, not Rosemont Valley." Nan's voice held a glimmer of amusement.

"Yeah." She tugged on the puppies' leashes to move them farther down the sidewalk.

"What's wrong, Kat?" Nan murmured.

She stepped out of the way of a woman pushing a gigantic double stroller as she tried to think of a cheerful way to answer Nan's question. She didn't want her friend knowing how miserable she was.

"Have you seen Aiden?" Nan asked gently when she didn't respond.

"No," she said, her voice coming out almost as a whimper, giving in to Nan's sympathy. It killed her to be in the same city and not see him. She'd never admit she looked for him, wherever she was, hoping for a glimpse of him. But half a million people lived in Miami, and Aiden wouldn't visit the neighborhoods where Kat could afford a place to rent.

She walked her dogs to a small park, and she sat on a sticky bench. She was on her way to look at another potential space for her store and was grateful for the small break.

The puppies lay under a tree in the shade, resting their heads on their paws. Not used to the humidity, Kat wiped her forehead with the back of her hand, her dress clinging to her sweat-covered body, the bracelet Aiden bought her in Serenity Bay sliding down her tanned arm. She hadn't taken it off since the day he fastened it around her wrist.

"What are you waiting for, hon?"

"What if he's with Samantha?" Kat voiced her worst fear.

"Does that matter?"

Nan's question took her off guard.

"What do you mean, does it matter? Of course it matters." She wished she had something to drink to wash away the tears. She always felt like crying, but only her determination to start living the kind of life she wanted held them at bay.

She hadn't found an apartment to rent, instead spending her time working with a real estate agent, looking for storefronts that were in her price range but would still be in part of the city that would attract customers who had the disposable income to shop for clothes they didn't need. It was a difficult combination.

She'd reasoned with herself staying at the hotel was prolonging her vacation.

It wasn't, not really.

She was giving herself an easy out by not signing a lease for an apartment.

"Why are you in Miami, Kat? If Aiden isn't available, would you leave?"

"I'm not sure," Kat said honestly.

"No, you wouldn't," Nan said firmly. "You've always wanted to live near the ocean, and you have always wanted to open your own shop. Your mother's house brought in a good price, and now you can afford to do both. Aiden isn't the only reason you're in Florida, so stop believing he is. If he's not available, for any reason, that would suck, but you would be okay because you'll finally be living the life you want."

In the two weeks Kat had been in Miami, she'd spent several hours on the beach, and when Nan said that, it all clicked into place. If she found Aiden married to Samantha, or engaged, or simply dating to get to know each other again, it wouldn't be the end of her life.

It would only be a different kind of beginning.

She needed to face her fears and find out if Aiden missed her —or if he was just fine without her.

Because as much as her heart would break, she would be okay without him.

"You're right."

"Good girl," Nan said, her approval clear through the phone line. "Let me know how it goes."

She tucked her phone into her purse and gathered the puppies into her arms.

She'd go talk to Aiden—but she had to find him first.

Aiden took another sip of scotch and toed off his dress shoes.

It'd been a long day.

He unknotted his tie and let it hang around his neck, and he was unbuttoning his shirt when his cell phone rang.

He wasn't in the mood to talk to anyone. His family treated him with kid gloves since he'd been back, but he didn't blame them. Surly and heartsick, he'd turned into a recluse, snapping at anyone who dared to visit him.

His brother's name flashed on the screen, and Aiden bit back a frustrated sigh. Dylan checked on him because he cared, but no amount of caring would help.

Aiden fell asleep wanting her, woke up cradling his pillow in his arms, dreaming of her.

It'd been months, and he was no closer to forgetting about her than the last day he saw her.

The call went to voicemail, and Aiden brushed off the guilt that tingled down his spine. He knew how it felt to be helpless, to be states away and wanting to do something, anything, but unable.

In the kitchen, Aiden added more ice to his glass and three fingers of scotch. He hadn't gone on another bender. No. Somehow, he hurt more than when Samantha left him, and he lived like a zombie—alive, but dead inside.

The bell to the elevator chimed, alerting him to a visitor, and Aiden frowned. His building's attendant was professional, always announcing if someone was on their way to see him.

It was probably Samantha coming back to look for something else. That had been her mode of operation into gaining access to his condo—claiming she forgot something or saying she left something behind.

It had been true the first few times she stopped by—a stray pair of earrings, or a necklace. Even going so far as to ask if she could keep the painting they found together at a flea market.

He'd given it to her, of course.

Aiden didn't need any of their memories.

He'd made new ones.

"Samantha," he said without turning around. "What else did you forget?"

When she didn't say anything, he thought maybe he'd find her undressing or selecting music for the stereo, always trying to entice him back into a relationship he didn't want.

He took another sip of scotch, let the burn calm him before he flicked a glance over his shoulder.

What he saw made emotion clog his throat and tears burn his eyes.

The idea had never entered his mind he'd see her again.

"Kat."

"Hello, Aiden."

His eyes hungrily traveled over her body, taking in the sandals on her feet, her shapely legs tanned bronze, her light pink sundress.

"You cut your hair," he said stupidly, unable to think of anything else to say.

"A little," she said, reaching for the ends of her hair that now only reached her shoulders.

Two golden retriever puppies bounded to his feet, but they couldn't decide if they wanted his attention or to play with each other and explore unfamiliar territory, their bright blue leashes dragging behind them.

"Cute dogs," he said, his mind numb from the sight of her standing inside his living room.

He wanted to rush to her, pull her small body into his arms and kiss her senseless, but he held himself in check; he didn't know why she was there.

"They're Portia's."

"Who's Portia?"

"Jack's dog."

"Jack?" He lost the thread, but only because he couldn't stop staring at her. Kat's eyes were as he remembered, soft, but radiant, long lashes framing beautiful golden-brown irises. Her lips sparkled with gloss, and her skin glimmered with sun and health.

She didn't wear glasses.

Her smile fell, and he wanted to kick himself for dimming the light in her eyes.

"Maybe I should go," she murmured to the floor, her shoulders slumped.

"No!" Aiden's skin pricked with fear, and he began to sweat despite the central air. He couldn't let her leave. He cleared his throat. "I mean, stay for a drink. If you want."

The puppies chased after him to the kitchen. Reluctant to take his eyes off her, even for a few seconds, he quickly poured her a glass of red Moscato and joined her on his couch. "How long have you been in Miami?"

"A couple of weeks," she said, then sipped the wine.

Aiden's stomach dropped to his feet.

She wasn't here for him.

He'd been foolish to think so.

Draining the scotch, the ice cubes melted, he let the bitterness and disappointment wash over him.

God, he'd missed her, but all she was doing was stopping by to say "Hi."

"What are you doing here?" he asked, trying to keep the anger out of his voice. She didn't need to know every day they'd been apart was pure agony for him, that every day over these past months just saw him one day closer to . . . well, nothing he wanted to form into words.

Her lips quirked. "Here in your apartment? Or in Miami?"

He could have gotten the hurt out of the way, ripped the Band-Aid off and dealt with the aftermath later, should have taken the bad news like a man, but he said, "In Miami."

Kat stood from the couch, carrying her wine with her.

"Miami is my last stop," she said, staring out his balcony doors. "You weren't lying when you said you lived near the ocean."

"I didn't lie about anything," he said.

She gave him a sad smile, the corners of her mouth barely lifting. "I didn't either." Kat sucked in a breath. "What am I doing in Miami? I live here now."

Fighting for nonchalance, he leaned back against the cushions. "Really."

"Yeah. What about you? Did you and Samantha fix things?" Kat set her wineglass on his dining table and twisted her fingers together, turning her knuckles white.

He noticed her bracelet then, the one he bought her in Serenity Bay, the white and pink stones matching her dress. Aiden refused to let the piece of jewelry give him hope.

"No." He looked into his empty glass. He needed another drink.

"Do you, I mean, did she tell you why she left?"

"She got pregnant," he said, his voice clipped. "She lost the baby and came back, pleaded with me to give her a second chance."

"I'm sorry. Was it—"

"Mine?" Aiden poured another scotch, less than an inch this time. He should stop drinking or he'd do something he regretted.

Like beg her to stay.

Or force her to go.

"I don't know. *She* didn't." His eyes zeroed in on her belly, remembering their time in the motel. Yellow sunlight. Soft sheets. Searing kisses. Whispered secrets.

Making love.

Without protection.

"How about you?"

Kat covered her stomach, her hands splayed against her dress. "Oh, no. No."

Aiden nodded. He'd believed her when she said the timing of her cycle wasn't right, but he stared at her, freezing his expression, hoping she couldn't see the disappointment.

Rubbing his eyes, Aiden was suddenly dragged down with fatigue. "Kat—"

"I found a place to rent," she broke in.

"For a store?"

Kat smiled. "Yeah. It's a little out of the way. I couldn't afford anything on the main strip, or even close to it, you know? But there's a dance studio down the street from my place. I poked my head in, and I'm going to help with her toddler class. Madam Lucette asked if I could bring the puppies; some of the kids have trouble fitting in right away, separated from their parents. She'll pay me a little, and she's giving me a room over her studio for free. It will help until my store starts making a profit."

Aiden loved the look on Kat's face as her features lit up in pleasure. "It sounds like you'll be happy here, Kat. I'm glad for you."

"And you? How are you, Aiden?" she asked, creases of worry framing her eyes. "You and Samantha broke up. What about your job? How did that turn out for you?"

"I quit. I couldn't take it anymore."

Emptying his desk had been bittersweet. He wouldn't miss the office, the long hours, the heavy workload. It'd been his dream, to be an attorney, on the fast track to the cushy DA's office, but the weight fell from his shoulders as he strode to his car carrying a cardboard box containing the few personal things he hung on his walls.

"Are you okay? What are you doing now?" she asked, her lips trembling.

He wanted her to be worried about him; he wanted her to be asking these questions, trying to figure out how she'd fit into his life. But more than likely, she was only asking to make sure he would be okay when she left.

Aiden would never be okay unless she was in his life.

It had only taken Samantha's lips on his to know he would never be happy with another woman.

"I teach law at the University of Miami. It's not as lucrative, but it's a lot less stress." And he'd have time to be a father. Something, through his conversations with Kat, Aiden realized was important to him.

Kat nodded. "That's great. I'm happy for you."

Suddenly, a wave of anger washed over him, and he wanted her to leave. He'd had enough of seeing her and not being able to touch. Only her memory kept him company during these past months, and dreams of her would haunt him for the rest of his life.

Making a show of pulling his phone from his pocket and checking the time, he said, "If there's nothing else, I'm exhausted. Maybe we can meet up for coffee sometime."

The offer slipped out of his mouth before he could tell himself no. Why prolong the agony by spending time with her?

Miami was big enough they could certainly live in the same city and not bump into each other.

Unless he looked for her.

Which he would not.

"There's one more thing," she said, picking up her wineglass. She took a long swallow.

He rolled his hand in the air, in a gesture that said, "Get on with it," and sipped his own drink.

Kat set her empty glass on the table and approached him, the heels of her sandals clicking on the kitchen tile.

Standing between his knees, she gripped the ends of his tie and licked her lips. "I love you, Aiden."

He wanted the words. He would have traded his soul for the words, but now he finally had them, they pissed him off.

"Are you sure, Kat? Because you've been in Miami for two weeks, and you're only now telling me." He pulled away from her, yanking his tie from her grasp, his heart thudding behind his ribs, his blood slowing in his veins, turning to ice. His brain screamed to shut the hell up, to take what she offered.

But he wouldn't be her second best.

"Just what in the hell have you been doing?"

Chapter Thirteen

K at hadn't expected Aiden to be angry at her, but dammit, she'd needed the time, and she wouldn't apologize for taking it.

And maybe she shouldn't have, but she read his anger as a good sign.

If he didn't care about her, he wouldn't be showing any emotion at all.

"You know for the past six years I've been living my life for someone else," she said, drawing a nod of agreement from him.

"Living my life to keep a promise to my mother, living my life to make Neil's mother happy. Living my life how Neil wanted me to live it. After you dropped me off, I lasted two days. Not because I'd fallen in love with you, because I had, but because on our road trip, you taught me I needed to live for myself, that if I wasn't happy, nothing I was doing would be worth it."

Kat turned to the balcony doors. "May I?" she asked, placing her hand on the glass.

Aiden nodded.

She slid the doors open and stepped onto the balcony, looking over her shoulder to check the puppies wouldn't follow, but they were sleeping under Aiden's dining table.

He stepped outside with her, and with him by her side, she scanned his view, the water turning pink in the sunset, the sounds traffic from below traveling to her, faint and far away.

"I took some time," she said, continuing her story, leaning against the railing. "I broke up with Neil and told his mother. I put my mother's house on the market, sold it, actually, for a fair price. I missed you, but I needed a little time to myself, so I traced our steps. No, I didn't stop to help anyone, and I didn't spend the night in jail, even once."

Her heart skipped when a faint smile crossed his lips.

"I went by the motel in Serenity Bay, and I stopped at the gas station TJ held up."

"Kat—"

"No, I'm okay. I needed to see it," she said, relieved by the concern in his eyes. "And what took the longest was my visit to Danny and May's. She had her baby—a little girl, but I guess you know that. I spent time with Jack, and he gave me two of Portia's puppies. I needed to figure out who I was. Who I would be by myself."

She wanted to touch him, but she didn't want him to pull away, not again. She would finish what she had to say and then let him decide.

"When I got here, it took me a while to find my courage because, Aiden, I didn't know. I didn't know if you and Samantha got back together; you loved her. So much. At least, I thought you did. Nan accused me of hiding, and I guess I was. But I also needed to know that if you didn't love me, didn't want me after all, I would still have a life. And I will. You could tell me to leave, and I would be okay. My heart would be broken, but I would be okay. I've already made a friend; I have a place to live, and I found a place to work part time doing what I enjoy. I found a lovely little space for my store, and for the first time in a long time, I'll be excited to wake up and go to work. I needed those things, all those things, in case you didn't need me." She met his eyes. "Do you understand?"

She worried the stones of the bracelet fastened around her wrist and finally let the tears run tracks down her cheeks. His eyes were cool, a cool, crisp blue, and she couldn't read any emotion in them.

Aiden remained silent for so long she lost confidence things would work out between them. Maybe she wanted him so much she ignored the signs.

Bad signs.

Aiden's anger swooshed out of him as he expelled his breath. How could he be mad at her for doing what he wanted her to do?

He sank onto a patio chair and ran his fingertips through his beard.

Wiping her cheeks, Kat said, "I'm sorry about you and Samantha and her pregnancy. I'm sorry it didn't work out between you."

"I'm not." He said it honestly, his voice ringing firm and true. "Since the day you bumped into me in the airport, all I've wanted is you."

She let out a small whimper, and he opened his arms.

Kat felt how he remembered: small, curled in his lap like a cat, the scent of vanilla catching his nose.

Aiden buried his face in her hair, and he wrapped his arms around her, pulling her close. God, he'd missed this, missed holding her.

He stood, and anchoring her to him, her face pressed against his neck, he opened his balcony doors and stepped inside.

One of the puppies opened a lazy eyelid, but it drifted shut, the dog too worn out to do anything but go back to sleep.

He carried her to his bedroom, turned down his comforter, and gently laid her down on his bed.

She looked up at him, her brown eyes sparkling with tears, but a smile lifted the corners of her mouth. With her hair fanned on his pillow, the skirt of her dress riding up her thighs, she looked gorgeous, and she was his.

With the mattress dipping under his weight, he sat next to her, and nudged her shoulder. Kat rolled onto her side, and he undid the zipper of her dress.

It'd been months since he made love to her, each week sheer hell remembering how she felt, how she'd enveloped him in her heat, giving him all of her.

He hadn't realized it then. Maybe he'd been too sick from those goddamned tacos, or maybe he'd been too heartsick at having to let her go, but she'd told him, over and over again during those four days at the motel, how much she loved him.

How could he have ever doubted she would come for him?

He unclasped her bra and slid the flesh-colored panties from her thighs. Kat looked just as he remembered: full breasts, her belly dipping into a valley before melting into her pubic bone. She added a tan to her skin, evidence she spent time in the sun since she came to Florida.

She sparkled, like the diamond he planned to place on her finger.

"Are you going to get undressed too, or are you going to look at me all night?" she teased, raising a hand to his face and trailing her fingers down his cheek.

Aiden turned his face to her palm and kissed her. "Let me take my time," he murmured. "I've missed you too much not to take my time."

He slid his tie from around his neck and unbuttoned his shirt. He was in the process of undoing his pants when she echoed his earlier thoughts: "Would you have ever come for me?"

Naked, the tip of his erection brushing his abdomen, he slipped between the sheets next to her and sighed when she wrapped her body around his.

"You needed to find your own way, but I was afraid it wouldn't lead back to me. I'm not sure how much longer I could have lived without you." He kissed her, breathed in her scent. The time they'd been apart taught him to never take her for granted. Every minute, every second, he would cherish, because saying goodbye had been the easy part. Living with it was the most difficult thing he'd ever done.

"I had to figure out what I wanted. I knew I wanted you, but I needed to have you in my life on my own terms, or I wouldn't have been able to make you happy. Because *I* wouldn't have been happy. And I want to make you happy, Aiden."

He took her mouth with his, nudging her teeth apart to tangle his tongue with hers. As he devoured her lips, he spread her thighs and dipped his fingers into her, finding her ready for him.

"You make me happy, Kat. You will always make me happy." He settled between her legs, and he met her eyes before pushing into her.

Gently, he settled his weight on top of her, and she wrapped her arms around his neck, a moan escaping her lips in a wispy breath.

"Marry me," he whispered into her ear. "We'll travel, we'll buy a lake house in Minnesota. We'll see Mount Rushmore."

"I want to go wherever you go," she murmured.

Her muscles clenched around him, and he tensed, pushing them over the edge.

After he caught his breath, he slid off her and spooned her, pulling her close, his hand splaying against her belly.

Kat's laugh startled him, and he grinned, knowing what caught her eye.

"You printed this out?" She grabbed a silver-framed picture off his nightstand.

"It's all I had. I didn't take any pictures of you."

The photo he framed was the shot taken by the rookie photographer in LAX.

Kat's hands were braced on his chest, and he had his arm around her, steadying her. He'd studied the picture a million times, memorizing every pixel, and every time he looked at it, he saw it. How close he held her, how intimate their gazes were staring into each other's eyes.

"I look so different," she murmured, running a finger down her body.

Aiden smoothed his fingers through the tangles in her hair. "You've always been you."

She set the picture onto the night table and kissed his lips. "But you brought out the best in me."

"You would have done that for yourself. One day. With or without me." Aiden believed that. He believed that one day, Kat, tired of being a caterpillar, would have found her way to transforming into the butterfly she was meant to be.

"But your way was so much more fun," she said, brushing his hair from his forehead.

Aiden chuckled. "You call scorpions, finding lost kids, getting arrested, and almost dying of food poisoning fun?"

Resting against the headboard, Kat pulled the comforter up and covered her breasts, tucking the edge under her arms. Aiden almost protested but reminded himself she was his, and he'd get to see her every day for the rest of his life.

Giggling, her lips swollen by his kisses, her cheeks pink from making love, she said, "Yeah, don't you?"

"Yeah." Aiden sighed. "I love you, Katrina. You never said you'd marry me." In anticipation, his heart picked up speed, and he nuzzled her shoulder as he waited for her answer. The scratch the old woman gave her at Blackout was completely healed, and now a faint spattering of freckles dotted her glowing tanned skin.

"Of course I'll marry you. It's what I came here for. I didn't want to spend any more time without you."

"Good. I have the perfect honeymoon planned."

Kat laughed, wrapping her arms around his neck. "Oh, you do, do you? And what's that?"

"Road trip."

Acknowledgments

As always, thank you to my friends who have my back, believe in me, and want to read my stories. Be it my friends on this side of the screen, or the ones I have never met in person, your support is valuable to me.

Thank you to my family and friends who give me the space and time I need to write.

I couldn't do this without you.

About the Author

Vania Rheault has lived in Minnesota all her life. In 2003, she graduated with a BA in English with a concentration in creative writing from Minnesota State University, Moorhead.

When she's not writing, she's reading, playing with one of her two cats, or going to movie night with her sister.

www.ingramcontent.com/pod-product-compliance
Lightning Source LLC
Chambersburg PA
CBHW021007120726
47905CB00009B/2896